PATHSIDE PREDATOR

RAVES FOR *PATHSIDE PREDATOR*

Christine Noyes weaves a tale of suspense and psychological intrigue drawing readers into a dark and complex world where the line between hunter and prey blurs. The narrative unfolds with a meticulous blend of procedural details and character development, keeping the reader hooked from the first page to the last. *Pathside Predator* is a riveting crime thriller that goes beyond the conventional boundaries of the genre. Surprising twists and turns made it one of my favorite reads.

—Natalie Soine
Readers' Favorite 5 Star

Noyes explores the story of a killer with a distorted sense of justice. Delving into grief, betrayal, and scandal, it had me challenging my own sense of right and wrong. *Pathside Predator* prompts reflection on who deserves sympathy—the predator, the FBI team, the victims' husbands, or anyone who is in pain. Fast-paced and intriguing, *Pathside Predator* is a highly engaging thriller and a recommended book for lovers of murder mysteries.

—Mimi Odigwe
Readers' Favorite 5 Star

Pathside Predator will have lovers of whodunit, mystery, and sleuth novels riveted. An intriguing plot and enthralling twists along with the subtle tone of the storyline kept me hooked. I felt as if I were right there next to every character helplessly watching the scenes unfold. There is adventure, thrills, wit, and so much more to enjoy in this book.

—Keith Mbuya
Readers' Favorite 5 Star

Christine Noyes is a master storyteller. She is so skilled at bringing her characters to life that I became totally invested in them. I worried about them, celebrated with them and shared their pain as their story created a web of mystery. *Pathside Predator* had me intrigued from the beginning and guessing until the end.

—Brenda Anderson
administrative assistant, retired
Orange, Massachusetts, Police Department

CHRISTINE NOYES

Pathside Predator

a Bradley Whitman novel

Haley's

Athol, Massachusetts

Haley's
488 South Main Street
Athol, MA 01331
haley.antique@verizon.net • 978.249.9400

Proof read by Richard Bruno.

Cover designed by Christine Noyes. Cover photo by Christine Noyes.

International Standard Book Number, trade paperback: 978-1-956055-70-2

International Standard Book Number, eBook, Kindle: 978-1-956055-56-6

Library of Congress Cataloging-in-Publication Data pending

To my family, friends, and supportive readers.
You continually lift me into the light.
And always, Al.

CONTENTS

BUTCHER

Relishing the last bit of life leaking from her body as the crimson-coated knife slid from her throat, the killer faced a nagging question. *Did I put the trash out this morning?* The thought that the unusually warm autumn day might cause discarded red snapper from the previous night's dinner to steam in the plastic bag evoked a queasy reaction. Turning attention back to the task at hand and careful not to damage the woman's areola, the butcher used the razor-sharp blade to remove her right nipple. As it always did at that point in the process, the euphoric mood deadened—much like the torn flesh from the defaced breast.

SERIAL KILLER

Sergeant Donovan Doyle of the Revere Police Department held a red paisley handkerchief to his face. As sun beat down and evaporated the early morning dew, Doyle wiped fresh sweat from his brow.

"Well? What do you think?" Doyle asked the medical examiner.

Doctor Maria Reyes sent him an impatient glare. "I'll let you know what I think as soon as I am done, sergeant."

"Maria. Is it? Or isn't it?" Doyle asked, equally impatient.

Both turned their heads as tree branches snapped on the hiking path to their right. Detective Harold Reed approached, accompanied by two patrol officers. Like Doyle not wanting to disturb the area surrounding the victim, they kept a distance.

"Hello, Detective Reed," Doctor Reyes said. "It looks like you have a victim of the Pathside Predator."

Doyle threw up his hands in frustration. "You couldn't tell me that?"

"Relax, Donovan. Not everything is about you," Reyes responded.

Detective Reed cast Doyle a questioning glance. Doyle shrugged his shoulders and shook his head in response.

"What do we have, doctor?" Reed asked.

"Female, Caucasian, approximately thirty-five years old. She shows signs of sexual assault, although there's no semen. She has defensive wounds on both arms and legs, and it looks like she was punched in the face at least twice. But the knife wound to her throat is what killed her. I'd put time of death somewhere between seven and ten o'clock last night."

"What about her breasts?" Detective Reed asked, knowing the killer's unique signature.

"The right one. A clean cut," Reyes responded.

Reed lowered his head and took a deep breath. He examined the victim from a distance. Her appearance showed similarities to those in photographs distributed to police departments around New England. The most recent reported kill took place in New Hampshire nine weeks prior. If the killer followed the pattern, law enforcement would find four more victims in Massachusetts before the murderer moved on to another state. Reed turned to Doyle.

"Call Gaston."

Federal Bureau of Investigation Supervisory Special Agent Nick Gaston picked up his ringing phone. "Are you sitting down?" Doyle asked.

"Sergeant Doyle. It's been a long time. What can I do for you?" Nick asked.

"I hate to put a damper on this fine day, Agent Gaston, but we have a serial killer in our backyard."

Nick sat back in his chair. "Go on."

Doyle described the crime scene, relayed the coroner's findings, and reminded Nick of the pattern that the media-named Pathside Predator adhered to. "There will be four more unless we catch this bastard."

"I'm sending a team," Nick said.

"We could sure use Whitman on this, but I don't think there's an easy way to get him to the crime scene," Doyle replied.

"I'm calling him anyway."

Agent Bradley Whitman sat in his home-based office that consisted of a large corner desk, top-of-the-line computer system, all-in-one printer, and three overhead monitors. File cabinets lined the wall to his right. Beyond the cabinets sat his bed and then bathroom, the only room in his home with walls.

Bradley had bought the abandoned industrial laundry-service building ten years before just after taking the job with the FBI straight out of Massachusetts Institute of Technology. He shared his home with Rusty, a black-and-rust-colored Doberman Pinscher who had once saved his life as Bradley worked on a case.

Many doubted his ability to land a job with the FBI, but only those who did not know him well. As a boy, Bradley struggled with his physical limitations. An enterovirus struck him when he was six years old leaving both legs paralyzed. Instead of throwing himself into sports as he would have preferred, he threw himself into books, research, and problem-solving. When he was twelve, Bradley's parents took him on a cruise. The trip, having become more of an adventure than anticipated, gave him his first opportunity for independence and furnished him with the confidence that he could make a difference in the world. His position as an analyst with the Chelsea, Massachusetts, division of the FBI provided the perfect opportunity. His career had not always gone by the book, but he always strove to be the best and most reliable analyst in the bureau.

When he saw Nick's name pop up on his cellphone, Bradley answered.

"Bradley, I'm going to give you a chance to test that new wheelchair of yours."

"What have we got, Nick?"

"The Pathside Predator has made it to Massachusetts and struck in Revere last night," Nick sighed.

Silence.

"The cool-down period is getting much shorter. Send me the location," Bradley said and hung up.

Since the realization eight years prior that a serial killer roamed Connecticut, Bradley had followed the case. The murders seemed to stop after authorities found the fifth victim within the span of two years. Then, a year after the last Connecticut murder, another spree began in Rhode Island with five more victims in twenty-two months.

Once again, a year passed before a woman walking her dog found a body off the South Woods Trail in New Hampshire's Pisgah State Park, bringing the investigation in the purview of the Boston division of the FBI. After the coroner's examination and consideration of similar circumstances, police and FBI investigators concluded the murder connected to those in Connecticut and Rhode Island.

FBI officials assigned the New Hampshire cases to the Portsmouth, New Hampshire, field office with assistance from the Chelsea division.

Bradley remembered it being only nine weeks since the fifth body turned up in New Hampshire, indicating to him that the length of time had diminished for what investigators had called the one-year interstate cool-off period. If the idea of a standard cool-off period meant anything, apparently something or someone had made the killer move up their timeline.

Bradley hoped that, by rushing into another murder and changing their apparent modus operandus, the perpetrator made a mistake.

Bradley had received his new 4x4 all-terrain power chair three weeks before and had not yet tried many of its features. His new chair could climb stairs and slopes, ride on sand, and travel through snow, the perfect New England ride for an adventuresome paraplegic. With four oversized nubbed tires, he could use it on everyday floor surfaces and still take it through mud and negotiate bumpy roads. But, the chair came equipped with a smaller fifth wheel in back to use specifically on flat surfaces. As the fifth wheel lowered to the floor, the two large back tires lifted off the ground, allowing the chair to run on three wheels to save battery power.

West of Massachusetts Bay, Broad Sound collects the Atlantic Ocean and snakes its bounty through the bogs of Revere. City-owned Sea Plane Basin boasts two-hundred-twenty-seven acres of marshland, split almost through the middle by Salem Turnpike running from Revere to Saugus. Overgrown in some sections, Sea Plane Basin Trail winds through the tranquil northern section of the picturesque parcel. Stopping only because the Revere coroner's vehicle and a police cruiser blocked him from going further, Bradley drove his custom truck along the area's gravel path.

Using his truck's mechanical lift system, he lowered himself in his chair to the gravel, then rode the path on four wheels toward the police officer who stood a hundred feet from the vehicles. Showing his credentials to the officer, he turned the chair off the path and up the slight slope to follow the patrol officer to the scene. Bradley could feel the gyro system in the chair adjust the angle of his seat as he moved through the tufted terrain. The soft, sandy turf would have given him incalculable trouble in his old chair, but he moved smoothly and effortlessly despite the obstacles. The idea of such newfound freedom of travel exhilarated him.

The feeling soon waned as he spotted the blue tarp covering the victim's body. The forensic team continued their examination of the surrounding area as Doctor Reyes stood off to the side, alone, waiting for the go-ahead to remove the body. Bradley gave her a quick nod as he approached the scene, then turned his attention to Doyle. "Sergeant Doyle. It's been a while," Bradley smiled.

"Nice rig you've got there. Has it got a Hemi?" Doyle snickered.

Bradley smiled. "Where's Detective Reed? Nick said he'd be here."

"You must have taken different paths. He just went back to the car. He wanted to radio the chief. Are you ready to see her?"

"Yeah, let's see what we've got."

She wore only her socks and running shoes. Her matted long brown hair splayed across the moss-covered soil. Her bruised right arm lay outstretched as if she reached for something and her left arm rested across her body, her hand covering the offended breast. Spurts of blood from her throat, stabbed not slashed, painted her pale skin as if an abstract piece of art—*controlled chaos*, Bradley thought.

The position of her legs suggested extreme effort on the part of her attacker as they lay unusually wide open to show a small amount of blood that trickled down her inner thighs, evidence of penetration.

Bradley began to feel nauseated. Although he had seen many dead bodies, the woman's plight hit him hard, perhaps because she reminded him of his own fiancée, Doctor Laney Weaver, who shared physical likeness with the victim.

"Have we found any of her clothing or personal items? "Bradley asked Doyle.

"Nothing. Either everything got hauled out or nothing came in."

"What about footprints? One set? Two?"

Doyle shrugged. "It looks like the area's been cleaned. We'll have to wait and see what they come up with."

"Doctor Reyes," Bradley called, "were her legs moved into position pre or postmortem?"

"My best guess is postmortem. It's a strange detail. The way the blood dripped on her thighs suggests her legs were much closer together when she was sexually assaulted and judging by the light amount of blood, I'd say that also occurred postmortem."

"It is a strange detail, and a new one," Bradley whispered.

Bradley noticed a sweeping mark in the dirt near the victim's legs. He recalled seeing the pattern when he was a child, before his own legs became useless. Back then he would lie on his back in the snow, flap his arms, and spread his legs wide open again and again. Then he would stand up and look back at the angel imprint he had left behind.

To the doctor he said, "What do you make of this?" as he pointed to the angel skirt scraped into the earth.

"Very good, Agent Whitman. I planned to include it in my report. Look at her right sneaker."

Bradley saw what looked like a shoe print on the side of the woman's sneaker. He imagined how that might have happened.

Then he noticed a large bruise the size of a grapefruit on her left thigh.

"The killer placed a foot on her right shoe and pushed on her left thigh to spread them apart?" he questioned.

"As near as I can figure, yes," Doctor Reyes answered.

"But why?"

"That's not my area, agent. I only worry about when and how. It's up to you to discover the who and why."

"Thank you, Maria. Would you let me know when your full report is ready?"

"Of course, Bradley. I like the new chair." Doctor Reyes smiled, then prepared to take the body to the morgue. Bradley and Doyle moved out of her way and out of earshot.

"Of course, Bradley. I like the new chair." Doyle mimicked Maria's tone to Bradley.

"What's the matter with you?" Bradley asked.

"Ah," Doyle gruffed, "she won't give me the time of day. All because of a little misunderstanding."

Bradley's eyebrows raised. "What kind of misunderstanding are we talking about?"

"Just a wee bit of a mistake, a miscommunication, that's all." Doyle spat.

"I'm hearing a lot of misses here. What exactly happened, Doyle?"

"I asked her out to a nice dinner at Fork and the Knife, you know, the Italian place on West Broadway."

"Yeah, I hear it's great."

"It is. So, we decided to meet there at seven o'clock," Doyle said.

"Okay, so what happened? Were you late?" Bradley asked, sorry he got himself involved in the conversation.

"Sort of. I thought the date was for last night, Thursday, but she said it was on Tuesday. She waited for me for over an hour before she realized I wasn't coming. Then she left a nasty message on my cellphone."

"Oh, that's bad, Doyle. That's really bad. You stood her up!" Bradley's mouth formed an involuntary grin.

"Not intentionally. I tried to explain, but she wouldn't listen to me."

"Do you blame her? Jesus, Doyle, you're a cop. Details should not elude you." Bradley started to chuckle.

"Dammit, Whitman. This isn't funny. She's really mad. What should I do?"

"Move to another county," Bradley laughed.

Doyle clenched his fists as blood rushed to his face and his pale cheeks turned the color of rosé wine.

"All right, calm down. You're going to have a coronary, and I don't think Maria would tend to you right now." Bradley paused. "Here's what you do. Tomorrow, send her flowers with a sincere apology letter. The day after, send her chocolates with another apology letter. The day after that, send her a fruit basket with yet another apology letter."

"Jesus, Whitman, I'm a cop. That's a week's salary for me," Doyle said.

"After the fruit basket, she will want it to stop. She'll call you. That's when you really lay it on thick. Tell her what an ass you are and how badly you wanted to get to know her better. Tell her you know you don't deserve another chance but hope she will consider it."

"For chrissake, Whitman. You want me to get on my knees and beg, too?"

"If that's what it takes," Bradley said.

"I'm all done here, Agent Whitman," Maria Reyes called out.

"Thank you, Maria. I look forward to your report," Bradley called back. She flashed him a bright smile.

"Yes, thank you, Maria, ah, Doctor Reyes," Doyle stuttered.

The doctor shot him a steely-eyed glare. Doyle dropped his head and stared at the ground.

"Jesus, I felt that from here," Bradley smirked.

"I'm glad my misfortune amuses you," Doyle growled as he walked down the hill.

For multiple reasons, Bradley paid great attention to his surroundings as he made his way back to his vehicle. First, he wanted to make sure the investigators didn't miss anything. Second, he didn't want to run into an overgrown stump, and third, he wanted to see what his chair could do. The electromagnetic braking system never needed to kick in, as the terrain didn't allow Bradley to move swiftly. He guessed the slope of the hill at a mere fifteen degrees, and the chair specifications said it could manage up to thirty. He also didn't get the opportunity to use the four-wheel-drive feature, something he thought he might need to engage. All in all, the chair performed well for its off-road debut.

His white custom Silverado pickup truck had only needed minor modifications to accommodate the new chair. Already equipped with hand controls and a large enough lift for his chair to elevate him into the driver's position, the truck required alterations to the center console to fit the chair's larger tires, repositioning of the seatbelt system, and adjustments to the hand controls to suit the higher chair frame. He had been back on the road in less than two days after acquiring the new chair.

"Call Nick," Bradley said to his vehicle's handsfree cellphone system. Nick answered at the first ringtone.

"Are we sure it's the Pathside Predator?" Nick asked.

"As sure as we can be. The media still doesn't know about mutilation of the breasts, so it's highly doubtful we're looking at a copycat," Bradley replied. "That fact hasn't been reported anywhere, as far as we know."

"Alright. I'll let Davis know," Nick said.

Bradley and Executive Assistant Director Davis hadn't always been on the best of terms, but Bradley respected Davis's position in the department and hoped, in return, the director respected his. In Bradley's earlier days, he incurred multiple reprimands and, more recently, a six-month suspension for not following procedure and almost getting himself and a civilian killed. If it weren't for Bradley's former boss and good friend, Supervisory Special Agent Derek Richards, Bradley would no longer work for the FBI. Unfortunately for Bradley, Derek Richards retired two years earlier, and Davis had assigned Derek's job—the job everyone thought Bradley would inherit—to Nick Gaston.

Bradley liked Nick. They worked well together. Nick largely owed success in his position to Bradley, and Nick knew it. As awkward as Nick felt taking the position, he knew it the right thing to do for the team. If he had refused the promotion, Davis would have brought an outsider into the Chelsea headquarters, an unappealing prospect.

"Where are you headed?" Nick asked Bradley.

"Home. I'll wait to hear what the director's plan is. I have some reports to wrap up, and then I'll clear my schedule. When we get the go-ahead, I will be ready to give this my full attention. Whose team are you thinking to take lead?"

"Morrison's. He should be on the scene any minute," Nick said.

"Mara's not going to like that."

"Tony's team has more experience. She'll understand. Besides, we're going to need all of us to nail this bastard," Nick said. For a man who once constantly spoke crassly, Nick had usually managed to tame his vocabulary. Only when with Bradley did he allow himself to revert to his former unfiltered self.

"Call me when you're done with Davis," Bradley said.

Bradley no sooner hung up with Nick than his cellphone rang. The monitor on his dashboard showed the name, Derek Richards.

"Hey, Derek," Bradley answered.

"Is it true?" Derek asked.

"Is what true?"

"Is it the Pathside Predator?"

"Jesus, Derek. How the . . . where did you . . . ?"

Derek interrupted. "Is it?"

"I can't . . . you know I can't . . . How the hell did you hear about this?" Bradley asked.

"It doesn't matter. You just answered my question."

"For the record, I didn't say a word."

"It's too soon," Derek continued. "There's usually a year before the killing starts in a new state. Something changed."

"For a retired agent, you seem to know a lot about what's going on, Derek. Should I be worried about a leak in our operation?"

"No. You should be worried about one of the most prolific serial killers of our time operating in your backyard."

"Yeah, well, I am. We've got nothing concrete. Sixteen murders and not one piece of physical evidence. All we have is a profile."

"Hey, don't let yourself get overwhelmed. It's a murder investigation. You already know more about this unknown subject than if it were an unrelated crime. You're ahead of the game. Now, go work the case."

"Jesus, Derek, I miss your pep talks."

"I'm just a phone call away."

"How's Cate doing? I'm sorry I haven't been in touch. You know how it is."

"Yes, I do. Cate is doing great. She started back at her volunteer job at the REACH community a week ago."

"Wow, that's fantastic news. Zayt must be happy to have her back. Wait, so what do you do these days now that Cate is fully recovered?"

"I've got a couple options that I'm mulling over. What are you doing tonight? Can you meet me somewhere?" Derek asked. Bradley detected an edge to Derek's voice that suggested more than a social visit.

"Ah, it depends on Director Davis. We're waiting on the official word that the FBI will take lead on the case. A formality, I know, but I'm all about following procedure these days," Bradley said.

Derek chuckled. "That's good to hear. Meet me at O'Malley's at five o'clock." Derek disconnected the call.

Aside from being the former supervisory special agent of the Chelsea FBI headquarters, Derek Richards was like an older brother to Bradley. Derek's history with the bureau made him well respected throughout the country. Largely known for capture and conviction of two notorious New England-based mob bosses, Derek could also boast elimination of a corrupt group of elite politicians and businessmen and women responsible for multiple murders, high-stakes fraud, money laundering, and black-market activities. Bradley had been with Derek for both investigations.

Two years earlier, Derek and his wife, Cate, rode in a limousine with five friends on their way to celebrate Bradley's thirtieth birthday. They never made it. An angry ex-convict had planted a bomb in the tailpipe of the vehicle. That turned out to be Derek's last day working for the FBI. He retired to care for his wife, who suffered major injuries in the blast.

So, when Derek asked to see him, Bradley found it impossible to refuse. Not that he would ever want to.

Rusty greeted him at the door. Bradley knew Rusty hated to be alone, but he sometimes couldn't avoid it. He had not known how long he would be at the crime scene, and with the weather so hot, he couldn't leave Rusty in the truck.

"Hey, boy. I bet you want to go outside, don't you? Hang on a minute."

Feeling nostalgic, Bradley reached for a scrap of paper from his desk and wrote a note in black marker. It read, "Give Cate a hug for me." He attached the note to Rusty's collar with a red clip and opened the slider doors to his backyard. Rusty bounded out the doors and down the steep banking into what used to be an abandoned sandpit but more recently hosted the REACH community.

Revere Enhancement and Community Housing developed due to the need for housing the homeless, with an emphasis on veterans. The idea originated with Bradley's friend Zayt, a former Navy Seal and former homeless veteran. With the help of many, the idea came to life, housed more than seventy people, and provided more than three hundred meals daily to residents and homeless citizens. Cate managed the kitchen while Zayt worked security and another friend, Shea, handled the housing arrangements.

Before Zayt had a cellphone, he and Bradley communicated using Rusty and his collar as their messenger. They met through one such message. Not knowing to whom the dog belonged, Zayt—who then lived in the abandoned sandpit with other homeless people—sent a note with a plea for help after finding a fellow homeless friend murdered. Bradley answered the call. They'd been close friends ever since.

Bradley had just completed and emailed the reports he promised to his agent colleagues when his cellphone rang. Zayt apparently did not wish to communicate through Rusty that day.

"Give her a hug yourself. She's right here," Zayt said.

"Bradley, come see me. I miss you!" he heard Cate yell through the phone.

Bradley smiled. "There's nothing I would more like to do, but I can't. Listen, Zayt, I need to ask you a favor."

"Sure, dude. What is it?"

"I think I'm going to be quite busy for a while. I was wondering if I could count on you to take care of Rusty when I'm not around. I don't really know what to expect."

"You bet. Just let me know what you need. Hey, is everything okay?" Zayt asked.

"Yeah, just a big case. You'll be hearing about it soon enough. Thanks, man. I appreciate it. And, seriously, give Cate a hug and tell her I love her."

"Will do. You take care of yourself and be careful."

Bradley sat at his computer and searched the bureau's case files on the Pathside Predator. Knowing it possible that the killer might one day end up in Massachusetts, he had kept himself informed.

Attractive Caucasian women with well-toned bodies, the victims shared some physical traits. Their ages ranged between thirty and forty-five, although the older victims could have passed for younger. Financially categorized as upper-middle to upper class, the social status of each victim also showed similarities. Most of the early abductions took place on running paths or deserted side streets, but as time progressed, the unknown subject grew bold. Victims disappeared from parking lots, beaches, airports, and one from a crowded theatre.

Updated two years prior, the official FBI profile of the unidentified subject or unsub suggested a male age twenty-five to forty and in good physical condition. The report went on to state that the killer was organized, had an engaging personality used to disarm his victims, and presented as quite intelligent.

Bradley sighed as he read the profile. He could guess the rest without reading it. "The unsub is sexually motivated. He targets, stalks, stabs, and then sexually assaults his victims without remorse. He is a psychopath playing God."

"This tells us nothing." Bradley spoke out loud, a habit he had when he worked from home.

Derek is right, he thought. *Just work the case.* Bradley began to build his own profile of the current victim's killer. He closed his eyes and envisioned the crime scene. When he opened his eyes, he scribbled down the first thoughts that came to mind, a practice he had relied on many times in the past: *organized, persuasive, tidy, obsessive, smart, impulsive, confident, collector.*

When he compared his list to the official profile, two things stood out. First, according to the existing profile, one would not think the killer impulsive, yet Bradley felt sure that the positioning of the victim's legs fell into that category. The second and quite disturbing for Bradley concerned the report's omission of sexual overtones. Bradley had clearly seen evidence of sexual violation, yet sexual motivation did not register as a major trait in his mind. *Probably because the act was performed postmortem. Interesting*, Bradley thought.

Nick's name displayed on Bradley's phone before it began to ring.

"Hey, Nick."

"Sometimes I really hate this job," Nick said.

"Yeah, you say that at least once a week, Nick. I get it."

"Well, it should be you dealing with all this bureaucratic shit, not me."

"That's why they pay you the big bucks," Bradley chuckled. "What's going on?"

"I don't know. Davis is stalling or something. I can't figure out what he's thinking."

"What do you mean? It's our case, isn't it?"

"Yes. But that's all he's saying. It's like he's testing me or something. Like he knows something that I should know, and I'm supposed to figure out what it is. Jesus, I don't know."

"Nick, you're not making sense." Bradley said.

"No shit. I know that. But . . . fuck, I don't know what to tell you."

"What exactly did Davis say?" Bradley asked.

"He said it's our case. Get on it."

"That's it?"

"Yeah, that's it."

"Why did it take you so long to get back to me, then?"

"It took me this long to get that much out of him!" Nick said, exasperated.

"He didn't say anything about sending out a warning to the public?" Bradley asked.

"I asked about that. He wouldn't give me an answer. I think there's something wrong with him. Maybe he's losing it."

Bradley grew quiet.

"Hey," Nick said, "are you still there?"

"Yes, I'm here. I don't think we can waste any time, Nick. The media will get hold of this soon. Maybe you should have the public affairs office prepare a statement. Acknowledge the similarities but stress that it is early into the investigation. Then have them write a public warning. That way we will have it ready when we need it."

"Yeah. Good. I'll do that right now. We've got a lot of information coming in from Connecticut, Rhode Island, and New Hampshire. Not surprisingly, we didn't have all the details from those cases in the FBI files. I'm calling a meeting for two o'clock this afternoon. You'll be here, right?"

"Yes, I'll be there. Stay steady, Nick. Work the case."

"You sound like Derek."

Bradley chuckled. "I'll see you at two."

MOVING FORWARD

Bradley dreaded making the call he knew he should. Bradley's fiancée, Doctor Elaine Weaver, worked as a trauma specialist at Massachusetts General Hospital. Her close friends call her Laney. Undoubtedly this case would cut into the precious little time they got to spend together. Both understood the responsibilities of the other, but it didn't make things any easier.

They had become engaged a year and a half before and still hadn't discussed a wedding date. Bradley's mother, Lynn, continued to nudge Bradley on the issue. Both she and Bradley's father, Doug, loved Laney. And, as Lynn was prone to suggesting, grandchildren would be a wonderful addition.

He picked up his cellphone and called Laney.

"Hi, honey," Laney answered.

"Hi, how's your day going?"

"It's pretty quiet today. But, as you know, that can change quickly."

"Yes, I know. Speaking of that . . ."

"Oh, no. Nothing good ever comes after that phrase," Laney said.

"You're right, it's nothing good. I can't give you details, but you'll be hearing about it soon, I'm sure. It looks like I will be very busy for the foreseeable future."

"Should I be worried?"

"Not for me," he said somberly.

"Does this mean tonight's dinner is canceled?"

"I'm afraid so. If I can manage, I'll let you know. But I wouldn't count on it."

"Bradley," Laney sighed, "are we ever going to have enough time?"

Bradley glanced at the ceiling. "I hope so, Laney. I'll try to call you later." Feeling disappointed, he hung up the phone.

Bradley and Laney made a wonderful couple. But the things that made them completely compatible were the same things that kept them apart—devotion to duty, compassion for others, and an intense need to save and protect others. Nothing short of a drastic career change for one or both would alter their situation. Bradley didn't see that as an option for either of them. Which led him to think about Derek.

He wondered how Derek made the transition from his demanding job as supervisory special agent to stay-at-home caregiver. Bradley understood the immediate need that had arisen, and he would most assuredly have done the same if he were in Derek's shoes. But what about during the past seven or eight months since Cate became stronger and self-sufficient with her back to work and him not. He wondered how Derek handled it.

Bradley felt bad he never talked to Derek about it. In their conversations, he always asked about Cate. Aside from the standard "How you doin'?" greeting, he couldn't recall ever asking Derek how he was actually doing. He made a mental note to ask Derek that night when they met at O'Malley's.

At one forty-five, Bradley pulled his truck into the Chelsea Federal Bureau of Investigation parking lot at 201 Maple Street. He met Carl, the security officer, sitting at the lobby desk, despair pasted across his face.

"Carl? Is everything alright?" Bradley asked.

"Oh, hey, Agent Whitman. Yeah . . . I mean . . . ah, yeah, everything's fine."

"Come on, Carl. Spill it. What's the matter?"

"My wife's pregnant . . . again."

"That's great, Carl. Congratulations. Why the gloomy face? You love kids. How many have you got?"

"I have five, soon to be six kids. Six!"

"Ah." Bradley understood his anxiety. "Well, what does your wife think about the news?"

"She comes from a family of ten. She thinks we're just getting over the hump!" Carl said with a heavy sigh.

Bradley chuckled. "Come on, Carl. You should be celebrating. What's going on?"

"I don't know if I can afford another one. They're not cheap, you know."

"Let me ask you something, Carl. When is the last time your kids went hungry?"

"Never."

"When is the last time your kids didn't own any shoes?"

"Never."

"When is the last time your kids had to sleep in the streets because they didn't have a roof over their head?"

"Never."

"When was the last time you hugged your kids?"

"This morning, before I left for work."

"And, when is the last time your kids made you smile."

"This morning, before I left for work."

"Seems to me you and your kids have everything you need, Carl, except for one thing."

"What's that?"

"Another kid. Congratulations, Carl. Don't worry, things have a way of working out."

"Thanks, Agent Whitman." Carl smiled.

Bradley took the elevator to the eighth floor. The doors opened into a conservatively decorated foyer. The floor boasted the FBI seal with the agency's motto, Fidelity, Bravery, and Integrity. The long hall straight ahead led to the end of the building and Nick Gaston's office. On the immediate left, a pearled glass partition created a false sense of privacy for the four teams of agents who shared the large room referred to as the bullpen.

Beyond the partition came the two interrogation rooms, each with one glass wall to allow viewing from the hallway, separated by a room not visible from the hall and used for listening to interrogations through a speaker system. A conference room, briefing room, and bathrooms lay across the hall on the right. Outside Nick's office sat his executive assistant, Hazel Hadley. Hazel had been with the bureau for more than thirty years and worked for Derek as well as others before him.

Because Nick had sounded a little frazzled on the telephone, Bradley decided to check on him before the meeting.

"Hello, Hazel. You look lovely today," Bradley said as his chair quietly moved down the carpeted hallway.

"Agent Whitman, thank you. How nice to see you. Is he expecting you?" Hazel asked.

"No. I just thought I would see if he needed anything before our meeting."

"Let me tell him you're here." Hazel picked up the phone, pressed a button, softly spoke into the phone, then hung up.

"You can go right in, Agent Whitman."

Bradley had tried to get Hazel to call him Bradley, but she insisted on using a person's formal title when conversing. *Maybe that's why Derek would never call her by her first name,* Bradley thought. She was Hazel to everyone in the building, other than Derek. He always called her Mrs. Hadley.

"Hey, Nick," Bradley said as he rolled into the office then noticed Nick rubbing the back of his neck and pacing behind his desk. "Uh, oh, what's wrong?"

"Davis has fallen off the face of the earth, Bradley. The guy who's in my face 24/7 is a ghost just when I need him most. I don't know what's going on."

"I'll admit, that's odd. But maybe he's busy with another case. Just give it a little time, and he'll be driving you crazy again before you know it. In the meantime, we've got a serial killer to catch. Do you need me to do anything in this meeting?"

"Yeah. I want you to describe the crime scene and give the profile," Nick said.

"Okay, I can do that. But, about the profile . . . " Bradley paused, trying to think of the best way to word what he wished to say.

"What about it?"

"I don't trust it. I mean, most of it is okay, but I don't think our unsub fits into the Ted Bundy mold," Bradley said, referring to a notorious 1970s serial murderer dubbed the Campus Killer by the media. "And that's what the current profile is."

"Why?" Nick had learned to give Bradley a wide berth. Bradley tended to see things differently than most others even if those others were the best in their respective fields. Nick didn't know how Bradley did it, but he knew to respect that he could.

"Just a couple of minor things, really. But I'd like to scrap the pre-existing profile and work this as a solitary case. There may be a danger here of pre-formed opinions of the type of suspect we are looking for. I don't want to rule out any possibilities."

"Just work the case," Nick smiled. "Alright, give us your profile as it stands now. Let's go."

Bradley and Nick made their way to the crowded briefing room. Not one chair sat empty, and several agents stood in the back of the room.

"It looks like there is some interest in this case," Nick smirked as he walked to the podium in front of the whiteboard.

"Okay," Nick began. "I'm sure you are all aware of the woman found murdered along Sea Plane Basin Trail. And to answer the question I'm sure is coming; yes, we do believe this is the work of the so-called Pathside Predator. The FBI has jurisdiction in this case because the killer has crossed state lines.

"Agent Whitman is going to tell us about the scene and give us an early profile of the unsub. But before he does, I want to make this very clear. All communication to any outside source will come from my office or the public affairs office. No one speaks about this case to the media, to their spouses, parents, or dogs. Am I clear?"

Quiet mumbling circulated the room.

"I'm sure I don't have to tell you how serious this is. Sixteen women have already died, and our killer shows no sign of stopping. Agent Whitman, tell us what we've got so far."

Bradley moved his chair closer to the podium. He didn't use notes.

"At seven ten this morning, we received a call from the Revere Police Department regarding the discovery of a woman's body in a sparsely wooded area off the north side of Sea Plane Basin Trail. Our Jane Doe victim has yet to be identified. She is a white female, approximately thirty-five to forty years old, brunette, with a single knife wound through her carotid artery. Bruises on her face suggest her attacker punched her multiple times, killed her, then assaulted her sexually in what looked to be a brutal fashion although no semen could be found on the victim. Bruises on her arms indicate she fought for a short time before becoming incapacitated. The coroner determined the time of death between ten o'clock and midnight last night. And yes, PP did take a trophy: her right nipple."

Bradley stopped to collect his thoughts. He hadn't intended to include the next bit of information, but he couldn't see how it could hurt.

"The positioning of her body, postmortem, differs from existing PP victims. Our perpetrator went to great lengths to forcibly spread our vic's legs to a specific position resembling a gymnast move called the splits. This could mean either our victim or our unsub relates to something to do with gymnastics, cheerleading, or anything that would require this move.

"Now, I'm sure you have read the existing profile of the Pathside Predator, but I would caution you not to exclude any possibilities based on that profile. This is a smart, highly organized and persuasive individual who obsesses over details known only to our unsub, and as you probably know given the profile, likely plans to kill four more Massachusetts women before moving on."

Bradley backed his chair away from the podium to allow Nick to move back in.

"Tony's team will take lead on this investigation, but we will need everyone to do their part. We've got stacks of reports to go through. There's a pile on the table here for each team, pick them up before you leave. All information will funnel through Tony and Bradley. Mara, get with Tony. I'm going to need you to take his existing case load. Okay, let's get to work."

When Nick said Tony would take lead on the case, Mara's lips pursed and she began to tap her foot on the floor. But hearing the news she would be taking Tony's existing case load threw Mara to a place Bradley had never seen her go. She slowly stood and, extending her five-foot-eight-inch frame, crossed her arms across her chest and glared at Nick with a clenched jaw and flared nostrils. Her reddened complexion corroborated Bradley's supposition about her emotions.

The room emptied, leaving only Nick, Bradley, and Mara. Bradley quickly stated, "Ah, I've got some things to wrap up," and hurried out of the room. He shut the door behind him.

It had taken Nick a long time to acknowledge his feelings for Mara. As with many FBI agents male and female, the job got in the way of having a meaningful relationship, especially early in a career. Nick and Mara had been together for nearly two years and managed to separate their work and professional relationships until then, thought Bradley as he left the room. He couldn't help but wonder if Nick's decision to keep Mara away from the case was personal.

Bradley made his way to Nick's office and waited.

"Can I get you anything while you wait, Agent Whitman?" Hazel asked.

"No, thank you, Hazel. But Nick may have a bit of a headache when he returns," Bradley grinned.

Minutes passed before Nick lumbered down the hall towards Hazel's desk. He stopped short when he saw Bradley waiting for him.

"Hazel, could I have some water and ibuprofen please?" Nick asked before advancing to his door.

"After you." Nick swept his arm as a gesture for Bradley to enter his office.

Hazel followed the two men into the room, placed a bottle of water and a foil packet containing ibuprofen on Nick's desk, then left.

"Well, that must have been fun," Bradley said.

"What do you want?" Nick said abruptly.

"I'm just here for support. You did the right thing. Mara is the junior agent. She'll get over it."

Nick sighed and tore into the foil pack. "If you need anything, I'm going to be here until four-thirty." Bradley said before leaving Nick to his misery.

As he made his way to his desk, Bradley saw Mara near Tony's station. Arms held out in front of her like a forklift, she stood at his desk while Tony filled them with file folders. Sighing heavily with each stack Tony added, she made no attempt at hiding her disappointment.

"Thank you, Mara. I know this sucks, but there's no agent I trust more than you to take care of my cases," Bradley heard Tony say as Bradley made his way to his own desk on the far side of the room.

Mara's face softened. "Thank you, Tony. I appreciate you saying that."

"Well, I mean it. Let me know if you need anything else," Tony said.

Mara nodded and carried her load back to her desk. Bradley detected a faint smile on her face.

One of the reports Bradley completed to clear his workload earlier in the day had been assigned to Tony and thus belonged to Mara. The report concerned two Boston area schools that received letters threatening an act of violence on school grounds.

The vague text of the letters suggested the possibility of casualties. Bradley's report stated the letters, both received that morning, should not be taken lightly. He suggested that even though the typed notes held no specific threat, the carefully chosen words and tone held merit. He sent copies of the letters to the FBI Forensic Science of Communication department for further analysis.

Bradley turned his chair and made his way to Mara's desk just as she plopped into her seat.

Mara glared at Bradley before speaking. "I know what you're going to say. I'm the junior agent and this is standard protocol. But . . . excuse my language, this completely sucks!" She finished with a heavy sigh and slumped shoulders.

Bradley could not contain his boyish grin. "Actually, I came to talk to you about one of the cases you're inheriting from Tony."

"Oh," Mara frowned. "Sorry, Bradley. I guess I'm feeling a little bitter."

"Well, you know . . . " Bradley said, "you are the junior agent, and this is standard protocol."

Mara closed her eyes and dropped her head in defeat. "Sometimes you can be such an ass."

"Mara, don't let this bother you. We're going to need everyone on the Pathside case. It's not a one-man or one-woman job. Besides, you've got something more important to be thinking about right now. Which one of those folders contains the high school files?"

Bradley pointed to the stack she got from Tony.

"I don't know," she said as she rifled through the stack.

"Ah, here it is. Cambridge International High School and Charlestown Prep School. What's the case?" She opened the folder.

"Each school received a letter this morning. There." Bradley pointed to the top page in the file. "That's the note Cambridge International High School received."

"Wait. Why do we have this case? We don't have jurisdiction. Boston police do."

"BPD asked for our help. Actually, the headmaster at Cambridge International insisted on our involvement. Apparently, there are several children of highly placed foreign diplomats attending the school. Chief Hanson could hardly refuse."

"So the chief will want to take credit if things go well and can blame us if they don't."

Bradley shrugged his shoulders. "Go ahead, read it."

Mara silently read the all-caps, typewritten note.

THE MORE YOU TEACH THESE ALIENS ABOUT U.S. THE HARDER IT WILL BE TO STOP THEM FROM TAKING OVER. I'LL BE DOING U.S. A FAVOR.

"Huh. That's interesting how the writer used U.S.," Mara said.

"What is your immediate reaction to the letter?" Bradley asked.

"Well, the writer is educated, politically aware, serious in his or her beliefs, and seems intent on backing them up. He sees himself as altruistic."

Bradley nodded his head. "I always knew you would make a good profiler. How about the next note?"

SOMETIMES YOU GUT TO CULL THE HEARD. I'LL BE DOING U.S. A FAVOR.

Mara's eyes squinched. "If it weren't for the same second line, I wouldn't have thought it the same author."

"Why not?" Bradley asked.

"Well, it's much more to the point than the first. Not nearly as poetic. I don't get altruistic from this, I get anger. Maybe even revenge. And they spelled the words *got* and *herd* wrong. Not as educated as I thought."

Bradley leaned back in his chair and allowed a smile to grace his face. His eyes tended to sparkle when he was about to make a point.

"What?" Mara asked. "I know that look. What am I missing?"

"Read the first letter again and picture the person that wrote it."

Mara picked up the letter and re-read it. When done, she closed her eyes to help conjure an image of the author in her head.

"Okay," she said.

"Now picture that same person writing the second letter and read it again."

Bradley watched Mara's expression morph from skepticism to understanding.

"Oh, my God," she uttered.

"How does it read to you now?"

"Sometimes you need the guts to cull those who are being heard."

Bradley furrowed his brow. "Exactly. Poetic, altruistic, and educated. And probably determined. I sent both letters to the FSC for further analysis."

"Is this it? Is this all we have?" Mara asked.

Bradley nodded somberly.

"Where do we start?"

"With the profile. You said it yourself. He's politically aware and obviously upset about a sector of people who he perceives have been or are being heard. It screams white supremacy, but there could be another motivating factor."

"Are we sure our author is male?" Mara asked.

"Not one hundred percent, but if I were a betting man, I would put a chunk of cash on it. Start with the state house. Find out if there is anything happening that would outrage our guy. Then check the newspapers, both local and national. Concentrate on political processes that have occurred due to protests, rallies, etcetera. Find out which organizations are speaking the loudest and which are gaining momentum. As easy as it would be to think this is racially motivated, it could be politically, socially, or even financially driven."

"I'll see what's happening with immigration issues. That seems to be a high priority for him," Mara said.

"Absolutely. And make sure you keep BPD in the loop." Bradley reached toward Mara and placed his hand on her forearm. "I don't think we have a lot of time before he strikes, Mara. The police department has increased security at the schools, but they can only do so much. I'll give you as much help as I can, but you should wrangle an intern or two before they get eaten up by the Predator case."

"Good point. Thank you, Bradley." Mara leapt from her chair and hurried out of the room.

"See if Earl Waters is still working as an intern," Bradley yelled to her back.

Mara waved her hand in response as she rounded the partition into the hallway.

On the way back to his desk, Bradley wondered about Earl. He had worked with him almost two years earlier during the

Vincent Vega case. He remembered Earl as a bright, young, organized individual yet he had no idea if Earl still interned or worked for the FBI. After all those years, Bradley realized how little he knew about the daily activities inside Chelsea headquarters. For the first time, it saddened him.

Although not his responsibility to examine the documents, Bradley spent the next ninety minutes scanning police and coroner reports from Connecticut, Rhode Island, and New Hampshire. Nick would expect him to sit in on the briefings, so he would likely receive the same information again. But somehow, he felt superfluous repetition could be helpful. The more he knew about the crime scenes the better his developing profile of the unknown subject.

Just before four-thirty, Bradley texted Nick and reminded him he would be leaving soon.

What's so important? Nick texted back.

Meeting Derek. Bradley replied.

Damn I miss him. Nick replied.

A snicker escaped Bradley's lips. He understood exactly how much Nick missed Derek.

O'Malley's stood along Route 16 halfway between Medford, where Derek lived, and FBI headquarters. Bradley arrived ten minutes early to a packed parking lot. Having to find a space in the lot next to the restaurant, he trundled in his chair across the two lots wondering if there would be an unoccupied table inside.

"Mr. Whitman?" asked the hostess as he came through the door.

"Yes," Bradley replied, surprised to be expected.

"Please, follow me," she smiled and led him to a table in the far corner of the restaurant where Derek sat waiting for him.

"You're early," Derek smiled.

"Not so much as you," Bradley pointed out as he positioned his wheelchair into the space left open for him.

"I was in the area. I figured it didn't make much sense for me to go home and then come back. It's good to see you, Bradley."

"You too, Derek. You're looking good . . . rested. Maybe even relaxed." Bradley grinned.

"Yeah, well, two years away from the bureau will do that for you. How's Laney?"

"She's great. Busy as ever. How does Cate like being back to work?"

"She's loving it. It's all she's been talking about for the last few months. . . wanting to get back there."

"What about you, Derek? How have you been doing? I always ask you about Cate, but. . ."

"I'm good. It's been hard to watch Cate go through this, but I'm glad I could be there for her. More than glad—grateful."

"You gave up a lot," Bradley stated.

Derek shook his head. "All I gave up was a job. This whole experience has put things in perspective for me. I mean, I know the job is important, but you need to find balance. I learned that the hard way."

The waiter interrupted. "Can I get you something to drink?" he asked as he handed out menus.

"I'll have a Coke and a cheeseburger, medium rare," Derek said.

"Same here," Bradley replied.

Collecting the menus, the waiter smiled and walked away.

"I'm sorry I wasn't around more for you and Cate. I should have been." Bradley sheepishly looked down at the table.

"You've got to stop doing that, Bradley."

"Doing what?"

"Taking on the problems of the world as if they are your own. You've been doing that ever since I've known you. It's too much. I'm surprised you don't have an ulcer."

"Well, if it makes you feel any better, I have developed some digestive issues," Bradley smirked.

Chuckling, Derek decided to change the subject.

"What are the odds of catching the Pathside Predator?" he whispered.

"Not good."

Derek let out a sigh. "I've never heard you so pessimistic about a case."

"We don't have any evidence. Zero. All we have is a profile that could fit any of the dozens of today's active serial killers. And we're not getting any help from Director Davis. Nick is doing his best to coordinate between the state agencies, but without Davis, it's slowing us down."

Derek sat back in his chair and dropped his hands in his lap. He stared at Bradley as he tried to decide just how much to tell him.

"What? What is it?" Bradley asked.

"Director Davis is sick. He's leaving the bureau."

Bradley opened his mouth to speak, then paused to collect his thoughts. "When? Who's going to take his place?"

"I am."

Bradley's eyes darted open, wrinkling his forehead. Without saying a word, he leaned back in his wheelchair.

Derek asked with raised brows, "Speechless?"

"I guess I am. What does Cate think?"

"It was her idea that I reach out to the bureau to see if I could return. I think she's tired of me being home all the time." Derek grinned.

"But executive assistant director? You don't just step into that job, Derek. How long have you been talking to Davis?"

"I went to see him about two months ago. We were talking about other positions when he got the final word on his health. He recommended me to take his place. They offered me the job. This morning, I accepted it."

Derek watched as a broad smile replaced Bradley's shocked expression.

"Well, congratulations, Director Richards." Bradley reached his hand over the table to shake Derek's. "You're going to make one hell of a director. When do you start?"

"Right away. Davis is going to help with the transition as much as he's able. I'll have to be in Washington for a little while. But I took the job with the stipulation that I could mostly work out of the Chelsea office. I'll have to fly to DC once or twice a month, but Cate and I will work it out."

"What's wrong with Davis?"

"Stage four lung cancer. He's been sick for a while, going through treatments, but he's still been working hard. He just can't anymore," Derek sighed.

"Why did they wait so long to find his replacement?" Bradley asked.

"Davis told me that until I called two months ago, they had a replacement in mind. He's been trying to talk me into taking the job for the past month."

"What finally made you decide to take it?"

"The Pathside Predator."

Their burgers arrived, and they ate while catching up on each other's families. When the waiter cleared the dishes, Bradley leaned forward.

Gingerly, Bradley asked, "So, when we spoke this morning, had you accepted the job yet?"

"No. I hung up with you and phoned Davis."

Bradley didn't know how he felt about that. "Derek, I didn't force you into that decision, did I? I mean, I know I must have sounded frustrated, but I hope you didn't. . ."

"Jesus, Bradley." Derek shook his head. "No, it had nothing to do with you. I'm doing this because it's what I want. You are not responsible for other people's decisions." Derek paused, leaned forward, and then continued. "I thought we were beyond this. I thought after the Joshua incident you took the weight of the world off your shoulders. But you haven't, and it's not healthy, Bradley."

"Come on, Derek. It was just a question."

"No, for most people it's just a question. For you it's a slippery slope. And you know it."

Bradley sat quiet, averting his eyes from Derek's.

Derek continued, "I need to know you can keep yourself in check. I need to know I can trust you."

"Yeah, I know." Bradley showed a faint smile. "You're right, slippery slope. I did ask you to let me know if I ever skated the edge. Sometimes in my frustration the boundaries close in on me. Thanks for the reminder."

"You're a pain in the ass, Bradley Whitman," Derek grinned.

"I'm having a good day. That's only the second time today I've been called an ass," Bradley laughed.

Bradley hadn't thought about Joshua in months, but he did as he drove away from the restaurant. Sometimes, when showering and soaping over the knife wound on his shoulder or the gunshot wound on his leg, he relived those frightening moments. But he didn't usually think about how he put himself in that dangerous predicament. He did after his conversation with Derek. At the time of the Joshua incident, he had hidden his intentions from Derek—lied about his plan to use himself as bait for the murderer. He almost got himself and his friend Zayt killed that night.

He met Laney while working the Joshua case. He couldn't help but smile as he thought about her. "Call Laney," he said using his truck's handsfree cellphone capabilities.

"I didn't expect to hear from you," Laney answered.

"I wasn't sure how the day would go. Are you busy?"

"No. I'm just sitting down to eat. Are you hungry?"

"I just had dinner with Derek. Can I come see you?"

"Well, I don't know. You canceled dinner with me to have dinner with Derek? How should I feel about that?" Bradley could tell Laney held a faint smile as she spoke.

"I'll explain when I get there, and I promise to make it up to you."

"Ah, dessert," Laney laughed.

"I'll see you in about half an hour."

Bradley disconnected the call and said, "Call Zayt."

"Hey, dude. What's up?" Zayt answered.

"Can you take care of Rusty? I may not be going home tonight." Bradley said.

"Yeah, sure, no problem. Do what you have to do."

Bradley smiled, "Thanks, Zayt."

Bradley stopped at Mike's Pastry, known for Italian sweets, and bought an assortment of their famous cannoli.

Laney's face brightened when she saw the cardboard box on Bradley's lap.

"You didn't," She smiled.

"I did. I told you I would make it up to you," he grinned.

"Don't think you're getting off that easy."

Laney lived in a two-bedroom apartment on Canal Street, a mile from Massachusetts General Hospital. Her contemporary décor, the visual appearance Bradley did not care for, was well suited for his purposes. Her white chairs and couch had no arms, and the firm cushions made it easy to maneuver from his chair to a seat.

The black and white tiled floor gave the space a clean and elegant feel, although it sometimes made Bradley feel like a pawn traveling across a chess board. The floor-to-ceiling windows in her eighteenth-floor living room provided a beautiful view of Boston Harbor. Bradley never asked Laney how much she paid for the apartment, but he concluded it would probably take his entire month's salary to cover the rent.

"Are you staying?" Laney asked casually.

"If you want me to," he smiled.

Laney lifted the box of treats from Bradley's lap and placed herself there instead.

She leaned into him, her breasts cupping his chin, then tilted her head down to reach his lips. Bradley wrapped his arms around her, pulling her to him, their tongues twirled together like a dance-floor waltz.

When they came up for air, Laney whispered, "Take me to bed."

Bradley eagerly reached for the throttle on the chair, knocking the box of pastries from Laney's hand and landing the box upside down but unopened onto the floor. He did not stop to pick it up.

Laney climbed off Bradley's lap and onto the bed. She watched as Bradley lowered the arm of his chair and swiftly, using his exceptional arm strength, moved his upper body onto the bed. He then lifted each leg and placed them on the mattress before using his arms to position himself beside her. He made it look effortless, Laney thought.

Each grappling with the other's clothing, stopping only for tongue trysts, their breathing grew quick and full of anticipation. Bradley stripped Laney of her undergarments. He placed her on her back, covered her with his body, then tickled her nipples with his wandering tongue. His thick biceps flexed as he lifted his body, slid down her slim, toned abdomen and scattered tender kisses on her silky smooth skin.

Inching lower, he then swept her inner thighs with his lips before gently spreading her legs wider, leaving her womanhood unguarded from his intentions. A light touch of his tongue brought a moan to her lips, a gentle kiss sent chills to her spine, and then his skillful oral onslaught caused her body to tremble with desire. His cadence, determined by her arousal, ceased as her climax sat at the tip of his tongue.

"Oh, God, Bradley," she whispered in sensual agony.

Another light touch, another jolt through her body. He controlled her crest until the wave broke free. Then he devoured her.

Having completely satisfied her, Bradley laid his head on Laney's thigh, and she stroked his hair. He rested for a moment before retracing his journey—sliding himself up her satiated body, his tired tongue leaving swirls on her pelvis, stomach, breasts, then neck.

Laney felt his readiness as he leaned in for a kiss. She wrapped her arms around him and rolled him onto his back. His legs not completely following, she gently moved them to lie flat. She straddled him and eased herself onto him, watching as his chest arched and his chin reached for the sky. Her motion matched his hunger as each discovered the other's longings. First slow and easy, contracting her muscles to increase his pleasure, then harder, faster. When the need to burst consumed him, he grasped the small of her back and pulled her tight until release coursed through him, and she climaxed for the second time.

She lay on his chest, the two still attached, a warm trickle flowing from her. The warmth of his body dug deep into her heart. She could not imagine living a life without Bradley by her side.

The thought remained with her when, soon after, they sipped Merlot and ate crushed cannoli. Laney said, "What about August?"

"What about August?" Bradley asked.

"For a wedding." She glanced at him, surprised that she'd needed to explain what she had only thought in her head.

"This August?" Bradley's eyes widened. "Like, three months from now?"

"More like four months, but yes, this August."

"Okay. What did you have in mind?" Bradley asked.

"Just a small gathering, family and close friends. We could get a justice of the peace and have the ceremony at your house."

"My house? In the middle of an abandoned industrial park? Laney, I think we can find a more appropriate place than that to get married. Although, it *is* only three months away."

"Four," Laney reiterated.

"Have you talked to anyone about this? Your . . . friends?"

"Bradley, who would I talk to besides you? My parents are gone, I have no brothers or sisters, and most of my friends are doctors and nurses who have the same type of time constraints I do."

"Talk to my mother. She's been hounding me about when we are going to set a date. She would love it if you asked for her help." A thought occurred to him, and Bradley stopped himself. "Unless you wouldn't want her to help."

"Of course, I would. I love your parents. Do you think she would really like to?"

Bradley laughed. "Are you kidding? Other than giving her a grandchild, this would be the highlight of her life."

"Alright, I'll call her tomorrow," Laney smiled as she popped a crushed piece of espresso cannoli into her mouth.

DEREK TAKES CHARGE

Bradley left Laney's at six o'clock the next morning. He planned to get to the office early because he suspected Derek would do the same. He knew Derek wanted to tell Nick and the others about his new job before the official announcement.

On the way home to shower and change, Bradley called Zayt.

"Hey, did I catch you during your morning run?"

"Yeah, me and Rusty are on our third lap around the sandpit. Are you home?"

"No, on my way, but I'm only stopping to shower and change."

"Long night at work?"

"I spent the night with Laney. I may not see her for a while, so I wanted to spend some time with her."

"I heard about the Pathside Predator. It's all over the news this morning."

"Yeah. We're going to have to be at our best for this case. Can you keep Rusty for a while?"

"No problem. He'll be fine here with me."

"Thanks, Zayt. Oh, before I forget. Don't make any plans for August. Laney and I are getting married."

"The whole month?" Zayt laughed.

"I'll try to narrow it down for you," Bradley chuckled. "Thanks for your help."

"Be safe," Zayt said.

Bradley made it to the office by seven fifteen. The lights were on, and Mara sat at her desk.

"Good morning. Have you been here all night?" Bradley asked.

"No, I got here a couple hours ago. Hey, have you got a few minutes?"

"Of course. Let me get some coffee. Do you need one?"

"Yes, please."

Bradley noted that Mara sounded stressed, but he couldn't tell if it had to do with one of her cases or Nick.

He placed the coffee on her desk. "Here you go. What can I help you with?"

"It's the high school threats. We've scoured the statehouse records and the news feeds, and the only thing that stands out is the immigration tuition rate bill. It's being debated in the house and senate again, and it's still pretty controversial."

"Yes, I know about it. The bill would allow Massachusetts undocumented immigrant high school graduates to attend public colleges and universities at the lower in-state tuition rate."

"Right. Well, the opposition argues the bill rewards undocumented immigration. Both the house and senate have routinely stayed away from backing this type of legislation, but this time around it seems to have teeth."

"Who is leading the opposition?"

"They call themselves, get this, DAMIT—Dads Against Massachusetts Immigrant Tuition. Apparently, they figured moms did so well with the Mothers Against Drunk Driving MADD acronym," Mara scowled.

"Well, it does make its point," Bradley grinned. "Who's in charge of DAMIT?"

"A man named Bill Fowler, age forty-two. Lives in Somerville. He's married, has three children—a high school senior, a sophomore, and a middle schooler. He owns Fowler

Road Construction. You've probably seen his green trucks on the Mass Pike. He holds a lot of state highway contracts."

"Is this a real organization or just a bunch of guys who want to make some noise?"

"They numbered approximately six thousand at their last rally in front of the state house. They're already challenging the bill as unconstitutional on grounds it would be unlawful to use the citizens' tax money to subsidize undocumented immigrants."

"What else do you know about the group?" Bradley asked.

"It's rather loosely defined. Fowler is the most prominent figure. It doesn't look like there is an actual chain of command. Fowler leads, the others follow."

"So, you've got a guy who isn't shy about voicing his opposition to a cause, who also has access to construction materials, which I assume would include destruction materials. I'd say that's a damn good place to start."

"Oh my God, I didn't think about the dangerous materials, but you're right."

"Call his office and find out where he is going to be today. This is a guy you need to speak with face to face. Who have you got working with you?" Bradley worried about Mara going alone.

"Maybe I could get Jim. He would know what to look for, as far as explosives go. Do you think you could work that out with Nick for me?" Mara squinched her eyes.

"Me? Why not you?"

"Because I'm not speaking to him."

"Mara, you know he is just doing his job."

"Yes, I know. But it doesn't mean I can't make him squirm for a while." The corner of Mara's mouth tilted up.

Bradley smiled. "I'll take care of it."

Nick walked out of the elevator fifteen minutes later. Bradley followed him to his office.

"I like it better when you work from home, Bradley. Then I can at least drink a cup of coffee before you start bothering me," Nick said.

"Mara needs Jim to go talk to a potential suspect in the high school threat case. She asked me to clear it with you," Bradley stated.

"What? Are we back in high school? She couldn't ask me herself? Are you passing me the proverbial note? For chrissake, Bradley, this is the FBI, not Phi Kappa whatever," Nick growled.

"Are you done now?" Bradley elevated his eyebrows. "Because this is serious. We likely don't have a lot of time to figure this case out. Can she use Jim today or not?" Bradley asked, firmly.

"Yes, she can have Jim. What's the lead?"

"A construction company owner who has a bug up his ass about the immigration tuition rate bill. It's a good lead."

Nick rounded his desk and sat. He ran his hand through his hair and yawned.

"Are you alright?" Bradley asked.

"Yeah, just tired," Nick said as he looked up to the ceiling. "Hey, you talked to Derek last night, right?"

"Yes, we had dinner at O'Malley's"

"Did he say anything to you?"

"You'll have to be a little more specific than that, Nick. He said a lot of things."

"About me. Did he say anything about me?"

"No. Why?"

"He called me last night. Said he wanted to come in and talk to me this morning. He's coming in at eight o'clock."

Fifteen minutes, Bradley thought as he checked his watch.

"Okay. Why do you look so worried?" Bradley asked.

"Jesus, Bradley. Davis won't take my calls, and now Derek is coming to see me? This can't be good. Maybe Davis doesn't have the balls to fire me himself? Maybe Derek wants his job back and Davis told him to get rid of me? Either way, I can see the writing on the wall." Nick slumped in his chair.

"You didn't sleep last night because you think you're getting fired this morning?" Bradley chuckled.

"What else could it be?"

"Oh, I don't know. A thousand other things?" Bradley laughed. "When did you become so paranoid? Where did the confident egocentric Nick go?"

Nick's phone buzzed, which meant Hazel had arrived at her desk.

Nick pressed a button. "Good morning, Hazel."

"Good morning, sir. You have Derek Richards here to see you." Nick could tell she smiled as she spoke his name.

"Send him in, please," Nick responded. Then to Bradley he said, "He's early."

Derek came through the door wearing a freshly laundered navy blue suit, starched white shirt, and striped gray and blue tie.

"Nick, how are you?" Derek said as he held out his hand and smiled.

Nick stood and shook Derek's hand. "I'm doing great, Derek. You look well. Almost like you never left."

"Excuse me, I'll leave you two to talk about whatever it is you need to talk about," Bradley grinned, hiding his expression from Nick but hoping Derek could see.

"Thank you, Bradley," Derek said.

Bradley winked at Hazel on his way by, feeling good about the future of his FBI family.

He found Mara nervously checking her watch at her desk.

"Well, what did he say?" she asked Bradley.

"He said you can have Jim today."

"Great. What's Derek doing here? He looks great. I don't think I've ever seen him looking so healthy."

"I don't know. I guess you'll have to ask Nick," Bradley said.

Back at his desk, Bradley delved deeper into the case files for the first five Connecticut Pathside Predator murders. He believed the murders in Connecticut would hold the key to solving the present case.

The Pathside Predator's first confirmed kill, as far as the authorities could determine, had disappeared eight years prior while jogging on a quiet back road in Connecticut. When she didn't return home from her early morning run, Janet Marston's husband had gone looking for her along her usual route. He found his wife in a ditch beside the road, her body naked, throat slashed, and right breast mutilated.

Bradley stopped reading. While envisioning the husband finding his wife in that state, Bradley had developed a lump in his throat that made it difficult to swallow. He absently placed his hand on his neck and tilted his head back to stretch the muscles, then returned to the report.

The coroner determined Janet died quickly. According to the coroner's report, there was no sign of sexual assault. The investigators never found her missing clothing nor any physical evidence of her attacker. The report did conclude that blood would have splattered on the killer, as the crime scene itself held a large splatter pattern.

Barbara Baker, the second Connecticut victim, went missing from a wooded path forty miles from the area where the first victim died. Barbara's murder shared the exact details of Janet Marston's death, although the coroner noted Barbara displayed some defensive wounds on her arms. Barbara habitually walked the path with her dog Barlow, but the Labrador retriever had passed away three weeks earlier.

According to Baker's husband, the loss of the dog had sent his wife into a mild depression, and he had finally convinced Barbara to get back to her daily exercise routine. She never returned home. The investigator had written a note in the margins of his report. It simply read, *suicide watch for husband*. As it turned out, the note became a prophecy. The husband hung himself in the couple's backyard next to the empty doghouse.

Bradley placed the file on his lap and closed his eyes. The reports played out like a horror movie in his head, and he needed to purge it of the pictures. He knew if he expected to catch the killer, he would need to detach his emotions. But he found it more difficult to do these days, especially in this case, maybe because he would soon be a husband.

The coroner's report stated that Claire Dunston, Pathside Predator victim number three, had received multiple blows to the head and face to render her incapacitated but not unconscious, allowing her attacker to gain the advantage before stabbing, not slashing, her once through the neck severing the carotid artery. The investigators noted the blood splatter area significantly reduced from the previous two victims. Bradley guessed it a conscious decision made by the predator, altering the kill method to better suit his or her needs.

It wasn't until victim number four that sexual assault became part of the predator's modus operandi. Teresa Givens had not only been beaten, stabbed, stripped of her clothing, and relieved of her right nipple. The coroner found evidence of brutal sexual penetration which the killer performed after Teresa had died. Small amounts of blood and tissue stained her inner thighs, but no semen or DNA could be detected. Teresa had been last seen walking home from her gym two miles from her house, as was her custom. The authorities found her three days later in a remote wooded area, seven miles from her home.

Bradley felt a presence and looked up from the files. Derek stood at his desk. He wore a concerned expression.

"Are you alright?" Derek asked Bradley.

Bradley tossed the file folder onto his desk and ran his hands through his hair.

"Jesus, Derek. This is . . . I can't imagine . . ." Bradley swallowed hard, then resumed. "Have you read these?"

"Just this morning." Derek reached for a chair from a nearby desk and sat with Bradley. "I found it very . . . extremely difficult to detach emotionally. I count my blessings every day that Cate is still here with me."

"Derek, I'm sorry. I didn't think."

"Bradley, If I've learned anything in the last two years, it's how to talk about what's going on in my life. Cate and I have never been closer. You and I, we've butted heads a couple of times, but I want you to know you can talk to me anytime about anything. Not only you, but everyone in this building." Derek hesitated before continuing. "I'm bringing in an FBI psychologist, Doctor Kumar. She will be working with us on this case."

"A psychologist?"

"She's a consultant. She's an excellent profiler, Bradley. You told Nick yourself that you didn't trust the current profile."

"Well, yes, but I'm already working it. I'm off to a good start."

"That's great. You can fill her in when she gets here. That should be in about . . . " Derek looked at his watch, " . . . twenty minutes. I'll send her to you as soon as she gets in."

Bradley's face resembled that of a Boston cod about to swallow bait.

He usually worked alone. Occasionally he teamed up with Mara or Nick before Nick became his boss, but he preferred to work solo. But before Bradley could object, Derek stood to leave. "I've scheduled a meeting in one hour right here in the bullpen."

Bradley swore he saw a grin flash across Derek's face as he walked away.

Reaching for the final Connecticut file, he read about Diane Trindle. She disappeared when bicycling home after a yoga class along the Farmington Canal Trail running through the backside of her property on New Britain Avenue. The Farmington police found her bicycle leaning against a tree next to her defiled body in a wooded area fifty feet from the bike path. The forensic unit dusted the light blue mountain bike for prints but found only those of Diane Trindle, her husband, and her young daughter.

As in the four previous cases, Diane's husband found himself at the top of the suspect list but not for long. While his wife drew her last breath, he sat in a conference room with his client pitching an advertising campaign for a new line of women's self-defense products.

Bradley read the coroner's report before closing the file. Diane and every Pathside victim thereafter had also been sexually assaulted postmortem. It seemed, Bradley thought, that the Pathside Predator's signature had become established with Diane Trindle's murder, since the assailant, when finished, placed Diane's left hand over her bloody right breast.

Still holding the file in his hand, Bradley closed his eyes and dropped his chin to his chest. He didn't know how long he had been sitting like that when his eyes shot open after he heard the raspy sound of someone clearing their throat.

She wore a smile. Not the kind of smile when greeting a great friend and not a smile shown when finding someone in an embarrassing situation, but a warm, nice-to-finally-meet-you smile.

"Hello. I hope I'm not disturbing you," she said. "My name is Sahani Kumar." She reached to shake Bradley's hand.

Bradley reached and shook.

"Doctor Kumar, hello."

"Please, call me Sahani. I find the title doctor a bit formal."

"And I am Bradley. Bradley Whitman."

"How nice to finally meet you, Bradley."

"Finally?" Bradley questioned.

Sahani smiled again. "Yes. Derek speaks of you often."

"Oh, really. How long have you known Derek?"

She tucked her long silky black hair behind her right ear. "Oh, a couple of years. He tells me you are an individual with unique insight."

"Well, I'm not sure how to take that," Bradley chuckled. "The word unique could be used to suggest so many things.

"Please." He pointed to the chair Derek had left behind. "Have a seat."

"I assure you Derek meant it in the most complimentary way."

Bradley noticed a sparkle in Sahani's dark eyes, as if they had been sprinkled with gold dust. He needed only look into her eyes to know she sported a smile.

"Derek tells me you are a brilliant profiler," Bradley noted.

"Derek is a kind man."

"Well, Sahani, if you are going to be working this case, you will probably be here for a while. Let me show you around."

Realizing he still held Diane Trindle's file in his hand, Bradley dropped the folder onto his desk. He then used the twenty minutes before Derek's meeting to show Sahani around FBI headquarters.

Minutes before Derek's briefing, the bullpen began filling with agents and analysts from each of the eight floors of the building. Bradley placed himself at the far end of the room by his desk as Sahani moved to the opposite end of the room where Derek stood with Nick.

The chatter slowly ceased, and Derek began to speak.

"Good morning. It's been two years since I stood in this building and I can tell you truthfully, it's good to be standing here again. I understand there are a few new faces working here since I left, so for their benefit, let me introduce myself. My name is Derek Richards. I am the former supervisory special agent of this facility but left the bureau two years ago for personal reasons. I have recently been offered a new position within the bureau, and that is why I am here. As I just explained to Supervisory Special Agent Gaston, Executive Assistant Director Davis has retired, and I am going to do my best to fill his position."

What started as murmurs became shouts of a congratulatory nature. Someone in the crowded room started clapping, which prompted everyone else to do the same. Derek tried to quelch the outburst but succeeded only when it had run its course.

"Thank you. I appreciate your support. As you all know, the Pathside Predator has struck in Revere. If you've been following the case, you also know that we can expect another victim unless we catch this person first. I've brought in a consultant, Doctor Sahani Kumar, an FBI psychologist, to assist in this case."

Derek nodded to Sahani, and she stepped forward to speak.

"Hello. I'm very happy to be here, and I look forward to speaking with each of you. As Executive Assistant Director Richards has stated, I am here to assist in the investigation into the deaths of the sixteen victims attributed to the Pathside Predator. But my position here is not limited to profiling this assailant. I am also here to assist you, each of you, during this most difficult task.

"My goal as a psychologist is to foster positive personal growth and mental health," she continued. "This case will subject us all to horrendous details, details the gruesomeness of which are not shielded by experience or mental fortitude. Details that, once learned, will be impossible to ignore. It is my job to help you live with those details.

"My door will be open to anyone who wishes to talk whether about the case, personal difficulties, family matters, or to just chat," She concluded. She noted disinterest in the faces before her as she stepped back.

Nick stood. "Doctor Kumar's office will be on this floor at the other end of the building, Room 8B. I will be scheduling fifteen-minute introductions for each of you, beginning with the agents in my department."

Grumbling rolled through the room as Nick's meaning became evident.

"Is this mandatory?" Agent Tony Morrison asked.

"Yes. The introductory sessions are mandatory. After that, it is up to you whether you wish to continue to make use of Doctor Kumar's expertise," Nick stated.

"Nick, we've got work to do. We can't stop to have a chat," Tony said.

Nick opened his mouth to speak, but Derek beat him to it.

"This wasn't Nick's directive, Tony. It's mine." Derek stared directly at Tony.

Bradley was not caught totally off guard with the announcement. He thought it odd that Derek would bring in a profiling consultant. Now he understood Derek's reasoning behind it.

Griping continued as the agents left the bullpen to return to work. Bradley worked his way through the exiting crowd to reunite with Derek, Nick, and Sahani.

Looking at Derek, Bradley grinned. "I didn't hear any clapping after that last announcement."

"They rarely do," Sahani frowned.

"I didn't expect it to be a popular idea. But it is a good one," Derek said.

"We'll see," said Nick.

Before leaving, Derek stopped by to inform Bradley he would be traveling to Washington early the next morning and would be gone for a week. He intended to spend the rest of the day with Cate but would be available if needed. Derek also expressed trepidation about leaving Cate alone for so long. Bradley promised to check in on her when he could.

After the meeting, Mara left the office with Agent Jim Jansen, an explosives expert, to meet with William Fowler, owner of Fowler Road Construction. Before leaving, Mara asked Bradley if he thought Nick would have to sit with Sahani Kumar as well. She sported a great smile when Bradley answered, "Yes."

Mostly empty, the quiet bullpen allowed Bradley to read the ten remaining victim reports. All read similar to the one about Diane Trindle.

He had not yet received the report from Doctor Maria Reyes. He knew it too soon for her to have finished her examination. Maria sometimes frustrated agents, making them wait until the smallest of details had been thoroughly examined. She wasn't the fastest coroner in the Commonwealth, but she was the best. Bradley didn't expect the report until midafternoon.

Laney dialed Lynn Whitman's cellphone number.

"Laney? Is everything alright? Did something happen to Bradley?" Lynn asked in a panic.

"No, Lynn. Bradley is fine. We are fine. I'm calling because I wanted to ask you for a favor. I'm sorry I worried you."

"Sweetheart, there's no need to apologize. It's just that I don't get many phone calls during the week from you or Bradley, and when I do, it's usually not good news. What can I do for you?"

"Well, I was wondering if . . . and please tell me no if you really don't want to . . . I wondered if maybe . . . no, it's asking too much, never mind."

"Laney, for goodness sake honey, spit it out. I would be happy to do anything for you, as long as it's within my power."

"Well, I was hoping you would be willing to help me plan a wedding . . . my wedding . . . our wedding. You know, mine and Bradley's."

Laney still stammered as Lynn screamed into the telephone.

"Ahhhhhh! Yes, oh yes, yes, yes. I would love to help you plan your wedding. Oh, Laney, you have made me so happy. Does this mean you have set a date?"

"Sort of. We want to get married in August."

"What a beautiful time of year for a wedding. We should research venues right away. Next year's schedule will be filling up quickly. I know of a wonderful place in the . . ."

Laney interrupted Lynn's excitement.

"This year, Lynn."

"I'm sorry, Laney. I was so excited. What did you say?"

"This year. We want to get married this August."

Lynn's excitement turned to momentary silence.

"You mean three months from now?" Lynn asked.

Laney smiled. "More like four months, but yes."

"But, honey, every place will have been booked by now. The venues, bands, and even clergy will be booked solid, especially in August."

"We don't want anything big, Lynn. Just a small gathering with close family and friends. I suggested we have the ceremony at Bradley's house. That's when he told me to call you."

"Well, thank God I passed on some good sense to my son. An industrial park wedding, Laney? I'm sure we can come up with a better place than my son's tin can of a house. We could have the wedding here in New Hampshire at our house. Or we could talk to Cate. I'm sure she would have some wonderful ideas. What do you think?"

"I think I would be happy getting married to your son in a soup can if we had to. But I am open to suggestions."

"What is your work schedule like this week? I don't have any plans. We could meet for lunch somewhere. Maybe even ask Cate to join us if you would like."

"I would love to have her help. I have the day after tomorrow off work. Is that too soon?"

"Oh no, honey, we need to get started right away. I'll see what Cate is doing and get back to you," Lynn said. "And, sweetheart, thank you so much for asking. You've made my dream come true."

After hanging up with Lynn, Laney texted Bradley:

Your mother is very excited to help with the wedding. She is going to try to enlist Cate's help also.

Bradley texted in return.

There's no turning back now!

He added a smiling emoji to the text.

Laney sat back in her office chair. She suddenly felt slightly nauseous. She grinned and wondered where that feeling came from. *It couldn't be nerves,* Laney smiled, because she had no doubt she would be happy with Bradley for the rest of her life.

DARKNESS

Bradley still sat at his desk studying the Pathside Predator files when Mara stepped off the elevator with two men, the younger of the two in handcuffs. Bradley watched as she led them directly into Interrogation Room A. Both men seemed anxious.

Twenty minutes later, when Mara emerged from the interrogation room, Bradley intercepted her.

"What have you got?" Bradley asked.

"He's our guy. Excuse me, he is our kid. He's Fowler's son, a senior at Somerville High School. He planned to place four pipe bombs inside backpacks, pose as a student from Cambridge International High School to gain access, and leave the packs in restrooms throughout the building. That's all I've got so far."

"What about the father? Did he know about it?"

"No. When I showed him the letters, he recognized the statement as his own. He bristled at the thought that it might be his son, but he brought us to his home where he allowed us to search for evidence. We found bomb-making materials in his son's bedroom." Mara's demeanor softened. "Fowler is very disturbed about this. He's blaming himself. He decided to retain a lawyer, so we are done questioning his son until his counsel gets here."

"That was great work, Mara. You should be extremely proud of yourself. Does Nick know yet?"

"I called him from Fowler's. Jim stayed behind with a Boston Police Department detective and several officers. I'm going to go fill Nick in on the details now. You want to come?"

"No. This is your case, your victory. Great job!"

"I couldn't have done it so quickly without you, Bradley."

"Sure, you could." Bradley smiled and returned to his desk.

Laney sat at her desk, her cellphone cradled in her hand. She smiled as she read Bradley's text—**There's no turning back now!** She didn't want to turn back. She felt as happy as she ever had.

Her hand began to tremble. She watched it with fascination and wonder for several seconds. *Strange*, she thought. *Why would I be . . .* The sudden stab of pain behind her left eye blinded her, its onset as quick as a bolt of lightning on a scorching summer night. Thunder erupted in her head as her cellphone spilled to the floor. Her neck stiffened, throwing her head back as if to look toward the heavens. Her torrent of suffering ceased almost as quickly as it began. She fell forward, flopping unconscious onto her desktop.

After meeting with Nick in his office, Sahani Kumar cradled a file folder as she walked down the hallway toward the bullpen. When she spotted Bradley at his desk, she detoured to speak with him.

"Excuse me, Bradley. I don't wish to disturb you, but Agent Gaston and I have almost finished the scheduling for our introductory meetings with this department. Because you mostly work from home, Agent Gaston asked me to check with you as to the best time to schedule your appointment."

The prospect of a short, informal session with Sahani Kumar did not concern Bradley. In his younger years, his parents thought it important to give Bradley an outlet, someone to speak to other than his small family. He saw several doctors, and he never minded the sessions. Mostly he studied each psychologist's technique. As a boy, Bradley guilelessly groomed himself to profile people.

"Well, seeing I am here now, why don't we get to it? That is, unless you have other things to do." Bradley smiled.

"Derek told me you like to jump right into things." Sahani's eyes betrayed amusement.

"It seems Derek has told you quite a bit about me."

"He's very fond of you, as I'm sure you know. But rest assured, he didn't tell me anything that I couldn't surmise from our first meeting this morning. Shall we go to my office?"

The bleak room radiated detachment. Walls the color of wet sand surrounded the twelve-by-twelve-foot space, and the only furniture in the room consisted of a tan rectangular metal desk with a walnut veneer top and two office chairs with bright red cushions to sit on and lean against. Four cardboard boxes sat stacked in the far corner.

"I apologize for the uninviting décor. In time I will unpack and requisition a bookcase and file cabinet. So, please try to imagine a warm, sunny space with pleasant pictures . . . and the smell of spring." Sahani laughed as she added the last.

She sat in the chair in front of her desk, and Bradley rolled his chair to face her.

"That's quite alright. It reminds me of home," Bradley said before thinking.

"Really? How so?"

"Not so much the inside of my house, but the outside. You see, I bought an abandoned commercial laundry facility in a largely deserted industrial park." Bradley scanned the room.

"It's almost the same color as your walls, a little lighter maybe, and it is much larger. But the impression is the same."

"What about the inside?"

"It's quite comfortable. The best part about a metal building is that you don't have walls to contend with."

"Why is that?"

"Because of the beams, the I-beams." Bradley saw a questioning expression cross Sahani's eyes as her trimmed brows sank toward her lids. "The walls and ceiling are constructed of very strong steel beams that can support the roof, so no need for interior walls."

"Well, it sounds very . . . industrial."

Bradley chuckled. "Yes, it does, doesn't it? It suits my needs."

"Derek tells me you two have known each other for a long time."

Bradley grinned remembering the first time he saw Derek. He pictured him standing next to the cruise ship *Perth's* dinner table with the maître d' and wearing navy blue slacks and a blue oxford shirt. He wondered if Sahani knew what Bradley had come to realize. Derek only wore a blue shirt when he was concerned about something. If only Bradley had known that back on the cruise ship.

"I was twelve when we met. So I guess that makes it twenty years. We met on a Caribbean cruise."

"I can't picture Derek relaxing on a cruise. He doesn't seem the type."

Bradley laughed. "He isn't. He wasn't on vacation like the rest of us. The FBI sent him there on a case. Of course, we didn't know that when we met him."

"Who's *we*. You said *we* and *us*."

Bradley smiled again. "Have you met Cate?"

"No, but I've heard wonderful things about her."

"That's where we all met. I was on the cruise with my parents, and we were assigned to a dinner table with Cate and her sister Sheila. Holly and her father, Mike, and then Derek joined us on the second night. A table for eight. We became lifelong friends, and in Derek and Cate's case, lifelong partners."

"How nice you have stayed in touch after all these years. But I gather it isn't coincidence that you came to work for Derek."

"No. Derek knew I planned to apply to the FBI. I never asked him directly, but I believe he did everything he could to insure I would work for him once I graduated from MIT."

"And you are an intelligence analyst?" Sahani shrugged her shoulders. "Forgive me. I haven't read your file. You caught me off guard by wanting to have this meeting today."

Bradley liked the fact that Sahani Kumar did not know everything about his FBI background.

"Yes. I'm an analyst."

"Did you always want to be an FBI analyst?"

"No. I wanted to be an FBI special agent. But, because of my physical limitations, analyst it is." Bradley made sure to keep eye contact with Sahani as he spoke. He watched her eyes shift from his to his legs and then back again. She made no attempt to hide her curiosity.

"What put you in the chair?"

"A virus when I was six. When did you know you wanted to be a psychologist?"

Sahani paused, deciding whether to answer the question. "Not until college. I take it you knew long before you went to MIT that you would join the FBI."

"I decided my career path when I was twelve years old sailing aboard a cruise ship through the Caribbean."

The one overhead light in the room shone down on Sahani. It cast a shimmer on her bronze skin, leaving Bradley with the feeling that if he touched her at that moment, she would float away like a silk sheet in a high wind. He liked her. He liked talking with her.

Bradley asked, "Have you written up a profile of the Predator yet?"

"No. I try very hard not to come at things from a known perspective. I received and read the files yesterday. I hoped we could work on the profile together."

"In between your sessions?"

Sahani wagged her forefinger toward Bradley. "Not sessions. Introductions," she corrected.

"Ah, right. Sorry."

"My meetings are scheduled between eight o'clock in the morning until noon each day with fifteen minutes in between each. The rest of the day is for the Predator and open office hours. But I need to be here in the office, so if we are to work together on the profile, you will need to come to me." She raised her eyebrows to ask the question she did not wish to voice.

"Or we could use technology and meet over the bureau's teleconference account," Bradley countered.

"Yes, that is an option. But I despise technology unless it is a last resort."

"How do you feel about dogs?" Bradley asked.

"Dogs? I like dogs. Why?"

"Because I despise leaving my dog alone, and if I need to come to the office, he will be coming with me."

"You have a dog?"

"I do. His name is Rusty."

"Hmmm. Interesting. I didn't peg you for a pet person. Is that it? A dog? Is there anyone else of importance in your life other than your cruise ship friends and family?"

"Very smooth, Dr. Kumar. That was a very nice transition for delving into my personal life," Bradley grinned.

"It's Sahani, and I did not maneuver the conversation that way. it just presented itself," she smiled in return.

"I have a fiancée. Her name is Laney. Well, her actual name is Elaine, Dr. Elaine Weaver. She's a trauma specialist at Massachusetts General Hospital."

"Wonderful. Congratulations. When is the big day?"

"In three months," he grinned, "if we can pull it off."

"Why do you say that?"

"Because we just decided this morning. We put off picking a date because we're both so busy. But we'll figure it out," Bradley chuckled. "I'm sure my mother is on it already."

"Good for you. You can't let work get in the way of your happiness. I think I saw that stitched on a pillow somewhere," Sahani laughed.

Bradley nodded, then looked to the floor. His gravest concern about his upcoming marriage had a place as a cliché stitched on a pillow. And he knew the Pathside Predator would certainly disrupt his personal life.

"This is an exciting time in your life. A lot going on. Not the best time for this Predator case to drop in your lap." Sahani sensed a slight darkening in Bradley's demeanor.

Bradley lifted his head, his sparkling eyes steely and cold. "Is there ever a good time for a case like this?"

"No. There isn't. But it's much more difficult to think clearly when you see yourself in the victims. And when I say victims, I mean the women, the husbands, the children, and families of the Predator's chosen. And that is exactly what will happen in this case. To all of us. There's no getting around it. The best way to keep it from having long-term effects is to talk about it. Don't let it fester. If you let it fester without tending to the infection, it can destroy you."

Bradley softened his expression. He knew Sahani to be right. But he also knew he would not be seeing her in her office again unless it had to do with the Predator's profile. He glanced at his watch.

"Well, it seems our time is up," he said.

Sahani shared a sad smile. She, too, knew Bradley would not engage her help. It just didn't fit his profile.

The bullpen sat empty when Bradley's cellphone rang just as he finished packing the files from his desktop into his briefcase. He did not recognize the telephone number that appeared on his phone screen, but that was not unusual.

"Hello?"

"Hello. Is this Mr. Bradley Whitman?" the male voice asked.

"Yes, this is Bradley."

"Mr. Whitman, my name is Dr. Benjamin Abrams. I work at Massachusetts General Hospital with Elaine Weaver."

"Oh, hello Dr. Abrams. What can I do for you?"

"Mr. Whitman, I'm contacting you because you are listed as Elaine's emergency contact. I'm afraid I have some terrible news." A short pause followed. "We found Elaine in her office. She was slumped over her desk and unresponsive. We did everything we could. I'm sorry, sir. She's dead." A heavy grey cloud filled Bradley's head. He felt the denseness of it, the cool droplets of water it held. A thunderhead of vapor squeezed his brain.

He shook it loose, shook his head until the clouds dissipated, and determined he must have misunderstood what the voice on the phone had said.

"I'm sorry. I think I heard you wrong. Could you repeat that?" Bradley whispered.

"I'm sorry, Mr. Whitman. Elaine Weaver is dead. We did everything we could to revive . . ."

"No, that's not possible. You must be mistaken. You made a mistake. It's not Laney." Bradley's hands began to shake. The clouds returned and clapped with thunder at every word Dr. Abrams spoke.

"When we found her, she lay unconscious, and she never regained consciousness. Whatever happened happened very quickly. I'm so sorry."

Bradley could no longer control the muscles of his body. His cellphone dropped to the floor; the voice on the other end continued to speak but Bradley could not hear it. His breaths grew quick and labored, his face went the color of an unbleached bed sheet. He didn't notice when Nick came to his side, picked up the phone, and spoke to the man on the other end.

Bradley swayed in the storm's wicked winds. The relentless tornado-like swirl had him dizzy and disconnected from the world below—or was it above? He couldn't tell. Did he wish it to stop, or did he wish it to pick up speed and sling him into the heavens?

His face—something flew onto his face. He could see nothing but darkness, and his arms would not obey his mind's command to remove the offending blindfold. His neck craned back with the force.

Several moments passed before the squall grew weak and the tornado in his head reduced to a mere windstorm, yet darkness persisted. He willed his hands to move, making fists as his arms hung by his side, releasing the fists and repeating several times. He then reached for his face to clear away the debris.

When Bradley reached for the paper bag big enough to cover his entire face, Nick removed it. Bradley's breathing slowed, and a pink hue returned to his skin. He blinked his eyes to clear the clouds and saw Nick standing over him.

"Bradley. Can you hear me?" Nick asked frantically.

No response.

"Bradley. Come on Bradley. Can you hear me?" Nick repeated.

Bradley slowly nodded his head, his eyes glazed, his body spent.

"We need to get him to the hospital," Sahani said. "His heart rate is at a dangerous level. I'll call an ambulance."

"It will be quicker if we drive him. I'll get the lift van and meet you out front," Nick told Sahani.

Nick called Carl at the front desk to make sure the van wasn't in use by any of the departments in the building.

Harried and uneasy, Nick told Sahani, "It's in the garage. Meet me at the front door," before he opened the door and ran down the stairwell.

He quickly descended eight flights of stairs while thinking, *I can use the lift gate to get him in the truck, yeah, that will work. We've got tie-down straps for moving stuff. I can strap his chair down. Shit . . . I've got to call Derek.*

Back in the bullpen, Bradley blinked his eyes quickly, trying to regain control of himself. He felt numb as if he didn't have a body at all, as if the rest of his physical self had just then fallen victim to the enterovirus that took his legs. *Is that possible?* he thought. Then his brain began to remind him of his telephone conversation with Dr. Abrams. He shook his head, willing his brain to stop.

"No," he yelled. Surprised he could move his arms, he pressed the palm of his hands into his eyes. "No. Stop." He began pounding his forehead, hoping to eradicate the recent conversation from his memory. *If I don't remember it, it didn't happen*, he thought.

Sahani placed her hands one on each side of his head, covering his ears, to shield Bradley from his own beating. "Bradley. Can you hear me? You need to breathe. You need to concentrate on breathing. In. Out. In. Out." Bending over in front of him, she placed herself at his eye level. "Breathe. Breathe," she repeated.

Bradley's arms, numb once again, fell to his side. He suddenly heard a voice drowning out his brain. "Breathe," it said. "Breathe."

His response, "Why?"

Using the joystick, Sahani slowly directed Bradley's wheelchair toward the elevator. As they waited for the doors to open, Bradley looked up at Sahani and said, "She's dead. He said she is dead. I'm going to be sick."

He looked pale and clammy. He continued to have trouble breathing, and she knew he had an elevated heart rate. Leaving the wheelchair in front of the elevator, Sahani hurried to Bradley's desk to retrieve the small, empty, rarely used wastebasket and set it on Bradley's lap.

The elevator doors opened, and Bradley moved himself inside, followed by Sahani. He didn't know where he planned to go, but instinct told him to get into the lift. Sahani pushed the button for the first floor.

Carl stood waiting for them when the doors opened.

"Nick will be out front in a minute," Carl said to Sahani. "You hang in there, man. Just hang in there," Carl said to Bradley as he walked alongside them to the front door.

Nick screeched the tires as he stopped the van in front of the automatic glass doors. He quickly jumped out of the driver's seat, ran to the back of the van, and opened the doors. He pushed a button, and a lift gate folded down, then made its way down to the pavement.

"Okay, Bradley. Let's go," Nick directed.

Barely above a whisper, Bradley said, "I can take my truck."

"Nope. No way, buddy. You'll have to put up with my driving today," Nick said, trying to make light of the moment.

Nick expected pushback from Bradley, but it never came. As if in a hypnotic state, Bradley followed Nick's instructions and moved his chair onto the lift gate. Using the tie-down straps, Nick secured Bradley's chair.

As Sahani prepared to settle into the passenger seat, she asked Nick, "What about the office? I didn't see anyone left upstairs."

"Hazel is there. She can hold the fort until someone gets back. I'll call Tony and Mara when we get to the hospital. It'll be fine," Nick answered.

They hadn't traveled more than a mile before Bradley made use of the trash bucket in his lap. Sahani unbuckled her seatbelt and crawled into the back of the van to assist him.

"Is he alright?" Nick asked.

Sahani looked at Bradley. "Are you? Nick wants to know. He's worried about you."

"I'm fine," Bradley answered. His breathing grew more regular, and color returned to his face. "Just get me to the hospital. I have to see Laney."

"We're taking you to the emergency room." Sahani said.

"Whatever. Just get me to the hospital," Bradley snapped.

The emergency room sat mostly quiet as it was barely noon. There stood a man with a galvanized nail protruding from his face, a young girl with a dislocated arm, and Bradley who couldn't comprehend just how much his life had changed.

"Where's Dr. Abrams?" Bradley asked as they approached the emergency room reception desk.

"I'm sorry. Dr. Abrams doesn't work in the emergency room," the receptionist replied.

"I don't give a damn where he works. I want to see him now," Bradley growled.

Sahani stepped in between Bradley and the desk. "Excuse me. I'm sorry, but Dr. Abrams called Mr. Whitman about his fiancée, Dr. Weaver."

"Oh, yes. I'm sorry." The receptionist looked down at her hands. "I'll call him right away."

Bradley wouldn't budge. He insisted he would wait for Dr. Abrams right where he sat.

Sahani spoke quietly, "Bradley, we need to have someone examine you. You don't look well.

"Bradley ignored the assertion. His eyes focused on the hallway leading from the examination rooms to the receptionist's desk. His fingers gripped the arms of the wheelchair like eagle talons on a fresh catch.

"Yes, he's here in the emergency room right now." The receptionist spoke into the telephone. Her eyes darted in every direction except towards Bradley. "Yes, doctor," she stated to the muffled voice on the other end of the conversation.

"Dr. Abrams will be here as soon as he can," the nervous receptionist said to Sahani.

Reading her name badge, Sahani responded, "Thank you, Diane. But Agent Whitman needs to be examined. He had an episode. He hyperventilated and then became nauseous and sick. I'm afraid his blood pressure is at a dangerously high level."

Diane handed Sahani a clipboard and pen. When Sahani attempted to hand the clipboard to Bradley, he knocked it out of her hands and onto the floor, never averting his eyes from the hallway.

"Hey," Nick yelled. "Easy there, Bradley." Nick moved between Sahani and Bradley. "I know you're hurting, Bradley, but she's just trying to help."

Bradley turned his head and glared at Nick. His cold vacant blue eyes contrasted with his hot red brow. The veins in his burning temples pulsated to the sound of a distant hospital monitor.

"I don't need her help. I need Laney. I need to see Laney," Bradley snarled. "Just stay the fuck away from me," Bradley said as he forcefully pushed Nick with his right hand, catching Nick off guard and causing him to stumble into the receptionist's desk.

Before responding to Bradley's strike, Nick whispered to Sahani, "Go call Derek."

Sahani walked away.

"You get one, Bradley. And that was it." Nick planted himself in front of Bradley's chair, legs spread wide. His angry voice muted so only Bradley and the receptionist could hear, he bent down to meet Bradley face-to-face. "You've just assaulted two federal officers. Now it's time to listen to me. You will be examined by a doctor, now." Nick glanced at the receptionist as he stressed the point. "Then you will see Laney. I will make sure of it. Get your shit together."

Nick took a step away and stood to his full six feet. His gaze remained on Bradley's. Bradley slowly lowered his eyes to the floor.

"Diane," Nick said. "we would like to see a doctor now. Please send Dr. Abrams in to see us when he arrives."

The phone rang several times before Derek answered.

"It's Sahani Kumar. I'm afraid I have some terrible news." She paused. "Agent Whitman's fiancée has passed away."

"Laney? No." Derek went silent as his chest filled with dread. He asked, "What happened?"

"I don't have any specifics. We are at the hospital now. Nick and I are here with Bradley."

"Jesus. Bradley. How is he?"

Sahani could feel the concern in Derek's voice.

"He had some sort of episode. He hyperventilated and then got sick. We're getting a doctor to look at him."

"Yeah. His blood pressure will be high for a little while. It usually takes close to an hour before it's back to normal."

"This has happened before?" Sahani asked.

"Yes. He'll be somewhat disoriented. Please, Sahani, stay with him until I get there. Has anyone called his parents?"

"No. We didn't have any time."

"I'll take care of it. I'll be there as soon as I can." Derek hung up the phone. Derek sat with his head in his hands as Cate walked into the room.

DISSOLUTION OF DREAMS

The only thing worse than making the phone call to Bradley's parents would be if it were Bradley lying dead in the hospital, thought Derek.

Tears streaming down her face, Cate tenderly placed her hand on Derek's shoulder.

"Lynn? It's Derek. I'm afraid I have some terrible news," Derek said.

Lynn gasped before her trembling voice uttered, "Bradley?"

"Bradley is fine, Lynn. He's fine." Derek swallowed hard before he continued. "It's Laney. Lynn, Laney is dead."

"No. That can't be. I just spoke with her, Derek." Lynn's breathing grew unsteady.

"Lynn, is Doug with you?" Derek asked.

"It's not possible. No. What are you saying?"

Derek could hear her anguish. He envisioned Lynn processing the awful news.

"Lynn, is Doug with you?"

"He's outside. Mowing. This can't be . . ."

"Go get him, Lynn. Please. Go get him now," Derek pleaded.

Standing next to Derek, Cate placed her hand over her lips to prevent the sound of her grief from traveling through the phone. Derek reached for Cate's free hand and held it while he waited.

Moment's later, Doug's nervous voice asked, "Derek? What's going on?" Derek could hear Lynn uncontrollably weeping in the background.

"Doug, Laney is dead. All I know right now is she collapsed at work. Nick brought Bradley to the hospital. On the way there, Bradley went into hyperventilation. They brought him to the emergency room to get his blood pressure under control, but he is resisting. He's distraught, Doug. I'm heading to the hospital now."

Doug found it difficult to respond because of the lump that had formed in his throat. As he held the phone in his left hand, he reached for Lynn with his right and pulled her close to him.

"We're on our way," Doug said before hanging up.

Derek stood and wrapped Cate in his arms. Her body trembled, and her tears moistened his shoulders.

"We need to be with Bradley," Cate sobbed.

Derek cupped her face with his hands and swept his thumbs to clear away her tears. He knew what he had to say would be difficult for Cate.

"Cate, I think you should stay here. Bradley is going to need time to process what's happening. And . . . " he took a deep breath before continuing, " . . . someone needs to tell the others."

"Oh my God, I've got to call Sheila. And Holly." Cate dreaded the idea of delivering the news to her sister and friend.

"And Zayt," Derek added. "I'll call Zayt on the way to the hospital."

Derek held Cate close as memories of how he almost lost her raced through his mind. Only then did tears form in his eyes, thinking of Bradley and how much he had lost.

One year younger than Cate, Sheila experienced life with much buoyancy and adventure. While Cate cherished her role as wife to her one and only husband and her volunteer work with the homeless, Sheila found her match with her third husband, David Carson, and the shimmering world of Hollywood movies. Born into a wealthy family, David chose the entertainment business as his calling, and he became well suited for it.

David's most recent movie, *Maker's Mark*, held the honor of the Number 1 box office hit for thirteen consecutive weeks and might soon become one of the top ten grossing pictures of all time.

After transforming herself from a stay-at-home mother and Hollywood wife with maids, chef, and pool boy attending to her every need, Sheila found her footing in the Hollywood fashion scene. Her new boutique and salon, Elegance by Sheila on Rodeo Drive, provided top-notch individual pampering to women with considerable disposable incomes. Among the Hollywood elite. it had become the preeminent place to shop. But it was Sheila's lesser known offshoot business that she was most proud of.

Fashion Cents, a small store in lower-income outskirts of the fashion district of Los Angeles, featured bargains. Stocked with new and previously worn garments, shoes, and accessories, Fashion Cents offered individual outfits for any occasion: job interview, school dance, wedding. The cost depended on how much the individual could afford. Sheila hired two local women to run the place in her absence but made a point to work in the shop at least one day a week. Both of her businesses thrived, but only Fashion Cents gave her the deep entrepreneurial satisfaction she had craved for many years.

Sheila had just walked into the boutique on Rodeo Drive when her cellphone rang. The caller ID read, *Cate*. Usually happy her sister called, she wondered why something prompted her stomach to sour.

Holly sat back in her office chair. She stared straight ahead, silent, focused on nothing, with tears streaming down her face. Her conversation with Cate lasted only minutes, but the blow of her words continued to strike. "Laney is dead."

They were so good together, she thought. *Why? Why, when Bradley has already endured so much heartache, would this happen?* Holly sunk her head into her hands. Sobbing accompanied her tears.

She thought of the last time she saw Bradley and Laney together. They had all attended the *Maker's Mark* movie premiere in Boston: Derek and Cate, Sheila and David, Mike and Olivia, Lynn and Doug, Holly and John, and Bradley and Laney. That same night, they watched Cate walk for the first time since the limousine incident—Holly preferred thinking of it as an incident rather than a bombing. Bradley had worn a midnight blue tuxedo with black lapels, and Laney chose a complimentary light blue gown. They made a stunning couple, but more importantly, they were deeply in love.

Holly found herself remembering the first time she met Bradley—she a shy twenty-four-year-old woman completely out of her comfort zone on a cruise ship, he a twelve-year-old boy in a wheelchair with more confidence than anyone she had ever met.

She wiped her tears and sat back in her chair. *I need to call Dad.* On the telephone. she had told Cate she would inform Mike of Laney's passing. Cate sounded relieved when Holly offered. Holly picked up her phone and dialed her father's number.

On his way to the hospital, Derek called Zayt.

"Is Bradley alright? Fuck, this can't be happening," Zayt said.

"He's having a tough time. I'm on my way to the hospital to

77

be with him. Can you take care of the dog? I don't know how long he will be."

"Yeah, of course. Jesus. Tell him I . . . I . . . shit."

"Yeah. I know." Derek whispered.

"Mara, I need you to man the office," Nick said into his cellphone. "Hazel is there alone. I need an agent there to take care of the phones and any emergencies."

"I'm only ten minutes away. I'll take care of it. Nick?"

"Yes, Mara?"

"Give him a hug for me," Mara said as she licked a tear from her lips.

When Nick went back inside the emergency room area, he found Bradley and Sahani absent from the waiting room. He asked Diane where he could find his co-workers. The receptionist showed him to Examination Room 3. Nick pushed the curtain back in time to hear the doctor say, "Your blood pressure is 180 over 120. That is dangerously high."

Bradley glared at the intern.

"Yes. We expected that," Sahani interjected on Bradley's behalf. "According to Mr. Whitman's history, his blood pressure will drop back to normal within the hour." Glancing back at Nick, Sahani added, "We just didn't want to take any unnecessary chances."

The young male intern promised to send a nurse in fifteen minutes to re-check Bradley's blood pressure, then added, "Try to rest comfortably," before he left.

"This is bullshit, Nick," Bradley spat.

"We have to wait here for Dr. Abrams anyway. There's no harm in getting you checked out. Jesus, buddy, you went from beet red to white as a sheet in a matter of seconds."

"I want you to leave. Both of you. I want to be alone." Bradley said.

Sahani began, "I don't think that's a good . . . "

Bradley interrupted, "I don't give a goddam what you think. I want you both out of here. Now."

"Alright, we'll go," Nick said as he put his hand on Sahani's arm. "We'll be in the waiting room. Have someone come get me if you need anything. Anything at all."

The two left Bradley alone in the examination room.

"Do you think it's wise to leave him alone?" Sahani asked.

"Jesus, he just lost his fiancée. He needs some space. Besides, I can watch from here to make sure he doesn't go anywhere."

"Nick, can you tell me about her? What was she like?" Sahani asked as they reached the waiting room.

Nick covered his face with both hands, then slowly slid them down his stubble-covered cheeks and chin before dropping them by his sides. With slumped shoulders and a weary voice, he responded, "She was perfect for him. I only saw her a handful of times, but it was obvious. I'd never seen him so happy. She worked here—right here in the emergency room as a trauma specialist. This is where they met."

Nick gazed at the floor, cleared his throat, and continued. "She was a beautiful woman. Intelligent enough to keep up with Bradley, and that's saying something."

"She sounds wonderful," Sahani smiled.

"Yeah."

Sahani's eyes shifted to the emergency room doors. "Derek is here." Sahani pointed toward the doors just as Derek rushed through them.

"Where is he?" Derek asked, hardly slowing his advance.

"Room 3," Nick replied.

Derek reached the curtained room just as Doctor Abrams arrived. Without exchanging words, Bradley and Derek waited for Abrams to speak.

"Mr. Whitman, I am Benjamin Abrams. We spoke on the phone earlier. Would you care to join me in my office?" he asked.

"No. Tell me now. Tell me what happened to Laney," Bradley choked.

"When we found Dr. Weaver in her office, she was unresponsive. We did everything we could to revive her, but she was already gone. I'm sorry. We will need to perform an autopsy to determine cause of death. That could take a couple of days. I asked the coroner to expedite her procedure."

Dr. Abrams glanced at Derek, then back to Bradley. "Would you like to see her?"

"Yes," Bradley whispered.

"Please, follow me," said Abrams.

Bradley and Derek followed Dr. Abrams through a service door at the back of the emergency room. A sign on the door read, Employees Only. The door led to a hallway, then to an elevator.

Once in the elevator, Derek asked Abrams, "Do you have any idea what happened to her?"

"I wouldn't want to speculate," the doctor replied.

"Please," Derek appealed. "Anything you can tell us."

Dr. Abrams peered down at Bradley slumped in his wheelchair. Although they had never met, Benjamin Abrams knew of Bradley Whitman. Elaine Weaver and he were about as close as colleagues get in a busy, most-times hectic hospital. They had often eaten a quick lunch together or chatted after a meeting. And even though Abram's position in the hospital had become administrative rather than treating patients, Elaine had consulted with him on some of her more challenging cases. He had seen for himself how happy she had been since Bradley entered her life.

As the elevator took them to the basement, Dr. Abrams responded to Derek's plea.

"Elaine was a healthy individual with no history of heart disease in her family. I would find it difficult, but not impossible, to believe that her death was related to her heart. Whatever the cause, it happened quickly. In my experience, if I had to guess, I would suspect an aneurysm."

Bradley hung his head, and his shoulders began to shudder. Derek placed a hand on Bradley's shoulder while tears reformed in his own eyes.

The elevator doors opened to a cool hallway, noticeably different in temperature from the tepid emergency room. Their work had brought both Bradley and Derek there before. They followed Dr. Abrams down the hall to the stainless-steel double doors.

"Please wait here for a moment," Abrams said before walking through the doors.

For the first time since he arrived at the hospital, Derek leaned down and looked into Bradley's empty eyes.

"Do you want me to go with you?" Derek asked.

Bradley shook his head from side to side.

A moment later, Dr. Abrams came out of the room followed by Dr. Maria Reyes and her assistant.

"Take as long as you need. She's just inside," Maria told Bradley as she gently placed a hand on Bradley's shoulder.

A chill encompassed his body as Bradley rolled his chair into the morgue.

It took nearly twenty-four hours to confirm Dr. Abrams's suspicions. Laney had suffered what Abrams called an intracranial aneurysm, meaning a weakened blood vessel between the underside of Laney's brain and the base of her skull had ballooned and then ruptured, causing bleeding in the brain. He explained she most likely lost consciousness almost immediately after the rupture, which left her vulnerable to the bleeding that followed. He concluded that, because she was alone when it happened, she had little chance to survive.

Those final words haunted Bradley. He sat in his wheelchair in his backyard overlooking the REACH community. It took every ounce of energy he could muster just to blink his eyes. Only one phrase filled his head. He recalled it over and over again: *Because she was alone . . .*

Laney used to joke about having an office in the hospital. "I never use it," she would say. "I barely remember what it looks like." Then she'd laugh. "It's the one place no one would look for me."

Because she was alone. Once he heard those words, Bradley knew that Laney's death was his fault.

LIFE GOES ON

Originally, Mara had looked forward to her eight a.m. scheduled appointment with Sahani Kumar. But Nick had made her nervous. While getting ready for work earlier that morning, Nick could not keep himself from listing topics of conversation Mara should avoid.

"There's no reason to mention you and me, you know, our personal stuff," he had started, "but, if she already knows about us and asks you, just say you'd rather not talk about your private life. Oh, and if she asks about how it is to work here, say something like, 'we make a good team,' or something like that."

Nick made it sound as if her introductory meeting had been intended as a psychological booby trap, but her conversation with Sahani had been anything but. They had talked about the path that brought Mara to the FBI and Mara's goals for her future. They spoke of Mara's love of puzzles, riddles, and mathematical games. And, before their time ended, Mara voiced her concern for Bradley and the sadness she felt, something she tried to do with Nick, but Nick found difficult to talk about.

By the time she walked out of Sahani's office, Mara felt better. She found it refreshing to talk to another woman who understood the job, who understood grief, and understood the need to sometimes talk about it.

"Nick!" Mara sighed and shook her head as she left the meeting with Sahani.

As she emerged from the hallway into the foyer by the elevator, she noticed Nick standing by her desk. He shifted his weight from foot to foot and looked at his watch. Just as he turned his head to glance at the hallway, Mara ducked back out of sight.

Damn him, Mara thought. *He's worried I talked about him—and us. Well, then. Let him worry.*

After letting out a quiet giggle, Mara replaced her calm, happy exterior with a flustered façade. Taking short, quick steps keeping her head down, she then emerged from the hallway. Without lifting her head, she peeked over to her desk and saw Nick watching her. He looked worried. She made a show of wiping her eye, as if whisking away a tear. She stopped abruptly halfway to her desk, turned on her heels, and raced to the ladies room. Without breaking stride, she pushed on the bathroom door and let it slam shut behind her.

She knew Nick followed her and stood outside the door. *Let him stew,* she smiled. Mara looked in the mirror and fixed her hair, drew herself a paper cup full of water, and sat in the chair by the window in the corner of the restroom. She checked her cellphone for messages and replied to two.

"Nick," Mara heard someone in the hallway call, then some mumbled conversation and footsteps leading down the hall toward Nick's office.

Mara smiled, tossed her paper cup into the trash, and returned to her desk.

Derek had delayed his trip to Washington by a day. As the ninety-minute shuttle flight was about to land at Ronald Reagan Washington National Airport, he realized he hadn't read a single word of the report he had pulled from his briefcase before takeoff. Thoughts of Bradley had consumed him.

He hadn't seen Bradley since his parents picked him up from the hospital. Before leaving for DC, he had called three times and spoken with Doug each time.

"Bradley hasn't said two words since we brought him home," Doug told him during one of the conversations. "Lynn isn't much better. They both just sit and stare at nothing. Lynn won't leave his side, and I can't tell if Bradley even notices she's there."

"Let me know if there's anything I can do," Derek told Doug. "Anything at all. I'll cancel my trip to DC."

"No. Don't do that. There's nothing you can do here. Not right now, anyway. It's going to take time," Doug said. "Go do what you have to do. I'll take care of things here."

Derek walked through the airport toward the arrival pick-up area where a car and driver waited to bring him directly to the FBI facility at 935 Pennsylvania Avenue.

Constructed of tan-colored concrete in the mid 1960s, the J. Edgar Hoover FBI Building, named for the first director from 1935 to 1972, is not much to look at. Two main eight-story buildings are set between Pennsylvania Avenue NW and connect to an eleven-story structure at E Street NW. Both buildings connect via a wing to create a courtyard in the shape of a trapezoid. The facility has an additional three stories below ground as well as a parking garage. Square windows in a bronze hue are set deep into concrete window frames.

It reminded Derek of unimaginative buildings he built with plastic bricks, his favorite childhood toy.

Less than a mile from the White House, J. Edgar Hoover headquarters houses executives, special agents, and professional staff responsible for coordinating FBI activities worldwide. In that building, policies are set, priorities recognized, and intelligence analyzed to ensure coordination at all levels, including operational support to field and overseas offices. However, in times of national crisis or emergency, the people in the J. Edgar Hoover Building take charge within the operations of the FBI.

Not until Derek walked through the doors did his new position as Executive Assistant Director of the Federal Bureau of Investigation Criminal, Cyber, Response, and Services Branch become real to him. Once inside the lobby, he stopped to take a deep breath and enjoy the moment. Then he thought of Bradley and how he wished Bradley could be with him.

"Hello, Director Richards," came the female voice.

Snapped out of his thoughts, Derek acknowledged the smiling, red-haired woman standing in front of him.

"My name is Madelyn, Madelyn Cross, your executive assistant. I came to help you navigate your way through this place."

"Hello, Ms. Cross."

"Please, call me Madelyn."

"Well, thank you, Madelyn. I'm feeling a bit like a country boy in a castle right now," Derek smiled back.

After exchanging a handshake, Madelyn handed Derek his new FBI badge and escorted him through security.

"Director Davis is waiting for you in his, I mean, your office. You are on the sixth floor. Would you like to stop anywhere before we head up?" Madelyn asked.

"No. I might as well jump right in," Derek replied. "Lead on."

Davis sat in a chair in front of the mahogany desk with a glass top. He read from a file. When he heard Derek enter, he placed the file on the desk and, with both hands placed on the chair's arms for leverage, struggled to get to his feet. He bore a full smile and extended his hand.

"Welcome home," Director Davis said.

While shaking his hand, Derek replied, "Thank you, sir. I only hope I can be half as good a tenant as you are."

"Was. As I was. It's all yours now, Derek. And I think we can dispense with the sir and Director Davis. The name is Paul. And you wouldn't be here if we weren't certain you were the right person for the job."

"Well, thank you, sir. Paul. How are you feeling?"

"Fine, fine. I just wanted to be here when you arrived. I know it can be a little overwhelming. I also wanted to tell you that I will be available as a resource for you for as long as I can."

"I appreciate that, Paul."

"You've got a good staff here. Lean on them. In time, you'll probably want to bring in some of your own people. Speaking of that, I heard about Agent Whitman's fiancée. How is he doing?"

Surprised the director already knew about Laney, Derek replied, "He's taking it hard. He's going to need some time."

"Please give him my condolences."

Derek nodded.

The director continued, "Well, I think we've discussed everything you need from me in the previous phone calls so, unless you have any questions I'll be on my way."

"Not right now, but I'm sure I will," Derek replied.

"Call anytime."

Davis slowly turned toward the door, then stopped, glanced around the office, and walked out.

Derek took a deep breath, laid his briefcase on his desk, and sat in the high-backed leather chair. The telephone displayed buttons on the left side of the receiver for four telephone lines, each clearly numbered. The call button below those informed Derek that pressing it would connect him to his executive assistant, Madelyn. An additional call button was not identified. Derek lifted the phone and pressed Madelyn's call button.

"Yes, sir," Madelyn answered immediately.

"Where would I find a cup of coffee?" Derek asked.

"I'll be right in." Madelyn hung up before Derek could say another word.

A few moments later, Madelyn opened the office door and delivered a steaming hot cup of coffee to Derek. He looked at it, took a sip, and said, "Light on the milk, no sugar. How did you know?"

Madelyn smiled. "It's my job to know, sir."

"Well, Madelyn. If I'm going to call you by your first name, you are going to return the favor. It's Derek. And, just so you know, I have no problem getting my own coffee as long as you show me where I can do that."

"Alright. Derek it is. But only for informal day-to-day occasions. The coffee room is through the white door just beyond my desk. You will find fresh milk and the occasional pineapple-macadamia nut muffin. My instructions were to keep those to a minimum."

"You've talked to Cate."

The corner of Madelyn's mouth curved up exposing a small dimple in each cheek. "I predict your wife and I will become good friends."

"I have no doubt," Derek replied. "What's on the agenda for today?"

"You have about an hour to settle in before introductions to your staff. Then . . . "

"Wait. I'm sorry to interrupt but, my staff? Aren't you my staff?"

Madelyn chuckled. "Derek, you're not in Kansas anymore. The country boy is now a prince. I, as your executive assistant, am your first line of defense. Many individuals will require your attention every day, but they need to get past me first. Before they get to me, they need to get past my assistant. In addition to us you have a handful of specialized individuals at your service, all of whom you will meet in," Madelyn checked her watch, "fifty-six minutes.

"You also have a meeting scheduled with Deputy Director Michael Mendez at one o'clock. I've arranged your lunch delivery for eleven-thirty. There is a mini refrigerator stocked with water and orange juice over here."

Madelyn walked around Derek's desk to the wall covered with bookshelves built above a full length of cabinets. The cabinet behind his chair and to the right held the mini fridge. Madelyn opened it as if to corroborate her claim. "The unmarked telephone call button below mine is for Cate's cellphone," she continued. "I can change that to your home phone if you would prefer."

"Uh, no. That's fine. Now I understand what Director Davis meant by overwhelming."

"Can I help you get settled in?"

"No, thank you, Madelyn. I appreciate your help."

"Sir. Derek, I just want to say I am honored to work with you."

Taken aback by the comment, Derek simply said "Thank you" as Madelyn left the office.

Derek sipped his coffee, unpacked his briefcase, and arranged his desk drawers the same as he had always done. Case files on the right, data and research materials on the left, writing implements in the middle drawer. Once satisfied, he picked up the telephone and pushed the unmarked call button.

"Are you settled in?" Cate asked as she answered her cellphone.

"How did you know it was me calling?"

"Who else would be calling me from the 202 area code?"

"Oh, I don't know. Maybe Madelyn Cross?"

Cate giggled. "She told you, huh?"

"Yes, she did. But what I don't get is why you didn't tell me she called."

"Why would I? She called to talk to me, not you. Do I need to tell you about every phone call I get?" Cate sounded amused.

"Only if it comes from arguably the second most powerful building in the country," he laughed.

"She sounds wonderful. Is she as wonderful as she sounds?" Cate asked.

"She's very thorough."

"You know she went to Harvard Kennedy School, right? Right here in Cambridge. And she's got a master's in public administration. And she's only twenty-nine years old. Oh, and get this. She's dating the personal assistant to the President of the United States. You know the nice-looking young man always standing behind the President? She's dating him. His name is Robert."

"What's her favorite color?" Derek asked wryly.

"Violet. What? Oh, wait. are you mocking me?"

Derek could only laugh.

Cate continued, "Well, I am looking forward to meeting her. And so is Sheila."

"Sheila? What does your sister have to do with this?"

"Are you going to mock me again if I tell you?"

"I promise not to mock."

"Maddie said she is having . . ."

"Wait. Maddie?"

"Yes, Maddie. That's her name, Derek. Anyway, Maddie is having trouble finding clothing that suits her to wear at the events Robert takes her to. She says all the women look the same. So, I told her about Elegance by Sheila. She loves the idea of a West Coast look as opposed to . . ."

"Okay, okay, I get it. I would love to chat fashion with you, but I should get to work. I just called to tell you I love you, I miss you, and thank you for the pineapple-macadamia nut muffins."

"I love you, too. Call me tonight?" Cate asked.

"I will." Derek couldn't help but smile as he hung up. He began to think Cate would fit right into the DC scene.

Derek picked up the file that Davis had laid down on the desk and began reading. He had almost forty minutes before he met the troops.

Other than the position of her legs, the latest victim's autopsy report looked no different than the reports of victims since the killer had perfected his or her kill routine.

Tony had read through every report twice and found nothing but frustration. Without a witness or any physical evidence, he could see no way of identifying the suspect.

When Tony slammed the report down onto his desk, the room quieted. Sahani Kumar had entered the bullpen in time to witness Tony's disturbance. She approached.

"Are you alright? Is there anything I can help you with?" Sahani asked Tony.

Tony glared at her. "I don't have time for a chat right now. Go jump into someone else's head."

Sahani captured Tony's glare with her own, then sternly replied, "I meant with the case. I'd like to help with the Pathside Predator case. That's why I am here."

Embarrassed and sure everyone in the room heard his outburst, Tony spoke loudly enough for all to hear. "I'm sorry, Dr. Kumar. I'm a little aggravated right now, but that's no excuse to jump all over you."

"I understand, Tony. Please, call me Sahani. I had hoped to work on the Predator's profile with Bradley, but he won't be available for some time. I'm told he shared a brief profile in the meeting held the day before I got here. Did you happen to record what he said?"

"I took notes, if that's what you mean by record."

"Yes, that's what I meant. May I see them?"

"Yeah, sure."

Tony's desk resembled a teenage boy's school locker. Crumpled reports and discarded fast food wrappers filled the drawers. Instead of neatly stacked folders, piles of pages from emptied folders co-mingled on his desktop without a thought of organization. How he intended to find his notes from the previous meeting baffled Sahani, yet Tony reached into a drawer, lifted a ketchup-stained paper French fry bag, and retrieved the notepad. He brushed salt off the pad before handing it to Sahani.

In black pen, Tony had written:

forget profile

org

obsessed in own way

"I'm sorry," Sahani said. "I assume the org means organized, but I don't understand this. Did he really tell you to forget the profile?"

"No, not in so many words. But I've worked with Bradley long enough to know when he says not to exclude anybody based on the profile, it means he doesn't trust the profile. And I trust Bradley."

"Okay. What about this, *obsessed in own way*. Can you remember exactly what he said about that?" she asked.

"He said the Predator obsesses over every detail, and those details are known only to the unsub."

"What about the sexual assaults of the victims? Did he mention anything about that?"

"Nothing," Tony replied.

"Well, that's interesting."

"Why?"

"Every autopsy I've read highlights the sexual assault and the fact that no evidence got left behind. Also, that the act itself was performed after the victims had died."

"That's right," Tony agreed.

Sahani glanced to the file Tony had slammed on the desk. "Is that the latest autopsy report?"

"Yes, it is, but it's not much help. There's still no physical evidence."

"May I take a look at it?" Sahani politely asked.

"Be my guest."

"I'll bring it back as soon as I've finished. And Tony?"

"Yeah?"

Sahani placed her hand on Tony's shoulder. "Remember to give yourself a break. The weight of the world does not rest on your shoulders."

"No, maybe not the world, but I feel every fucking ounce of the Predator sitting there."

Sahani lightly patted Tony's shoulder and walked down the hall to her office.

Thicker than the autopsy reports of any previous Predator victims, the file for the recently identified wife and mother of two, Grace-Ann Colson, left nothing to the imagination. Sahani noted that Dr. Reyes had examined every inch of the woman's body before surrendering her to her family for burial arrangements.

The bulk of the report read the same as those for previous victims, but Dr. Reyes had provided additional information. The report stated the examination of the victim's left hand, the one lying over her mutilated breast, revealed traces of substrate, isopropyl alcohol, and alkyl dimethyl benzyl ammonium chloride. Dr. Reyes concluded that the ingredients, common in disinfectant wipes, indicated that the victim's left hand had been wiped clean with a disinfectant cloth. The report went on to state that no such traces were found on the victim's right hand.

So, the unsub wiped the victim's left hand clean, then placed it over her cut breast, Sahani thought. *Was it a sign of remorse? Possibly respect for the sacrifice of her body part? Strange.*

Also, after a thorough examination of Grace-Ann's vagina, the doctor stated that the sexual assault took place using a foreign object with distinct striations. Although only faint ridges remained, the object tore her tissue and left markings inconsistent with the theory of penile-genital penetration.

Is this new? Why don't the previous autopsy reports mention this? Sahani wondered. *How could Tony say there's no new evidence. This is big.*

Excited, Sahani rushed back to Tony's desk and found him grimacing while typing into his computer.

"Tony," she called as she approached, "how can you say this report does not contain any new evidence? Didn't you read about the wiping of the hand and the use of foreign object to simulate sexual intercourse?"

Tony stood up, his lips pursed and eyebrows almost touching. "Who the hell do you think I am, some rookie off the street? Of course, I read that. What I said is there's no physical evidence. Nothing for me to work with. No lead to follow."

Sahani felt bad for the misunderstanding, "I'm sorry. I didn't mean to imply anything. I just got so excited. You were right! To trust Bradley, I mean. You were right to trust him in regard to the profile."

"Of course, I was right. But, just for the record, why was I right?" Tony asked.

Sahani smiled before she explained. "You said Bradley didn't trust the profile of the Pathside Predator, so he only spoke of the elements of the profile he was sure about. He left out the sexual aspect of the murders because he doesn't think it is the Predator's motivation. This report would suggest that the sexual violation is an afterthought. . . a crime of convenience. Bradley knows this, knew this, somehow."

"Okay. So what? What do we care what he used to violate her? We still don't have any evidence," Tony said.

"True, there is no physical evidence, but we have a much better idea of who our killer is—or isn't, I should say. The Predator is not a sexual psychopath. Our unsub has a much more personal reason for killing these women. All we need to do is figure out what that reason is."

"Oh, is that all?" Tony steeped the question in sarcasm.

"I need to keep this report for a while. Do you mind?" Sahani asked.

Tony threw up his hands and sat down in his chair.

Sahani walked down the hall to Nick's office.

"Nick, I need to see Bradley," Sahani said.

"What? No. No way. Give the man his space."

"I know it seems soon, but I think this is the right thing to do. Just a quick visit."

"It's only been two days."

"I know."

"What's so important that you need to see him?" Nick asked.

"It's complicated," Sahani answered. "What if I talk to Derek and he thinks it is the right thing to do? Would you back me up on this?"

"Derek? Well . . ., yeah, I guess if he thinks so."

"Thank you, Nick."

A SINGULAR PROMISE

"Dammit, I wish I could be there," Derek cursed through the telephone.

"It may be better that you aren't," Sahani replied. "He might try to use you as a buffer, and I think you would find it difficult to resist. Your instincts are to protect Bradley, as any true friend would. But if I am right about him, that could be problematic. I won't really know until I see him."

"Alright. I'll talk to Doug and let him know. But please wait another day or two."

"I can do that. You'll talk to Nick?" Sahani asked.

"I will."

Derek sat on the hotel room bed with his cellphone still in hand. He needed a moment to gather himself before he called Cate. He didn't want to sound the least bit tired, worried, or sad—although he felt all of those.

Sahani had called him just as he picked up his phone to call home. Her idea of going to see Bradley so soon had him worried. But he understood her reasoning. In fact, it was because of him she felt the need to do so.

Two years prior, when he almost lost Cate in the limousine bombing, Derek immediately went to Paul Davis and resigned his position as supervisory special agent of Chelsea FBI headquarters. Director Davis accepted his request with two conditions. Condition one was that he be officially on leave from the department, not retired as he told others, thus leaving the door open for an eventual return. Condition two was that Derek take advantage of the FBI's in-house therapists to help him cope with the changes in his life.

After a little pushback, Derek agreed. He began seeing Dr. Sahani Kumar twice a week and continued to do so for eighteen months. During that time when not talking about his work, himself, or Cate, he often spoke of Bradley and how Bradley was like the brother Derek never had.

It didn't occur to Derek that his psychotherapist and Bradley might meet one day. He talked of Bradley's intense need to protect people, how Bradley felt responsible for things he shouldn't, and how he would sometimes put himself in harm's way of a real or perceived threat. Sahani called it the savior complex.

Because of the conversations and her background on Bradley, Sahani called Derek to voice her concern that Bradley could be a candidate for experiencing chronic grief, a heightened state of mourning that keeps one from healing. She felt it important to evaluate him as soon as possible, and the coroner's report gave her the perfect opportunity. "Just a quick visit to see how he is doing," she told Derek.

Derek knew it to be the right move, but he still felt guilty about the backdoor approach. He'd rather be honest with Bradley, but he knew Bradley would never consent.

Closing his eyes, Derek imagined himself sitting on the edge of a rushing brook. Trees lining the banks of the water had turned the color of fall. He looked to his right where Cate sat beside him, reading a book. The sun lit her up like a spotlight in a darkened theatre. Her emerald eyes sparkled in the beam. Derek drew the surrounding clean, fresh air into his lungs, held his breath, then slowly exhaled.

When Derek opened his eyes, he was ready to call Cate.

"And how was the rest of your day?" Cate asked.

"Oh, Maddie and I went out for a late lunch. We had a few drinks before we popped into a local club and danced until the lights came on. How was your day?"

Unable to hold back her schoolgirl giggle, Cate laughed her way through her response, "I'm picturing you, Derek Richards, dancing in a Washington, DC, nightclub."

"And you find it that funny?"

Still laughing, Cate said, "I'm sorry, honey, but you wouldn't fit in at a Chelsea, Massachusetts, nightclub, never mind in the big city."

"Well, I guess that means you wouldn't be interested in accompanying me to the Children's Hospital Charity Ball in the Main Hall at Union Station next month. That's alright. I'm sure Maddie has a friend . . . "

"Oh, my God! Are you serious, Derek? A gala at Union Station? How on earth did you manage that?"

"Deputy Director Mendez asked if we would like to be his guests. I told him I didn't think you would be interested, but it sounds like maybe you are."

"Derek! Of course, I am. Do you think you could still accept his invitation? Do you think it's too late?" Cate asked nervously.

Then it was Derek who couldn't hold back his laughter. "I told the Deputy Director we would be honored to be his guests. He's looking forward to meeting you."

"Oh, Derek. Imagine you and me waltzing on the same floor that Jackie Kennedy once walked. I'll need something to wear, I need to call Sheila."

"You have nearly a month to get ready."

"I know. It's not much time, but I think Sheila can put something together for me."

"Not much . . . ?" Derek shook his head. "Would you like to hear about the rest of my day?"

"Yes, I would. I really would, but . . . can I call you back in a few minutes?" Cate asked.

Derek knew she would hang up the phone and call Sheila to tell her the news, and to brainstorm about what color and style gown she should wear. But he didn't mind. He loved being able to provide Cate with some excitement. Derek felt she had given up a lot of herself to be his wife, even though he knew Cate would never validate that feeling.

After hanging up with Cate, for the first time Derek thought about what their lives would look like if they moved to Washington.

On the evening of Laney's death, Doug Whitman had asked Mass General to forward his contact information to Laney's next of kin. All he knew was that Laney had an aunt who lived in Tennessee.

Three days later, when Doug received a call from a phone number he did not recognize, he answered.

"Hello. My name is Anise Jain. Have I reached Douglas Whitman?"

"Yes, this is Doug."

"I am Elaine's aunt, her mother's sister. The hospital gave me your number. I hope I am not disturbing you."

"No, not at all, Mrs. Jain. We've been hoping to hear from you."

"I'm sorry we didn't call sooner. My husband and I arrived in town late last night and have spent the morning making some arrangements, but we were hoping to get together with your family to discuss final details."

"That's very kind of you. My wife and I are staying with our son in Revere. We would love to have you over for dinner tonight if you don't have any plans. I could pick you up at your hotel."

"That's not necessary. We have our car. We drove in from Tennessee. Dinner sounds lovely."

Doug relayed Bradley's address and suggested a six o'clock dinner. He hoped it would be just the thing Lynn needed. She had made progress over the past two days but still showed little motivation.

When Doug told Lynn that Laney's aunt and uncle were coming for dinner, she snapped into action. She created a shopping list for Doug and began cleaning the house, moving Rusty from one spot to another as she swept and dusted. She felt useful again.

Bradley reacted minimally. When Doug explained that Laney's aunt and uncle wished to include him in the decision-making process, a single tear ran down Bradley's cheek. He could only nod his head. He did, however, promise to shower and change his clothes, something he had resisted the past three days.

Anise and Ari Jain arrived at six o'clock. Doug had warned them about the industrial neighborhood to ensure they wouldn't think they got the wrong directions.

Doug introduced himself, Lynn, and then Bradley to the Jains. Glancing at Doug like he forgot to introduce one of his own children, Lynn introduced Rusty.

"And I am Anise. This is my husband, Ari," Anise Jain said.

"Please, let's sit by the fire. I know it's not very cold out tonight, but I just love a fire, so I asked Doug to build one," Lynn explained.

"This is a very nice living space you have here, Bradley. Elaine told us you were practical. But she also said you were compassionate and exceedingly sweet," Anise said.

"Laney . . ." Bradley's voice sounded like paper scratching sandpaper. He swallowed hard and tried again. "Laney brings out . . . brought out the best in people. In me."

"I would say it worked both ways, Bradley. Elaine had never been so happy until she met you. We both noticed." Anise took hold of her husband's hand as he nodded.

Bradley's head dropped slightly.

"Ari and I never had children," Anise continued. "Elaine was as close to a daughter as we would ever get." Tears began to leak down her face. "I'm sorry. I told myself I wouldn't cry tonight."

"She was a wonderful woman. We already thought of her as our daughter." Lynn gazed at Doug, who also nodded.

Bradley's head sunk lower.

"Excuse me," Bradley uttered. Then he rolled his chair past his bedroom area and into the bathroom.

"He's not coping well," Doug explained. "I'm not sure how much help he will be with the arrangements, but Lynn and I will help any way we can."

"I just can't imagine what he's going through," Anise said through tears.

"I wish I knew what to say to him," Doug choked. "It's like he's six years old and lost the use of his legs again. I just don't know how to make it better."

Lynn wrapped her arms around Doug. "I'm sorry. I haven't been much help the last few days." She laid her head on Doug's shoulder. "But we will get through this. Because we have to."

Doug placed his hand on Lynn's head, and the four of them sat in silence.

Rusty jumped from the floor and ran to the bathroom door just as Bradley emerged. Rusty then followed Bradley back to the fire and lay on the floor next to him.

"What did you have in mind?" Bradley asked Anise and Ari.

Anise cleared her throat and began. "Well, as you know, Elaine was not a religious person, but she was a spiritual one. When her parents passed away, we had discussions about how each of us would like our remains handled. Elaine always said she wished to be cremated. She didn't care what happened to her ashes, but she didn't want anyone to hold on to them. She said she didn't like the idea of someone looking at a canister and getting sad."

"She told me the same thing," Bradley nodded.

"Alright. I'll call the funeral home and make arrangements," Anise said. "I really don't know what to do about services. We are the only family she has except for a few distant relatives she hardly knew. We thought we should do something here in Boston where most of her and your friends are. But we have no idea where or how."

"A memorial service in the hospital chapel," Bradley said. "Most of her friends work there. She would not want calling hours. But a small service in the hospital chapel would make her happy. And then a gathering here after the service."

Lynn and Doug shared an encouraging glance. Bradley had obviously thought it through.

"The hospital chapel is perfect," Anise sighed. "Why didn't we think of that? But wouldn't it be a lot of work and strain to have people come back here? Ari and I would be happy to rent a hall and have something catered."

"No," Lynn interjected. "Bradley is right. It should be here. But catering is a good idea, Anise. And we'll rent a tent, tables, and chairs. We'll toast her with her favorite wine."

"I'll speak with the hospital chapel to get available dates and times," Ari said.

"I'll get started on the tent setup," said Doug.

"Anise and I will find a caterer," Lynn said. "Doug, why don't you offer our guests a drink. I'll get dinner on the table."

"Let me help you," Anise said to Lynn.

Doug and Ari moved to the liquor cabinet, Lynn and Anise ambled to the kitchen, and Bradley rolled his chair out the sliding glass doors to the backyard with Rusty following behind. The sun had lowered in the western sky, leaving the sandpit and REACH community in the shadows.

Bradley tilted his head toward the sky and silently spoke.

Laney, I know what you would tell me. You would want me to go on, live my life without you, try to be happy. But I don't think I can. I don't think you know how torturous this is. I promise you I will get through the memorial and do my best to honor you. But I can't make any promises beyond that. I love you, Laney. And I failed you. I don't know how, but I know I did. And I can't live with that.

"I wondered why your light was still on," Nick said as he entered Sahani's office. "What are you still doing here? It's almost eight o'clock."

"I could ask you the same thing," Sahani replied. "I'm working on the Predator's profile. What's your excuse?"

"I'm doing what I always seem to be doing these days—paperwork."

Sahani pushed her chair back and opened the bottom left

drawer of her desk. She retrieved two glasses and an easily recognizable bottle of Blanton's bourbon.

Nick raised his eyebrows, then sat in the chair across from her. Sahani handed him a generous pour of the dark amber liquid.

They each raised their glass in the spirit of a toast, then sipped. Nick held the bourbon on his tongue for a moment before slowly letting it slip down his throat. His tongue tingled from the initial hint of spice followed by a faint vanilla and brown sugar essence and a fresh pear finish.

Nick hadn't realized he had done that with his eyes closed. When he opened them, he caught Sahani in a smile.

"Hits the spot, doesn't it?" Sahani asked.

Nick nodded. Then said, "I talked to Derek."

"And?"

"I don't like the idea of intruding. But Derek seems to think it's a good idea, so I won't stop you," Nick said.

"I promise you, Nick, I won't do anything to exacerbate Bradley's pain. I just want to check on him."

Nick glanced at the floor. "She was the real deal, you know. Bradley was crazy about her," Nick said.

"How well did you know Laney?" Sahani asked.

"Well enough to know Bradley will never be the same again," Nick said as he shot back the rest of his bourbon and stood. "Goodnight, Dr. Kumar."

"Goodnight, Nick."

Sahani took another sip before returning to her keyboard. Trying to focus on the Predator's profile proved fruitless. Her attention diverted to Bradley. She hoped her initial assessment of him had been wrong. After all, she had seen him at his most vulnerable when his emotions were raw. *But isn't that when we truly show who we are?*

Lynn glanced at the kitchen clock. Almost nine. Anise and Ari had gone back to their hotel for the night. Bradley had given the couple his key to Laney's apartment and told them they should stay there. It would be easier for them to get her things in order, he told them. The plan was for them to move to her apartment the next day.

Bradley had taken Rusty and gone to bed, although Lynn could not hear either one of them snoring. She surmised that Bradley wished to be alone.

"Doug, let's go sit outside. It's a beautiful night," Lynn said.

"Really? It's nine o'clock."

Lynn cast him a pleading gaze.

Doug then understood Lynn wanted to talk. "But it is a nice night. I'll pour us a glass of wine."

From the backyard where they sat, the scattered lights from the REACH community resembled fireflies frozen in time. That, Lynn guessed, was how Bradley must have felt the last few days.

"Well? What do you think?" Lynn asked Doug.

"I think they are very nice people," Doug responded.

"I'm not asking what you think about Anise and Ari. Of course, they're nice people. Anyone who could have given us Laney would have to be nice. I mean Bradley. He seemed to handle the conversation about the funeral arrangements well. I didn't know he had been thinking about it."

"He did handle it well—also, giving Anise and Ari the key to Laney's apartment. I don't think that was an afterthought."

"That's good, right?" Lynn asked. "I mean, maybe he's coming around? Maybe he's ready to talk?"

"Yes, I think so. Hopefully it will get easier after the memorial service."

AT FIRST GLANCE

The knock on the door the next morning surprised them. Neither Doug, Lynn, nor Bradley had noticed when the car pulled into the driveway. And with Rusty outside making his morning visit to Zayt and the REACH residents, he could provide no warning of a visitor.

"Good morning, Mrs. Whitman," Sahani said as Lynn opened the door. "I'm Sahani Kumar. We met briefly at the hospital."

"Oh, yes. I remember. Please come in," Lynn replied.

"I hope this isn't a bad time. I wanted to have a moment with Bradley if that's alright."

Bradley sat in his wheelchair by his dust-covered workout equipment, looking out the sliding glass door. He did not acknowledge Sahani's arrival.

Doug, who had been making a second pot of coffee, joined Lynn and Sahani at the door.

"I'm Lynn, and this is my husband, Doug. Bradley," Lynn called, "you have a visitor."

Bradley didn't respond.

Lynn spread her hands in front of her, palms up, and her sorrowful eyes met Sahani's. Sahani responded with a slight nod of her head and walked over to Bradley. She held a file folder.

"Hello, Bradley," Sahani said.

Without looking up, Bradley answered, devoid of emotion, "Dr. Kumar."

Sahani did not hear hostility, but she felt it. Bradley had been in the first stage of grief when she last saw him. It appeared he now felt anger, typically the second stage of grief after denial. Sahani had intended the visit to gauge where in the grief process Bradley stood so she would have a baseline to compare his demeanor within the coming weeks.

"I brought you the autopsy report from Dr. Reyes and my initial profile of the Predator. I thought you might want to see them," Sahani said as she placed the folder on the bench of Bradley's weight machine.

"Tony could have brought them or Mara," Bradley snipped. "Did they send you here to counsel me? Is that it?"

"They? They who?"

Annoyed by her question, Bradley responded, "The bureau, Nick, Derek. Any they!"

"Tony and the rest are very busy. I offered to drop these off. I'll go now," Sahani stated quietly and pleasantly. She turned and walked toward the door.

Bradley's eyes never left the glass door, and he didn't say goodbye.

Doug and Lynn followed Sahani out to her car.

"I'm sorry. He's having a difficult time with this," Lynn said.

Sahani reached for Lynn's hand and held it. "There's no need to be sorry. Bradley and both of you will need time. If there is anything I can do, please call me." Sahani handed Lynn her business card.

As Sahani drove away Lynn glanced at the card. The FBI logo appeared in the upper left corner. The card read—

Dr. Sahani Kumar, MS/PsyD
Forensic Specialist

A psychologist, Lynn thought as she understood Bradley's reaction to Sahani's visit.

Bradley didn't hold much reverence for psychiatric or psychological treatment. His parents had thought it a good idea to send him to a psychologist after he lost the use of his legs. He was eight years old when he visited his first. Bradley regarded the sessions as more of a classroom than therapy. He studied the process, tested responses, and managed to flummox several well-regarded professionals in the field before Lynn and Doug figured out his game.

The first doctor informed Lynn and Doug that Bradley suffered from oppositional defiant disorder, a condition where children routinely lose their temper, act resentful or spiteful, and blame others for their own outbursts and reactions. Knowing that Bradley never showed signs of hostility or resentment, Lynn and Doug immediately withdrew Bradley from the doctor's care. What they didn't know at the time was Bradley had exhibited those symptoms but only during his sessions.

After only two sessions, the second doctor diagnosed Bradley with obsessive-compulsive disorder. Bradley's parents hadn't seen any evidence of that, but Bradley made sure the doctor saw—and heard—plenty. In the first session, Bradley rearranged the doctor's desk as he placed all the desktop items in alphabetical order while whispering the alphabet over and over. Bradley repeated his action during the second visit, only then he arranged the doctor's items in descending alphabetical order from z to a and recited the alphabet backwards.

Lynn and Doug removed Bradley from the doctor's care as soon as she told them her diagnosis.

When Doug asked Bradley about his visits to the doctors, Bradley told his father that the doctors explained to him that his sessions were confidential, and he shouldn't talk about them.

"That's not what they meant, Bradley. They meant that they couldn't tell anyone else what you talked about, but you can talk about them if you want," Doug had told him.

"Oh, okay," Bradley replied, then rolled his wheelchair into his bedroom.

It wasn't until the third psychologist suggested to Lynn and Doug that they keep a close eye on the neighborhood animals and let the doctor know if any of them disappeared or turned up dead that they realized Bradley had found his own way to cope with the loss of his legs.

But both Lynn and Doug knew that Bradley's unpleasant reaction to Sahani Kumar was not contrived, which suggested that their optimism about Bradley's mental state the previous night may have been premature.

Cecile Boulanger lifted the grocery bags from the back of her SUV. The muscles in her arms and legs still burned from the early morning yoga class. She had hoped she would be home before her husband left to bring the kids to school if only to have help hauling in the groceries, but his Mercedes was already gone.

She still felt angry about their argument the previous night. She knew her parents never treated Jake well, but when there is a death in the family, she felt those things needed to be put aside.

Jake felt differently. Her mother's sister had died of breast cancer just two days before. It had been a long and painful illness, and Cecile's mother sat by her sister's side until the very end.

When Jake announced he would not go to the funeral on Friday, Cecile exploded. Whether the emotional wave of her aunt passing away or the tide of pre-menopause fueled her, she did not know. Cecile didn't often lose her temper and it took Jake by surprise. But he did not back down. He slept in the guest room.

Cecile made three trips carrying the groceries. With thoughts of her husband packed away, she could think only about stepping into a nice hot shower and washing the sweat off her before heading to work at the hospital.

She looks good, the Predator thought. *Look at that house. And that Escalade is bigger than my first bedroom.* The Predator watched as Cecile unloaded her groceries. *That's more food than we had in months! That poor, unsuspecting woman. If she only knew.*

She'll do.

"I'll be home Thursday night." Derek spoke into his desktop phone.

"Sheila and David are flying in Thursday morning, and I insisted they stay with us," Cate replied. "Holly, John, and Mike are going to drive in from Amherst Friday morning. Derek, have you talked to Bradley?"

"No. I don't think he's ready to talk to anyone."

"I don't know what I'm going to say to him," Cate sobbed. "I can't imagine . . ."

"I know, honey. I think the best thing we can do is let him know we are here for him. You know Bradley. He does things in his own time and his own way."

"I miss you so much," Cate sniffled.

"Me, too."

"So? Did you see him?" Nick asked Sahani when she got to the office.

"Yes, for a minute," she replied.

"How is he?"

"Angry."

"Shit. Is there anything we can do?"

"Yes. Let him be angry," Sahani answered.

The crisp Friday morning air seemed to slice the Predator's eyes. In rapid succession, tears slid from under both lids. Only the weather had the effect of producing tears from the Predator.

Heavy fog hovered four feet above the manicured graveyard and dew clung to the arriving mourners' shoes. The Predator watched as Cecile and her husband along with an older couple stepped out of the limousine.

When they entered Green Living Cemetery, the Predator chuckled and thought, *A bit premature, but let's go with it. And this is much more interesting than her everyday routine.*

The Predator parked on the lawn, away from the gravestones and mourners' vehicles.

It was a good turnout. Some twenty-five people stood under and around the green canopy. The few chairs provided seating for immediate family members. The casket lay on top of four evenly spaced webbed straps that would eventually lower the body into the ground.

Watching the funeral unfold, the prying eyes of the Predator noticed a distance between Cecile and her husband.

That won't do, the Predator worried. *Will I need to find a new subject?*

But as the casket lowered, the Predator smiled as Cecile's husband clasped her hand in his and kissed her on the cheek.

The stretch limousine found its way onto Route 99, heading north. Bradley, Lynn, Doug, Anise, and Ari rode in silence. None of them had been prepared for the number of people who attended the memorial. For an hour, Bradley sat responding to each individual's condolences, and as he sat in the limousine, he couldn't remember the face of one.

His tired brain told him he had seen Derek and Cate, Sheila and David, and probably Holly, John, and Mike. Zayt had been there too, he thought, but Bradley couldn't recall what he said to him. He felt as if the fog that had surrounded his home that morning wrapped itself around him and wouldn't allow him to break away. Even as he listened to the rhythmic sound of limousine tires rolling over pavement, every part of his being felt muffled.

He hoped for Laney's sake he had performed admirably, because, after all, that is what he had done—performed.

No canopy marked the gravesite where Laney's ashes would rest. A small pile of earth had been removed to create a planting hole for the biodegradable urn that held Laney's ashes in the bottom, and a four-foot white oak tree rooted on the top in potting soil. Black mulch sat nearby, the finishing touch of the planting process.

Fifty minutes after leaving the chapel, the limousine followed by a parade of vehicles turned into the only cemetery that agreed to allow the tree planting as part of Laney's burial, Green Living Cemetery.

Deciding it fruitless to watch Cecile, the Predator did not follow when Cecile and her husband drove by and out of the cemetery. When the last of the mourners drove through the exit, a new procession led by a black stretch limousine came through the entrance.

How fascinating, the Predator thought. Precise planning had always been the Predator's strong suit. *How inspirational to see the business of death being handled so . . . fastidiously.*

But there's no canopy. Had they planned everything else so well and then forgotten to dig the grave?

Completely caught up in possible drama about to unfold, the Predator turned off the car engine and watched.

The line of vehicles wound through the paved pathways amid thousands of moss-covered stones and dying flowers before stopping one section north of where Cecile had mourned and only twenty yards from where the Predator sat. Looking more closely, the Predator did see a small mound of earth in a pile. *Must be a cremation.*

Thinking about leaving, the Predator was about to start the car again when something unusual happened. The limousine driver opened the passenger door and the seat with the passenger still sitting on it slid out of the vehicle. As if on an electronic pizza paddle serving up a pie, the male passenger sat with his legs dangling from the seat.

A man in a black suit, white shirt, and black tie approached with a wheelchair and set it beside the dangling man. The Predator watched as, without much effort, the sitting man employed his arm strength by transferring himself from the extended limousine seat to the wheelchair.

What will they think of next? thought the Predator.

As the man rolled himself toward the small pile of dirt, the Predator examined his features. *Wait. Something about this is familiar. I've seen this man before.*

Others began to surround the wheelchair-bound man, and soon the Predator could not see him.

It was recently. I know it was. Was he at the . . . No, not there. On the news. He's the FBI agent I saw on TV. Instinctively the Predator sank lower into the car seat. *He was with Grace-Ann. I guess he's looking for me. I wonder who died. This can't be a coincidence. Hmm, I wonder if he feels it too.*

Bradley changed out of his suit as soon as the limousine delivered them back home. Then he got a beer from the bartender under the big white tent out front. People continued to arrive with food even though a caterer provided everything they needed. Someone had brought the flowers from the memorial and placed them around the bar.

Round tables with pink linen tablecloths and white folding chairs filled the tent. Easy listening music strayed from speakers behind the buffet table.

Bradley placed himself next to one of the tent poles in the corner opposite the bar. He didn't hear Derek walk up from behind.

Derek dragged a chair from a nearby table and placed it next to Bradley. The two watched as dozens of family and friends, some smiling, some sobbing, mingled in small talk.

Cate spotted them in the corner and joined them. Without saying a word, she sat on Bradley's lap, gave him a hug, and lay her head on his shoulder. After a few moments, she rose, dragged a chair from the same nearby table, and sat on the other side of Bradley.

Holly held John's hand as they walked toward the far corner of the tent. When they reached Bradley, Holly let go of John's hand and gave Bradley a quiet hug and kiss on the cheek. Each dragging a chair from the nearby table, Holly placed hers next to Cate. John sat next to Derek.

Sheila and David joined them moments later, again without saying a word. Sheila wrapped Bradley in her arms and kissed him on his left temple before taking a chair and sitting next to Holly. David sat next to John.

Lynn lifted her hand to her mouth as a feint, but an audible yelp escaped. Her eyes wide, tears began to stream down her cheeks. Doug and Mike turned their heads in the direction Lynn fixated and saw Bradley and his friends lined up in the corner.

"What is it, Lynn?" Doug asked.

"Don't you see?" Lynn sobbed. "That's their wedding party. Just like that, except Laney is missing." Lynn could not hold back her emotions. Her flowing tears spoke loudly and uncontrollably. Doug wrapped her in his arms, and he and Mike helped her into the house.

Seeing Lynn in tears, Cate, Holly, and Sheila jumped from their chairs and followed her into the house. Derek placed his hand on Bradley's knee.

"Another beer?" Derek asked.

Bradley nodded.

Nick's plate overflowed with lasagna, garlic bread, cookies, and pie.

"Jesus, dude," Zayt said over his plate of salad. "Don't you ever eat anything green?"

Mara laughed, and Nick scowled. Then Nick pointed out the parsley on his garlic bread.

"Here are my greens for the day. You know, not everyone is as health conscious as you, big guy."

"Health conscious. You're barely conscious, dude. You look like shit."

"He's right, you know," Mara agreed. "You do look a little worse for the wear."

"Great. Thanks. There's no place like a funeral to kick someone in the gut," Nick spouted.

"Sorry, dude. I just think you need to take better care of yourself. Shit's going to get worse before it gets better," said Zayt.

Nick dropped his fork and sat up straight. "What makes you say that?"

"History. This Predator dude is going to strike again and again. And you're going to be a man down, your best man. That's a lot of pressure."

"Yeah, well, we all have our crosses to bear," Nick said as he glanced toward Mara.

Mara hadn't notice. Preoccupied with the blue Toyota Camry that had parked up the street in front of one of the empty industrial park buildings, Mara found herself wondering what reason anyone would have to park there instead of pulling into the parking lot. *Maybe it is someone from the funeral who had to stop for a phone call. Happens to me all the time.*

"Right, Mara?" Nick asked.

"I'm sorry. What did you say?" Mara asked.

"Tell Zayt how good I am," Nick demanded.

Mara eyes shot open, and her lips curled. "Excuse me?" Mara replied.

"Tell him I run every morning and eat oatmeal for breakfast. Fuck the green stuff. I eat grains."

Zayt and Mara enjoyed a laugh at Nick's expense before Zayt steered the subject back to the Predator.

Lowering his voice, Zayt said, "Look, Nick. Bradley sometimes asks me to help him in certain situations where the bureau can't legally tread. I want you to know that I am here if you need me."

Nick grew serious. "I appreciate that, Zayt. I'll keep it in mind."

"Are we playing nice now?" Mara asked.

They both glared at her.

Derek stood fourth in line at the bar. Sahani fell in line behind him.

"So, how is he?" Sahani asked.

"You tell me. He hasn't spoken ten words," Derek replied.

"Is that very unusual?"

"No. I guess not. He's always been more cerebral than vocal. Except when he was a kid," Derek chuckled.

"Tell me about him as a child."

They moved a space forward in line.

"He was twelve when I met him. Full of confidence. I underestimated his intelligence back then. I never made that mistake again."

"How so? How did you underestimate him?"

"He noticed everything and then analyzed what it meant. He once told me that most people don't really see other people, they just see the shell of a person."

Sahani glanced toward Bradley.

"But he tries to concentrate on an individual's true intentions, not only their actions," Derek continued. "After he came to work for the bureau, he told me he had the ability to turn that cognizance on and off inside him. He likened it to flipping the switch of a lie detector machine. The first time I saw him do it was in St. Kitts a few days after I met him. Of course, I didn't know he was doing it at the time."

They took another step forward.

"The switch is off today," Sahani noted.

"Yeah, I guess it is."

"Derek, Bradley is not going to talk to me, not professionally anyway. I understood that after our initial meeting. It's even less likely now."

"You're probably right, Sahani. But with me in Washington and the Predator case keeping everyone busy, I'd really appreciate it if you would stick around and keep an eye on him. I would rest easier knowing you're here."

"Alright. I'll stick around."

"What can I get you?" the bartender asked as they reached the front of the line.

Watching from the Camry, the Predator pondered, *What am I doing here?*

But the answer was obvious. *I'm enjoying his pain, even though I didn't cause it. But it feels good. It feels like mine. It's always rewarding seeing my men in such agony. But this one. This one's a mystery. And he's looking for me. He is mine, completely. I wonder how much more pain he can take.*

The Predator decided to find out. With that thought, the Camry roared to life, made a U-turn, and headed home. Plans had to be made.

BLACK and WHITE and DARK and LIGHT

Unopened mail stacked high on the table. Most days Bradley never made it to the mailbox. Two weeks had passed since Laney's funeral. Each day resembled the previous one.

Bradley took care of Rusty's needs but lacked in his own care. He didn't eat much of anything, and he drank too much of everything. He pulled himself away from the outside world. He didn't answer his phone, open his door, or check his email. Dirty clothes hung from his state-of-the-art workout equipment, and the odors of two weeks of disregard hung in the air.

He had, however, spent the past ten days getting his financial affairs in order. He sat at his computer typing the last of a series of instructions having to do with his accounts.

Everything is taken care of. Now the letters, he thought.

He decided to write one letter and make copies. It would be hard enough to write, and the message was the same for everyone anyway. Once he got that done, he could make his final plans.

He began, *By the time you read this . . .*

Rusty jumped from the floor and let out a warning bark. Bradley looked at the monitor that displayed the camera image from the front of his home. It showed a silver sedan pulling into the driveway.

Bradley quickly closed the personal financial folders that sat on his desk and tucked them into a file drawer. He then put his computer in sleep mode.

It had been twelve days since Lynn and Doug, at Bradley's request, had left Bradley alone at home. *I should have answered the phone*, Bradley realized as they got out of their car. He met them at the door.

"Dear God, Bradley," Lynn exclaimed, "why wouldn't you answer your phone?"

"Sorry, Mom. I've been busy," Bradley lied.

Lynn squeezed herself between Bradley and the door jamb.

"Oh, my word, Bradley. Oh, no, no," Lynn said, waving her hand in front of her face. "What is that smell? This is . . . stench!"

Rusty rushed to greet them. Doug saw how happy Rusty was that they arrived. Lynn wove through the laundry-covered workout machines, opened the drapes covering the sliding glass door, then slid the door open to the backyard.

Rusty bounded out the open door, took a deep breath, then ran down the steep bank.

Without another word, Lynn shed her coat and headed to the kitchen. She retrieved a disinfectant cleaner and cloth and began cleaning the counter.

"Doug, put those clothes in the hamper. No, put them straight into the washing machine." Lynn pointed to the hanging attire.

Scrubbing furiously, Lynn continued, "Is this how you plan to live, Bradley? In squalor? Do you plan to ignore us for the rest of your life, too?"

"Lynn, I think you're . . ."

"What, Doug? You think what? I'm overreacting?" Lynn screamed. "Is that what you think?" With each word, her anger crumbled away, and fear leached through the cracks until she shook so badly that her legs buckled and she fell to the floor.

Bradley froze, horrified to have made his mother so upset.

Doug rushed to her and tried to help her up.

"No. Just leave me here," Lynn cried. Doug sat beside her on the floor as he leaned against the kitchen cabinets.

No one spoke. If pain had an odor, it would have matched the stench in the room.

Doug made the first move. He reached for his cellphone and made a phone call.

"Hi, it's Doug. Can you come to Bradley's? Yes, now. Alright. Thank you."

Derek met Sahani at the elevator.

"Leaving for the day?" Derek asked.

"No, just an errand. You?"

"The same."

"How's the new office coming?"

"Four walls and a bunch of boxes," Derek replied.

"Mine's finally coming around. At least you have windows."

"Yeah, but I can't see out of them. The contractors still have some work to do. I should be settled in by next week. Just in time to head back to Washington," Derek chuckled.

The elevator arrived, and they both got in.

"How's Cate? Is she getting used to the new schedule yet?" Sahani asked.

"Not really. She's coming with me on this next trip. We've been invited to a charity ball of some kind. She's been talking nonstop with Sheila about dresses, makeup, shoes, all that important stuff." Derek laughed.

"It is, Derek. It is very important to Cate," Sahani said in earnest. "I imagine she feels great pressure to make a good first impression . . . not for her, but for you. Your wife is extremely proud of you."

Derek squinted and turned to face Sahani.

"What is it you're not saying?" he asked.

Sahani chuckled. "Nothing, really. Let me just say that Cate is one of the most giving human beings I know. She always seems to think of others before she thinks of herself. So, it may be just a dress, shoes, and makeup to you, but I'm guessing her choices have more to do with how you look than how she looks."

Derek smiled and made a mental note to buy Cate flowers on the way home.

When Nick assigned Mara to take over Tony's caseload so he could head the Pathside Predator case, she was furious. In retrospect, she saw the advantage. Tony and his task force had gotten nowhere in their investigation. Meanwhile, Mara had closed four cases and was about to close another.

Someone had been crossing state lines to install bogus electronic credit card readers into gas station pumps. Normally, local officials would assume authority, but the information from one of the stolen credit card numbers had been used to purchase an array of firearms that landed the case in the FBI's lap.

Easily installed, the readers fit into the original credit card slots manufactured by a specific company.

Once the perpetrator identified which gas stations used those pumps, the perpetrator need only insert the device, wait a period of time, and remove the device to retrieve the personal credit card information of anyone who used the gas pump and paid with their credit card. The perpetrator would then sell the stolen credit card information to the highest bidder.

Identifying the culprit had been frustrating due to the time elapsed between collection of data and fraudulent use of card numbers. Mara had been working with the cybercrime unit on the sixth floor for only two weeks when they caught a break in the case.

One of the overnight employees of Sharp's Convenience Store in Kittery, Maine, had promised Mara to pay close attention to the gas pumps during his shift. Mara received a call from him at one o'clock that morning.

"I think I got him. He's already gone to two different gas pumps. What should I do?" the clerk asked.

"Nothing. Not a thing, I mean it, Duane. Just make sure the cameras are working. That's all you need to do. If he comes in the store, don't say or do anything out of the ordinary. Promise me. Just let him leave. We'll have everything we need from the cameras."

"Yeah, okay. I promise, Agent Thompkins."

"Duane, I'm going to call the local authorities to secure the gas station. Don't let anyone else use those gas pumps once he is gone. Understand?"

"You got it. Don't worry, Agent Thompkins. We'll get this guy."

Mara chuckled. "Yes, we will. I'll be there as soon as I can. Be careful, Duane."

The phone call had awakened Nick. He still lay in bed when Mara hung up.

"The gas pump guy?" Nick asked.

"Yes. We might have him—or one of them. I still think it's more than a one-man operation. I'm heading to Kittery. I'll keep you posted. Go back to sleep."

"Be careful. If it is an organized group, you don't know what you might be walking into," Nick said. "Maybe I should come with you." Nick got out of bed.

"Sweetie, I'm going to have the Kittery Police Department there with me. Go back to sleep." Mara walked around the bed, placed her hands on Nick's shoulders, and kissed him lightly.

Taking her by surprise, Nick wrapped his arms around her and kissed her hard and long. Then he took her head in his hands, gazed into her eyes, and said, "Promise me you'll be careful."

Stunned by his intensity, Mara simply replied, "I will."

With the roads void of traffic and her ability to skirt the speed limit, Mara arrived at Sharp's in an hour. Police lights flashed, and yellow tape cordoned off what Mara presumed were the offended gas pumps. She recognized Duane standing outside the store, smoking a cigarette.

"Nasty habit," she said to Duane as she approached.

"Yeah," he replied as he dropped the cigarette on the sidewalk and crushed it with his Nike. Duane combed his hair with his fingers and flashed Mara a smile. "Didn't take you long to get here. You must have been flying."

"Well, there's very little traffic this time of morning. And, if I'm worried about someone, I do tend to have a heavy foot."

"Worried? About me?"

"Absolutely. What you did tonight was valiant." Mara noticed Duane's eyebrows shrug. "Courageous," she explained.

Duane's posture improved as the compliment took hold. "Nah, I didn't do anything special," he replied as his cheeks began to redden.

Mara had become used to men and boys making advances at her. Mostly she ignored them, but she was acutely aware of

Duane's hormonal interest in her and wished to let him down easy. After all, he still needed to finish his senior year in high school, and she had no desire to attend his senior prom.

"Of course, you did. I was telling my fiancée about it while I got ready to leave. Well, he's also the supervisory special agent, so he knew about the case already, but he was duly impressed with your actions," Mara smiled. "So, why don't you walk me through what happened before we go inside and look at the recorder."

Mara watched as Duane's posture returned to sluggish form. Then he told her how the car, a Dodge Challenger, pulled up to the number four pump and filled up with gas.

"Wait. Did you say he got gas at the pump? The same guy who messed with the credit card readers?"

"Yeah."

"Did he pay with cash?"

"No, he never came inside."

"Wait here," Mara told Duane.

Mara went inside the store and found the owner speaking with a sergeant of the Kittery police department. She introduced herself and showed her badge.

"Excuse the interruption, but can you retrieve the information for the last credit card purchase on Pump 4, please?"

"Certainly," the owner replied.

In the six years Mara had been with the FBI, she worked some difficult cases involving extremely intelligent criminals. This would not be one of those cases.

Working into the late morning, Mara and her Kittery counterparts investigated the crime scene. An FBI IT specialist retrieved credit card readers from Pumps 4, 7, and 10. The camera footage clearly showed the Dodge Challenger with New

Hampshire license plate number VROOM2 stop in front of each of those pumps. At each pump the same man got out of the car, put a gas nozzle into his tank, and then inserted something into the card reader. Only Pump 4 actually dispensed gas into the vehicle, and that would prove to be a damaging mistake for the suspect.

"Nick, I'm begging you. Please put me on the Predator case. I feel like I'm investigating a kindergarten candy thief," Mara pleaded when she called Nick hours later to give him an update.

Nick laughed. "What are you talking about?"

"They're idiots, that's what I'm talking about. My grandmother could have caught these guys."

"Alright, calm down," Nick snickered. "Tell me what's going on."

"First of all, the moron who placed the devices into the gas pumps used his own credit card to gas up, giving us his name, address, and entire financial access."

"That's great."

"A quick look into New Hampshire Department of Motor Vehicles records revealed the car, a Dodge Challenger with New Hampshire vanity license plate VROOM2 is owned by a corporation called, you guessed it, VROOM. The corporation also registered vehicles with VROOM1, VROOM3, and VROOM4 plates."

"Well, that make things easy," Nick chuckled.

"The VROOM corporation lists New Hampshire resident Josh Kane as president, vice president, and treasurer. Long story short, this guy is a glorified gamer. He's been in and out of juvenile hall and county prisons for most of his life. He enlisted four kids to install and remove the devices, so he didn't get his hands dirty. By the looks of it, he's done pretty well for himself."

"So have you got them all in custody?" Nick asked.

"New Hampshire State Police just confirmed. They have Kane and the kid that drove the Challenger in custody. The kid spilled the names of the other three stooges. NHSP are on it."

"Is that it?"

"No. Now I have to go explain to a seventeen-year-old why I can't go out for pizza with him."

The laugh escaped Nick's lips before he could stop it. "Well, I did ask you to be careful."

"It's not funny, Nick. He's a sweet kid."

"Well . . . he's got great taste in women. See you soon?"

Mara paused. "Ah, yes. I'll see you soon."

Mara slowly lowered her phone, her arms loosely hanging by her sides. *There it is again.* Mara thought. *Uncharacteristic Nick.* Mara had noticed a difference in Nick the past couple of weeks. He had become attentive, loving, and vocal with his thoughts, all things he'd had difficulty with since she'd known him.

She couldn't help but think that Laney's death had something to do with it. But, whatever the cause, she decided to encourage it. On her way home to Chelsea, she stopped at an expensive woman's lingerie shop.

Doug opened the door.

"Please, come in," he said. "Thank you for coming. I didn't know what else to do."

"I'm glad you called," Sahani replied.

Lynn sat at the kitchen table with a cold cup of coffee in front of her. Dark rims shadowed her reddened eyes. Bradley had banished himself to the bathroom, his only means of escape.

"Hello, Lynn. Would you mind if I got myself a cup of coffee?"

Doug started to respond, but Sahani's eyes suggested he wait for Lynn to speak.

"Of course not. Let me get it for you," Lynn whispered.

"No, it's fine. You sit, I'll get it," Sahani said.

"There's sugar in the cabinet if you need it." Lynn added.

"Thank you, but I drink it black."

Sahani got a mug from the counter and poured herself some coffee before sitting across the table from Lynn. "So, do you want to talk about what happened?"

Lynn began to sob. "I don't know what to do. I don't know how to help him."

Sahani reached across the table and took Lynn's hands in hers.

"I'm pretty sure you do know how to help him, Lynn. I just think you are so worried about Bradley that you forgot the most important thing."

Lynn's bewildered frown prompted Sahani to continue.

"You need to help yourself first. You won't be able to help Bradley with his grief until you deal with yours. It won't work if you skip that step."

"But I am grieving. I have grieved." Lynn sobbed.

"That's good. I'm glad to hear it. Tell me. What have you been thinking about most this week?"

Lynn gazed up at the ceiling. "How Bradley lit up when she entered a room."

"I wish I had seen that," Sahani smiled. "What else?"

"The first time he invited her to dinner at our house. He was so nervous, he didn't tell her she would be meeting his parents. Something happened and they couldn't make it to dinner, but I thought it was adorable that he was so nervous."

"Oh? And why couldn't they make it? What happened?" Sahani prodded.

A light gasp escaped Lynn. She shook her head and lowered her gaze. "Oh, I don't remember."

Sahani glanced at Doug and saw him close his eyes. Sahani knew she had remembered the story correctly and pressed the issue.

"Think about it. What kept them from coming to dinner that day?"

Lynn began to quiver, and tears streamed down her face. Her voice cracked when she replied, "Bradley almost died."

Sahani used her eyes to motion Doug to Lynn's side. Doug stood by Lynn, his hand on her shoulder.

"That must have been very hard for you, seeing him like that. Tell me, Lynn. Who was there? Who kept him from dying?"

"Oh, my, God! Laney!" Lynn burst into tears. Doug kneeled beside her as she reached for him. He rocked her as she choked out cries of anguish.

"Let it out, honey," Doug whispered.

Sahani got up and moved to the opposite side of the room to give them privacy. She sat sipping her coffee at Bradley's desk. A moment later, she heard the bathroom door open. She knew it just a matter of time before Bradley would emerge. She just didn't know how she would handle it.

He rounded the corner and stopped, watching his mother cry. He had never seen her so distressed. It crushed him to see her hurting so much.

"What happened?" he asked Sahani.

"She's grieving."

"What did you say to her?"

"We just talked."

"I know how it works. What did you say?"

131

Sahani knew Bradley would show nothing but anger toward her, at that moment and maybe forever. She decided then how she would approach him.

"I just reminded her who she was grieving for," she answered. Then Sahani finished her coffee and returned to the kitchen table.

Bradley watched his mother and father give Sahani a hug before she left. Something inside his chest burned.

She wished to look elegant but understated. Her goal was to stand out enough to be noticed but not enough to overshadow the women around her. "It's a delicate balance. I don't want to be the leading lady. I want to be the girl next door," Cate had told Sheila.

The ensemble Sheila sent from her boutique in California could have easily been found in the armoire of Audrey Hepburn or Grace Kelly, two classically fashionable cinema actresses.

To complement Cate's eyes, Sheila had chosen a tasteful emerald-green chiffon gown with gold-beaded and embroidered v-neck bodice and capped sleeves. A thin green ribbon cinched her waistline. The matching shoes featured a modest three-inch heel, and the gold clutch purse filled to capacity with only a small package of tissues, lipstick, and makeup compact.

Cate's thick, wavy brown hair hung below her shoulders in loose, oversized braids with errant strands. A thin emerald ribbon intertwined throughout, framing her face. Although painstakingly fashioned, the hairstyle meant to look like a last minute afterthought.

Sheila had sent an array of jewelry for Cate to choose from. Although drawn to the necklace with a large emerald encased in gold, she chose a dainty emerald and diamond chip strand to hang from her thin neck with matching earrings.

Cate smiled as she inspected herself in the hotel room mirror. Sheila had struck the perfect note. Now it would be up to Cate to compose hers and Derek's foray into DC society.

As Cate entered the room, Derek stood staring out the window at the city's lights, his back to her.

"It's beautiful, isn't it?" Cate asked as she entered.

Derek turned. Before he said a word, Cate knew she had nailed it. Derek's eyes grew soft and wanting. "Yes, you are," he responded.

"And you look awful sexy in that tuxedo. Why is it you don't wear one more often?"

"Because I would spend all my time fending off women and not get a lick of work done. As it is, I lose half my day that way."

"I can't say as I blame the women," Cate said as she moved in for a kiss.

One kiss turned into two, then a lingering third.

"You know, I could call down to the desk and tell them that I fell in the shower and threw my back out and to send our driver away," Derek suggested.

"Not on your life, mister. This is your night to shine, and I am here to make sure you do. Besides, Sheila went through a lot of trouble to dress me tonight. And I'm just dying to meet your assistant, Madelyn."

"You can't blame a guy for trying," Derek said as he picked up Cate's shawl and draped it over her shoulders.

Only blocks from the Capitol building, Union Station could be considered the most iconic of Washington, DC, venues. The repurposed main hall, once a train station with barrel-vaulted ceilings and gold leaf accents seated more than two thousand guests. While the station itself still served as a transit hub, the main hall had transformed along with other parts of the grand late nineteenth-century building into shopping and other mixed use areas. Oversized semicircular windows placed high in alcoves line the hall guarded by Louis St. Gaudens centurian statues modeled after the Baths of Diocletian in ancient Rome.

"Hello, Director Richards. Aren't you looking handsome," Madelyn said as she greeted them at the door.

"Good evening, Madelyn. I thought we agreed you would call me Derek."

"I agreed to call you by your first name in informal settings. This is hardly an informal setting."

Derek raised his brows. "Ms. Cross, may I introduce my wife, Cate. I believe the two of you have already conspired about my well-being," Derek smiled.

Cate and Madelyn embraced as if old friends.

"It's so nice to finally meet you, Cate. You look positively stunning," Madelyn declared.

"Not half as stunning as you, Madelyn. My husband didn't let on just how radiant you are."

"You are too kind, Cate. It's your sister, Sheila, who pulled this off tonight," Madelyn said as she waved her hand from her head to her waist. "A couple of video chats and, voilà. You were so right about her. She is amazing."

Standing off to the side, Madelyn's date cleared his throat.

"Oh, I'm sorry, honey. Executive Assistant Director Derek Richards and Cate, this is Robert Harris, personal assistant to the president of the United States."

"Glorified office assistant, really," Robert said as he and Derek shook hands. "Madelyn has told me nothing about you,"

Robert chuckled. "But your wife and sister-in-law have been her favorite topic of conversation all week."

Madelyn put her arm through Cate's and smiled. "Follow me, I'll take you to Deputy Director Mendez."

The transition from cocktail hour to dinner spawned the first chance for Cate to excuse herself to use the restroom, although her need was not as great as her want. Staring into the mirror with her head spinning, Cate wondered how she would ever remember the names of those she had already met, not to mention of those she would soon meet. It wasn't often Cate felt overwhelmed, but she found herself lacking confidence.

"I remember my first Washington event," a voice came from a chair in the corner of the washroom.

Cate turned and saw Julia Mendez, wife of the deputy director.

"It was about this time in the evening when I went to the restroom because I thought I'd be sick. I was scared to death I was going to do something to embarrass my husband, fall on the dance floor, or drag toilet paper with my shoe."

Julia smiled.

"And? How did you manage to get through it?" Cate asked.

"I realized there was only one person in the room that I cared what he thought of me. And if I fell, I knew he would pick me up."

Julia got up and snaked her arm through Cate's. "Stick with me. It's taken me almost fifteen years, but I now know everyone's name and most of their embarrassing moments. After a few drinks, I may tell you some of mine."

"Wait," Cate said. She lifted each foot to check for toilet paper, laughed, then said, "Okay, I'm ready."

The two walked arm-in-arm to their dinner table.

Cate lost track of the number of partners she danced with. Reminiscing on the ride back to the hotel, Cate alerted Derek he should worry about Director Mendez.

"And why is that?" Derek asked.

"Because he is a marvelous dancer. I could get used to twirling around the dance floor with him."

"His wife couldn't say enough about you," Derek replied. "I think you may get plenty of chances to twirl with Mike."

"Mike? You're on a first name basis with the deputy director?" Cate's eyes ceased blinking.

Derek laughed at Cate's reaction. Then, turning sideways in the car's seat, he placed his hand behind her neck and drew her in. His tender kiss sent tingles down Cate's spine. When he withdrew, he said, "After all that dancing, you must need a warm shower."

Dimples formed in Cate's cheeks. "Indeed," she said.

SUBTERFUGE

Sahani waited four days before making her next move. She confirmed with Lynn and Doug that Bradley was home alone. When Lynn told Sahani that Bradley had begun having his groceries delivered so he wouldn't have to leave the house, Sahani knew the longer she waited, the harder it would be.

Before she knocked on the door, she heard Rusty bark, alerting Bradley to his guest.

Bradley opened the door halfway.

"What do you want?" he asked.

"I need to talk to you," Sahani replied.

"Talk."

"Bradley, let me in."

Bradley sat still for a moment before he sighed and opened the door. He rolled his chair to the kitchen table still topped with unopened mail.

"What is it?" he asked.

"Did you look at the files I left for you?" Sahani asked, knowing the probable answer.

"No."

Sahani lightly slapped her hand on the table. "I told him you wouldn't. He insisted you would help, but I told him you wouldn't."

"Who? Who insisted I would help?"

"Derek. He said nothing would keep you from this case. Not even Laney's tragic death. He didn't believe me when I told him I knew better."

"You? You think you know me?"

"Of course I do. It's my job to know you."

"You know nothing about me."

"I know I might as well take those files back."

"Get the hell out of here," Bradley yelled as he rolled his chair to the door and opened it.

"Alright. I have more copies," Sahani said as she walked out the door.

Fuming at Sahani's insinuation that she knew anything about him, Bradley angrily swept the contents of the tabletop onto the floor. Rusty jumped and ran toward the sliders.

"Shit, Rusty. I didn't mean to scare you, buddy. I'm sorry." Bradley moved to Rusty and stroked his back. Rusty looked toward the door. Bradley opened it, and Rusty happily trotted outside.

"You're a real shithead, Bradley," he said aloud.

Bradley considered that Sahani had been trying to use some form of reverse psychology on him but remembered how indifferent she had been to him a few days prior. He thought back to how he treated her at the hospital.

She thinks I'm an asshole.

Then he thought about what she said Derek had told her, that nothing could keep Bradley from this case. Bradley could see Derek saying that. *And,* Bradley thought, *isn't it the truth? Or, used to be the truth?*

Bradley went to his desk, moved the draft of his personal letter to his desk drawer, and picked up the file Sahani had previously dropped off.

The file contained the full autopsy report and Sahani's updated profile of the Pathside Predator.

Bradley began with the autopsy report. The use of a foreign object to simulate intercourse did not surprise him. The fact confirmed his original feelings that the sexual aspect of the crime was not a motivating factor.

Disinfectant on the victim's hand, not hands, raised curiosity. Certainly Grace-Ann could not have wiped her own hands before the attack, or her right hand would have held at least some traces of disinfectant. *No*, Bradley thought, *the Predator wiped her left hand clean for some reason.* Nothing in the remainder of the report suggested what that reason might be.

Bradley turned his attention to Sahani's updated profile of the Predator. She made no changes to age and physical attributes, but when Bradley got to the meat of the profile, he became enraged.

The unsub is a male sexual deviant who attacks targets of convenience. The act of sexual intercourse is the motivating factor. Victims are chosen in a seemingly random way suggesting the unsub is disorganized.

Bradley picked up his phone and stabbed at Nick's name in the contact list.

"Nick Gaston."

"You've got to throw out that profile Nick. It's bullshit. The team will be looking in the wrong direction."

"Bradley?" Nick asked.

"Yeah, of course it's me," Bradley answered.

"What's this about the profile?"

"It's bullshit. It's all wrong. She doesn't know her ass from her elbow, Nick."

"Who?"

"Sahani Kumar, that's who." Bradley breathed heavily.

"Wait. Are you telling me you don't agree with the profile we're using?" Nick asked.

"Not only don't I agree with it, but it's also dangerous. It's almost the opposite of who you should be looking for."

"Well, I don't know, Bradley. Sahani made a pretty good case backing up her profile. What makes you think she's wrong?"

"Because the sexual assault . . ."

Nick cut Bradley off in the middle of his sentence. "Bradley, sorry. I'll call you back later. Something just came up." Nick hung up.

Bradley threw his cellphone down onto his desk so hard that the cover cracked and popped off.

"Dammit." Bradley yelled.

He booted his computer and monitors. The computer began to sing with weeks' worth of notifications and alerts. He ignored them and went straight to his FBI login page.

"Holy sh . . . ," Nick caught himself. "What did you write in that profile?"

Sahani formed a mischievous smirk. "Everything I knew that would make him angry."

"He's going to find out about the real profile, you know. Then he's going to explode," Nick said.

"Yes, he will. But hopefully by then he will be entrenched in the case again. I had to do something. This way he'll only be angry at me for misleading him. He doesn't know you know about the fake profile because you just prevented him from informing you," Sahani smiled.

Nick shook his head. "Bradley must really be off his game if he fell for that."

"I don't know, Nick. I can be a pretty convincing bitch when I want to be." Sahani said, glancing back at Nick as she strolled out of his office.

Cecile Boulanger exited the yoga studio at 7:45 a.m., her normal time. The Predator knew her next stop would be her Weymouth home. Like most of the victims, Cecile stuck to a precise daily schedule, a trait the Predator looked for and admired.

The blue Camry parked on the opposite side of the street three houses away from Cecile's high-priced Stepford home. If all went according to schedule, Cecile would leave her house at 8:50 a.m. washed and dressed for her three-hour shift as activities director at the local nursing home. She would then return home and pick up the family dog, a small white puffy thing. Research informed the Predator Cecile's dog was a Bichon Frisé, and although the breed is known to be friendly and quiet, the Predator decided that when the time came, it would be best to eliminate the threat of the canine.

Cecile and the pooch arrived at Blue Hills Reservation by 1:00 p.m. and casually strolled the Skyline Trail. With most people still working, the Quincy trail provided peace and tranquility. She encountered only one other person on the walk, a slightly younger woman walking a Golden Retriever. Cecile and the Predator exchanged a pleasant smile but no words, just as both preferred.

On the way home, Cecile picked up her two young boys from elementary school and then returned home to prepare dinner for the family.

Just another typical Wednesday, thought the Predator.

Tomorrow the Predator looked forward to grocery shopping, work, and a visit to the hairdresser before returning to her victim's home after Cecile picked the boys up from school.

With details of Cecile's pending demise worked out, the Predator decided on a minimum of three dry runs.

After watching Cecile unload her dog and children from her SUV, the blue Camry carrying the Golden Retriever in the backseat, pulled away from the curb and drove away.

Before returning to the apartment, the Camry made its way to the neighborhood of Agent Bradley Whitman. Looking as if it had not moved from the spot in weeks, a white pickup truck still sat in the carport. With not much else to do, the Predator sat and watched from a distance.

After Sahani left his house, Bradley read and reread the bureau reports, autopsy reports, and newspaper articles from the Predator cases. He was certain about his version of the profile and worried the FBI used false criteria to weed out suspects.

Sahani had used Dr. Reyes's autopsy report to counter Bradley's initial profile. She noted the Predator as disorganized because the position of the last victim's legs did not conform to other cases. She suggested that the unsub acted spontaneously and recklessly in the act.

Bradley felt sure the act of spreading the victim's legs had to do with an obsession and not a sudden impulse.

Thinking about that, Bradley suddenly had a realization. "Son of a . . . ," Bradley said aloud.

He quickly flipped the pages of the Grace-Ann Colson autopsy report. When he found the part of the report he wanted, he reread it out loud.

"It appears the victim's legs were pushed apart by means of force. A footprint on the victim's right sneaker and a bruise on her left thigh suggest the killer placed their own foot on her sneaker-clad foot and a hand or hands on her thigh and pushed her legs as far apart as they were able."

Bradley stopped reading. Everything he knew about the Predator case circled his brain until it fell into place.

"Jesus," Bradley said. Then, "Rusty, we're going out."

Roused by Bradley's long absent enthusiasm, Rusty ran toward the door. Bradley retrieved his truck keys from the pile he had re-stacked on the kitchen table, and the two headed out to his truck. Before jumping in Rusty decided to relieve himself in the front yard. When he heard another dog barking, he stopped himself midstream.

No other dogs lived nearby, so it was not unusual that both Bradley and Rusty searched for the source of the bark. Bradley got a quick glimpse of what looked like a Golden Retriever in the backseat of a blue vehicle that had been parked but then made a U-turn to leave the abandoned industrial park that served as Bradley's neighborhood.

They're probably lost, Bradley thought.

"Finish up, Rusty. We have work to do," Bradley said.

Carl's eyes lit up when he saw Rusty prance through the front door of FBI headquarters.

"Agent Rusty, where have you been?" Carl smiled. "And you, Agent Whitman. It's nice to have you back," he added.

"Thank you, Carl. But I'm not sure I am back. I just need to fix something," Bradley replied.

"Well, it's good to see you and your sidekick."

Bradley started to move toward the elevator and then turned back to Carl.

"How's your wife doing, Carl?"

"She's into her craving stage. Last night it was pistachio ice cream. Do you know how hard it is to find pistachio ice cream at eleven o'clock at night?"

"I can imagine. Give her my best, will you?"

"I will. Thank you Agent Whitman."

"Someday I'm going to get you to call me Bradley, Carl. The heck with protocol."

Carl chuckled as Bradley and Rusty entered the elevator.

Rusty saw Mara and bounded to her desk. Mara let out a happy screech and wrapped her arms around the dog. The bullpen buzzed with activity despite the fact that only half the agents occupied their desks. Bradley noticed Tony was not at his.

Without going over to her, Bradley motioned to Mara asking if she would watch Rusty for him. She replied with a wave of her hand.

Bradley wheeled himself down the hall to Nick's office where Hazel sat at her desk. Bradley remembered seeing Hazel and her husband at the memorial service but couldn't remember anything he may have said to her.

"Agent Whitman, it's so nice to see you."

"Hello, Hazel. How have you been?"

"Just fine, thank you. Does Agent Gaston know you are here?"

"No, but I hope he has time to see me. It's rather important," Bradley stated.

"Oh, I'm sure he can make time for you."

Hazel picked up the phone and announced Bradley's arrival. Almost at once Nick opened his door. He couldn't hide his surprise.

"Bradley, I didn't know you were here," Nick said.

"I just got here. Have you got a minute, Nick?"

"Of course. Come in."

With the door closed behind him. Bradley didn't waste time getting to his point.

"It's a woman."

Nick elevated his eyebrows. "Okay, I'll bite. Who's a woman?"

"The Pathside Predator is a woman." Bradley let the statement hang in the air and observed as Nick's thought process played out.

Nick's expression settled on disbelief.

"Bradley, wait. I know Sahani's profile got you rattled, but I think there's something you should . . ."

"This has nothing to do with Sahani's profile. It has to do with facts: cognitive, behavioral, and demographic facts."

"Okay, I'm listening," Nick said as he sat at his desk.

"It's reported that there was evidence each victim was disabled before their death. This tells us that the killer most likely did not have a substantial weight or strength advantage over the victims."

"Okay, it could be a small man," Nick replied.

"Wait. Just wait until I finish Nick," Bradley barked, and Nick frowned.

"This latest victim, Grace-Ann, gave us more reason to look at a woman perpetrator. The way her legs were spread—using the unsub's whole body to force her legs apart—does not fit the profile of a male offender. Not to mention the size of the shoe print on the victim's right sneaker. Has forensics given you a report on the shoe print yet?"

"No, not yet. They've been pretty backed up."

"Well, I saw the print. In men's size shoes it was about a size six, maybe six and a half, I'd guess. How many full-grown men do you know who have feet that small?" Nick winced. "Never mind, don't bother. It's less than five percent from what I could find online."

"I expect the full forensics report within a day or two. We'll see what they say," said Nick.

"The areas where the women were killed are highly suspect. Any woman walking or biking alone would be wary of an approaching man. But an approaching woman? Not so much. And the victims were lured off the main path, not dragged. There's no evidence any of them got moved."

"Maybe our killer befriended his victims somehow."

Bradley, a bit irritated Nick wouldn't trust his assessment, continued. "The breast. It's extremely personal. I don't know why I didn't think of it before. I suppose it's not out of the question that a male subject might take the breast nipple for a souvenir, but that's all it would be, a souvenir. I think it means more. I think it is more likely a woman would find the mutilation the ultimate act of defeminizing their victim."

"On what grounds do you base that?"

"She places the victim's hand over her missing breast. It's like rubbing salt in the wound. But I'm not sure why she sanitized the victim's hand first. You need to talk to the doctors who did the other autopsies to find out if they noticed anything unusual about the hands."

"Not me. You." Nick said.

"What?" Bradley asked.

"I don't need to ask them. You do." Nick repeated.

"Wait, no. I'm not working. I . . ."

"Okay, if you need more time, I'll have Sahani do it," Nick said.

The veins in Bradley's temples began to pulse, and his cheeks turned crimson.

"Are you crazy? Did you read her profile? She's not qualified to analyze my dog, for chrissake."

"Bradley, I don't have anyone else. It's either you or her. We've got a lot of shit going on here!"

Bradley sat, his head down and shaking side to side.

"Alright, I'll contact the coroner's offices and see what I can find. But that's it."

Nick nodded.

"I'm serious, Nick. Tell Tony he's probably looking for a woman. I'll write up what I've got and send it to you."

As Bradley shut the door behind him, he couldn't see the big grin on Nick's face.

Bradley shared his profile opinion with Mara, who seemed to accept it much more easily than Nick. Bradley hoped she would use her influence to convince Nick to take his hunch more seriously.

What Bradley didn't know was that Nick had already called Tony to relay Bradley's message.

"It's a game changer," Derek said.

"For sure. I just hope his instincts aren't, you know, screwed up," Nick replied.

"I would rather follow Bradley's hunches on his worst day than most analysts on their best. If he thinks the Predator is a woman, I think it needs to be taken very seriously. How is he doing?"

"I don't know, Derek. He's different. He's angry."

"Can't blame him. His life has been pulled out from under him."

"That, yes, and Sahani has pushed his buttons. I don't know what will happen if they end up in the same room. I've never seen him so . . . agitated," Nick said.

"Sahani is taking one for the team. She knew exactly what she was doing, and it seems to be working. Don't worry about her. The funny thing is, those two are mirror images of each other."

"How so?"

"They are both highly intelligent, analytical, relentless, and extremely stubborn."

"Yeah? Well, I think the only reflection Bradley sees in Sahani is Cruella DeVille."

Derek chuckled. "Like I said . . . relentless. I'll be home in a couple days, and I'll check on Bradley. Send me his new profile when you get it and call me with any updates."

"You got it."

She wouldn't be needing him anymore, so she released the stolen Golden Retriever at her first opportunity.

"That was reckless," she said to no one but herself.

She had planned to go see Grace-Ann's husband to relish his sorrow, but instead she had made the spur-of-the-moment decision to check on Wheelchair Man in spite of her cautious nature. As she drove back to her hotel, she tried to understand what made her do it.

What is it about him? Why can't I get him out of my head?

But she already knew the answer. She had researched Bradley Whitman, whom she sardonically called Wheelchair Man, after first seeing him in the graveyard. That resulted in her first careless move— sending him a sympathy card for his departed fiancée.

Although generally written about in newspaper accounts as a boy wonder, she guessed Wheelchair Man's career as an

FBI analyst had been less than stellar. Otherwise, how could he account for the newspaper story citing a six-month sabbatical the FBI insist he take after they found a dead man in Wheelchair Man's home some years back.

She excelled at reading people. Very rarely did she miscalculate others' manners and motives.

He was broken. And he was broken long before he lost his fiancée. *But that could prove to be the final straw,* she thought. *Would he hang himself like Barbara Baker's husband, or would he shoot himself with his official FBI pistol?*

She felt aroused, and it took her by surprise. A man hadn't made her feel sexually aroused since she was fifteen years old, although that man didn't live long enough to satisfy her. Not directly, anyway. But what she learned from that experience steered her to her current path, a path of self approbation.

Enough distraction, she thought. Typically, nothing could take her thoughts away from her meticulous pre-planning or her post-reveling in her successes. Irritated with herself, she cleared her mind of everyone except Cecile Boulanger and, more importantly, Cecile's husband, Jake. Although he probably would not be a candidate for suicide, she knew his wife's murder would destroy him.

It took Bradley a couple of days to connect with all the doctors who performed autopsies on Pathside Predator victims. None could provide insight as to whether any of the other victims' hands held traces of disinfectant. Bradley couldn't be sure if it meant the act of wiping the hand was exclusive to Grace-Ann Coulson, the disinfectant somehow got wiped away at the scenes, or the coroners overlooked the detail.

He just finished talking with the last of the coroners when Rusty sprang from his bed and let out a bark. Bradley glanced at the monitor and saw Derek's vehicle pull up to his house. He watched as both Derek and Cate exited the SUV.

Not thrilled about having visitors, Bradley tried to paste a smile on his face as he opened the door.

"This is an ambush, I know," Derek said, "but I'm pretty sure if I called first, you would have come up with an excuse not to see us."

"Come on in," Bradley responded.

"It's my fault," Cate said. "I wanted to check in and see how you are doing."

"I'm fine, Cate. You don't need to worry about me," Bradley replied.

"It doesn't work that way, Bradley. You telling me not to worry about you isn't going to make it go away. What's all this?" Cate asked, referring to the table covered in unopened cards, letters, and bills.

"My mail," Bradley replied.

"How many weeks' worth? Are you on your own little mail strike?"

"I just don't want . . . " Bradley's voice trailed off.

"Okay," Cate said softly, then ordered, "You two go off in the corner and talk about whatever it is that Derek is dying to talk to you about. I'll take care of this."

Derek picked up a kitchen chair and carried it to Bradley's desk.

"So," Derek said, "how are you really?"

"How the hell do you think I am? My life sucks," Bradley said, then paused. "I'm sorry. I don't mean to be . . . I'm not angry at you. I'm angry at the world."

"I know."

"It's just . . . I don't have anyone to be angry with. It's not like it's anyone's fault except mine."

"Whoa. What? How the hell is Laney's death your fault?"

"I told her to call my mother. If she hadn't been in her office alone, she would still be alive." Unable to look at Derek, Bradley hung his head.

"That's just bullshit, Bradley, and you know it. Using that same logic, you would have to blame your mother for Laney's death. Are you prepared to do that too?"

Bradley's head shot up. "What? No. I'm the one who dismissed her idea of having the wedding here. I'm the one who suggested she call my mother. I'm the one who put her in that office. I'm the reason she is dead!"

Derek jumped out of the chair, knocking it over. The sudden movement and crash startled Cate.

"Jesus, Bradley. Who the hell do you think you are? God?" Derek yelled. "Things happen . . . all the time. Things we have no control over. None of us, including you." Derek reached for the chair, planted it firmly beside Bradley, and sat. "You're not God. You can't save everybody. Why is it I have to keep reminding you of that?"

"It's easier if I have someone to blame," said Bradley.

"It's not supposed to be easy." Derek took a deep breath, then continued. "Do you remember what you said to me the night I suspended you from the bureau?"

"No."

"You apologized, then said you were going to try to appreciate what you've got and not dwell on what you don't have. And you did. You're going to have to do that again, Bradley.

It will be much harder this time, but if you don't, you're going to destroy more than yourself. You'll destroy everyone who loves you, too. What happened to Laney was nobody's fault, especially not yours."

Losing the battle to hold back his tears, Bradley simply nodded his head.

Derek sympathetically held Bradley by the shoulders.

After a few moments of silence, Bradley spoke.

"So, what was it you were dying to talk to me about?" Bradley flashed air quotes when he spoke the word, dying.

Derek grinned.

"I want to know everything that leads you to believe the Predator is a woman. Walk me through it."

Bradley began with the sexual aspects of the crimes and laid out his reasoning. It felt good to express his thoughts aloud. Doing so convinced him even more that his hunch was correct.

When Bradley had nearly finished explaining to Derek, Cate interrupted.

"Hey, Bradley," she called.

"Yeah?"

"Who's PP?"

"What?"

"You have a sympathy card from someone who signed their name as PP. It's a little odd, too," Cate added.

"How so?" Derek asked.

"It looks like a child's handwriting, and it says, 'Your loved one is at peace. How do you feel now?' Who would ask that question in a sympathy card?"

Derek and Bradley exchanged a glance before joining Cate at the kitchen table.

"Let me see that," Bradley said.

Bradley examined the card with Derek looking over his shoulder.

"Where's the envelope this came in?" Derek asked.

"Here." Cate handed a white envelope to Derek.

Derek flipped the envelope over, back and forth. "There's no return address. The postage mark says it was mailed right here at the Revere post office."

Angels covered the front of the card along with the words With Sympathy. Inside, the handwritten inscription read "May you take comfort in knowing an angel is watching over you. Your loved one is at peace. How do you feel now?"

The handwriting looked as if penned by a child, but Bradley and Derek knew the writer went to great lengths to make it appear that way.

"What is it?" Cate asked. "Why do you both look like you've seen a ghost?"

"Cate, get a plastic storage bag from the kitchen drawer, please," Derek said.

Cate handed Derek the bag, and he placed the envelope inside. Bradley slipped the card inside before Derek sealed it.

"What is it?" Cate repeated. "Who is PP?" But just as she asked again, she understood. She knew by their reaction that PP stood for the Pathside Predator. "Oh, my God!"

"How?" Bradley asked.

"And why?" Derek said.

"She wants me to know I'm being watched. It may be a generic sympathy card, but the saying . . . "take comfort in knowing an angel is watching you." She doesn't mean that Laney is watching me. She—PP—is. And she's calling herself an angel."

"But how does she know about you, and why would she risk it?" Derek asked.

"That's what we need to find out," Bradley replied.

"You were on the news," Cate said.

"What? When?" Bradley asked.

"The day they found the body. Channel 5 showed a clip of you leaving the crime scene. The newscaster mentioned you by name."

"Okay, but what about Laney? We didn't even put a notice in the newspaper. How would she know about Laney?" Bradley asked.

"I don't know," Derek said as Cate shrugged her shoulders. "Have you noticed anything or anyone unusual?"

"No. But until I went to the office the other day, I hadn't left my house. I . . . no, it was nothing."

"What?" Derek asked.

"There was a dog in a blue sedan. He barked at Rusty when we were leaving for the office. But the car made a U-turn and drove away. I think they were lost."

"Would your profile suggest the Predator owns a dog?" Derek asked.

"No." Bradley shook his head. "But I would have bet money that the Predator would not take a chance like this, either. I'm not sure what to think."

"Maybe this is the mistake we've been waiting for," Derek said. "I'll get the card to the lab. I doubt we'll find fingerprints but maybe they'll be able to tell us something about the handwriting or pen."

"I'm glad you're back, Derek," Bradley said.

"I'm glad you're back, too," replied Derek.

BETRAYED

The next day, Nick called a meeting of the Predator task force. Knowing he would be back in town, Derek had told Nick he wanted to hear from the investigating team. The entire eighth floor crammed into the briefing room, including Mara who was not officially on the case but refused to be excluded. Derek, Nick, Tony, and Sahani stood together in front of the whiteboard. Tony was expected to outline the case, and Sahani planned to give the updated profile of the Pathside Predator.

Just as Nick was about to start, Bradley rolled through the door. Derek motioned him to the front of the room.

"Are you prepared to give the profile?" Derek quietly asked Bradley.

"Absolutely," Bradley responded.

Hearing that, Sahani took a seat at the side of the room. The move filled Bradley with satisfaction.

"Okay, let's get right to it. Tony, tell us what's happening with the case," Nick said.

"Right. Well, we've accounted for the victim's whereabouts for the two weeks before she was killed."

Derek interrupted. "Her name was Grace-Ann Coulson, Tony." Derek made it a habit—and insisted the same of his agents—to call the victims by name as a show of respect.

Unhappy with himself for the slip, Tony closed his eyes and pursed his lips as he began to speak.

"Grace-Ann and her family had a weekday schedule, and they stuck to it every day and all day," Tony said. "Her husband,

Todd, left for work each day at precisely 8:15 a.m. Grace-Ann put their two school-age children on the school bus at 8:25 a.m. The three-year-old daughter went to daycare Monday, Wednesday, and Friday from 10 a.m. to 2 p.m. During that time, Grace-Ann attended a yoga class at the gym followed by a shower, then lunch at the café next door. Sometimes women from the class joined her.

"She would return home after picking up her daughter and be back in time to meet her two other children as they came off the school bus at 3:15pm," Tony went on. "Tuesdays and Thursdays, the daughter stayed home with Grace-Ann. Their days consisted of house cleaning, grocery shopping, and household errands. Grace-Ann's husband returned from work at 6:30 p.m. when the family ate dinner. Every Tuesday and Thursday evening after dinner, Todd got the kids ready for bed so Grace-Ann could go for either a walk or a jog. She always went to the same place, Sea Plane Basin Trail. As you may recall, Grace-Ann was murdered on a Thursday night while presumably jogging."

Tony took a deep breath before continuing. "As I've stated, Grace-Ann's movements were predictable. A serial killer's dream. We've interviewed her neighbors, friends, yoga classmates, and everyone from the grocery store, pharmacy, and dry cleaners. Grace-Ann had not given anyone an indication that she was being followed or that she felt uncomfortable at any time. We've come up with nothing."

"Thank you, Tony," Nick said. "We got the forensics report. Grace-Ann's hand had been wiped with a disinfectant cloth. We hoped to get a brand name from the report, but I'm told it is impossible to distinguish, as the ingredients are much the same in each brand. However, we did get a hit on the shoe print from the side of Grace-Ann's sneaker. The print came from a New Balance 940v4 running shoe."

"Bradley, do you want to take it from here? Who are we looking for?" Nick asked.

Bradley cleared his throat before he began. "We're most likely looking for a woman in her thirties. The forensics report supports this suspicion. The report states that the New Balance 940v4 running shoeprint was from a size seven-and-a-half sneaker. New Balance does not make that size in the men's version of the shoe."

Bradley paused to let the murmurs in the room run their course. He glanced at Sahani, who wore a thin smile.

He continued. "This woman is smart, organized, obsessive, and persuasive. She is physically fit and blends in. She may have even participated in the yoga class or eaten at the café that Grace-Ann frequented.

"She is so confident," Bradley said, "that she allowed herself to be impulsive with the positioning of Grace-Ann's legs. That proved to be a mistake and could be a sign that she is feeling untouchable. Often, that leads to more mistakes. The sexual penetration is a ruse. She wants law enforcement to think the women were sexually assaulted by a male.

"The real prize for the Predator is the breast," Bradley informed the team. "In my original profile, I suggested the killer could be a collector. I don't believe that is the case. I think her act of taking the women's breast is to defeminize her victims. And it is possible she views herself as an angel of mercy. I hope to have a more complete profile for you soon."

Bradley chose to not share evidence of the sympathy card with the full team, although he did intend to share it with Nick and Tony if Derek hadn't already.

"Okay," Nick said, "so here's what we're going to do. We are going to go back to square one and look at Grace-Ann's murder from a new perspective. We are going to revisit the previous cases in the same way.

"Mara," he said to her, "I want you to talk to everyone at the yoga studio. See if anybody joined and then disappeared within our timeline. The same with the café. Interview the staff and see if they remember anyone hanging around at the same time as Grace-Ann."

Mara could hardly contain her excitement, which caused Bradley to crack a smile for the first time since he got the call about Laney. "I'll get right on it," she said as she left the room.

Derek asked Nick, Bradley, and Sahani to stay behind as the room emptied.

Bradley grimaced when he saw that Derek intended to include Sahani when telling the details of the sympathy card. Bradley had come to realize Sahani had duped him. What he couldn't decide was if he was more upset with her for doing it or with himself for falling for it. Either way, he wasn't happy.

"What I'm about to tell you stays in this room," Derek said. "It isn't only speculation that the Predator might make a mistake. It's already happened. She may be watching Bradley."

Nick and Sahani glanced at Bradley.

Derek described the sympathy card, including the handwritten note, then continued. "We think she may have seen him on the news and, for some unknown reason, latched on to him. Sahani, I think you and Bradley should brainstorm reasons why she might have fixated on Bradley. If we understand her reasoning, we'll have a more complex profile."

Sahani began to say something, but Bradley cut her off.

"I think if we work it separately, we may have a better chance of figuring this out," Bradley said.

"What makes you say that?" Derek raised his brows.

"Because I don't trust her," Bradley replied.

Derek turned to Nick and said, "Could you excuse us, please?"

Nick left the room. Derek took a seat and motioned Sahani to do the same.

"Let's deal with this right now," Derek said. "Sahani did what I told her to."

A lump lodged in Bradley's throat. He hadn't considered that Derek knew Sahani had deceived him. Suddenly his chest felt as if it were on fire, and it hurt deeply.

"You told her to lie to me?" Bradley asked. "To mock me and my job?"

Derek placed his elbows on his knees and cupped his hands. "No. I told her to do whatever it took to bring you back."

"Back? Back from what? From grieving the loss of my fiancée?"

Sahani again began to speak, but Derek held up his hand to stop her.

"Back from hell, Bradley. We both know you committed yourself to your own personal purgatory. And we both know why, as misguided as it was," Derek said.

"Who the hell are you to say what's misguided?" Bradley barked.

"Stop!" Sahani yelled. "I don't need you to fall on a sword for me, Derek. I decided my course of action knowing what the consequences would be. I deceived you, Bradley, not Derek. I took my best shot in hopes of snapping you out of your depression. I'm prepared to live with the fallout. What I'm not prepared to live with is another Predator victim, one I may be able to contribute to preventing. This isn't about you and me or Derek."

"How . . . how do I know this isn't part of your con? Your plan to save me from myself," Bradley asked.

"Because I'm telling you it's not. I promise I will never lie to you or mislead you again," Sahani said.

"One more question. Who else knew?" Bradley asked.

Derek exchanged a glance with Sahani, then answered, "Nick."

Bradley slammed his hand on the arm of his chair then glared at Derek.

"I thought we were brothers," Bradley said as he turned his chair toward the door. With his back to them both, he continued, "I'll work with you until this is over."

Derek watched Bradley leave, then put his hand on his chest and rubbed hard, as if trying to quell a cramp.

"Are you alright?" Sahani asked.

"Yeah. That one just hit a little hard," Derek said.

"He's still grieving, Derek. He's not himself. Give him some time."

"I don't know, Sahani. This feels different," Derek said as he left the room.

Sahani felt terrible for the rift she created between Bradley and Derek. *And now Nick is exposed.* She wondered about Derek's last remark, about it feeling different. She needed to know what Derek meant. *Why did he think things were different?*

Sahani left the room, strolled past Bradley who buried himself at his desk, and continued down the hall to the last office on the right. She knocked on the closed door.

"Come in," Derek called. He stood at his window looking toward the Boston skyline.

"What did you mean? Why do things feel different?" Sahani asked as she closed the door.

"Because I made it different."

"Explain that to me, please."

"A long time ago, I told Bradley I would always have his back. He could always count on me. And now he sees me as his Judas."

"That's a bit melodramatic, don't you think? Sure, he's not happy with you, but you didn't send him to his death."

"I did worse. I betrayed him. I betrayed his secret. That's how he sees it."

"And what secret is that?"

"That his brick house is made of straw, just like the rest of us. That he's fallible."

Sahani opened her mouth, but nothing came out.

"I know how that sounds," Derek said, "but you have to understand Bradley. He's been building that brick house since he was six years old. And he's done a hell of a job. Aside from the fact that he's brilliant and driven, he is profoundly loyal. When he connects with people, I mean really connects, it's for life. That's where the savior complex comes in. He becomes responsible for the people in his life. He just lost his fiancée, and I just blew down his house. What do you suppose happens when you crack the armor of a savior?"

"It's been cracked before. You said so yourself. The Joshua case. You had to suspend him, didn't you?"

"Yes, but he put himself in that position to try to save others. And I had to suspend him, but I also kept him from losing his job and he knew it. I always did. I always had his back."

"But this time it was you who caused the crack in his armor," Sahani understood.

"Not only did I cause it, I allowed you and Nick to see it. I didn't have his back. I stuck a knife in it."

"What you are describing is a person who is skirting the edge of schizophrenia," Sahani said.

Derek held her eyes with his, "We've got to pull him away from the edge. Far away. And now he thinks he can't trust me, so I'm in no position to help him. And that's why this is different."

Not a man of many friends, Nick found himself disturbed when he hung up from his phone call with Sahani. She told him that Bradley knew Nick deceived him. Sahani had wanted to prepare Nick in case Bradley approached him about it.

Other than Mara, Bradley was his closest friend. Not that they hung out together or met for a beer after work. It wasn't that kind of friendship. They shared a relationship based on mutual respect and, in Nick's case, complete admiration for Bradley's skill sets. They had always been honest and open with each other.

Until now.

Nick's phone buzzed. "Agent Whitman is here to see you," Hazel said.

"Give me a minute and then send him in," Nick replied through the speaker.

He sat behind his desk and rubbed his temples. Never one to shy away from confrontation, Nick did not look forward to battling with Bradley.

Bradley came through the door.

"Hey, Nick. I've been thinking about how the Predator picks her victims, and I've got a theory I think we should explore. Actually, you pushed the idea to the surface."

"Really? What did I say?"

"You asked Mara to check the yoga studio and café. It got me thinking. All the victims have been physically fit and, as far as we know, some exercised regularly. We know some jogged, bicycled, and some went to yoga class.

"I've profiled our unsub to also be physically fit," Bradley continued. "What if she is picking out her victims from gyms and yoga studios? I think you should expand Mara's investigation to include all of the past victims. Find out if they belonged to an exercise club or group of some sort. Maybe we'll get lucky."

"That makes a lot of sense. The Predator could blend into the crowd, watch someone closely, and if spotted, she's just another health nut. Yeah, okay, I'll get Mara on it. It's great to have you back, Bradley."

"Ah, yeah, well, I'm not really back," Bradley muttered as he turned to leave.

"Hey," Nick said.

Bradley stopped and turned back to Nick.

"I'm sorry about the profile thing and hanging up on you," Nick said.

"Don't worry about it. You were just following orders." Bradley turned and left the office.

Nick sighed in relief, then felt a little uneasy.

"Would you like to work here or in my office?" Sahani asked Bradley.

"I prefer we work here at my desk," Bradley replied.

Sahani found a chair nearby and sat down alongside Bradley's desk.

"Before we begin, I want to reiterate that Derek had no idea I intended to deceive you with the phony profile. He was worried about you and asked me to help if I could. When I saw your mother torn up and your father feeling helpless, I made the decision I thought best. Just me. No one else. Derek feels terrible about this."

Bradley did not return a comment, just a glare.

"Okay, then. Why do you think the Predator is watching you?" Sahani asked.

"Other than her telling me she is?" Bradley sniped.

"I mean, for what purpose do you think she is watching you?"

Bradley breathed a sigh of resignation before he spoke.

"It could be she just wants to stay close to the case to keep tabs on how much we know. The news channels captured me leaving the scene of Grace-Ann's murder and mentioned me by name. If she saw the news, she saw me."

"Did you see the clip? Maybe she was there watching."

"Of course, I did."

"And?"

"Nothing. The camera focused on me sitting in my truck."

"I don't understand. What would she gain by watching you?" Sahani questioned. "After a few days, she would have realized you weren't leaving your house.

"Maybe she meant it more metaphorically—watching our progress on the case or making a personal threat." Bradley suggested. "Besides, the card may have sat on my table for two weeks before Cate opened it. Maybe she was watching me and then gave up?"

"It still doesn't explain how she knew about Laney," Sahani said, "unless . . ."

"Unless what?" Bradley asked.

"Unless she was watching your house the day of Laney's memorial. She would be almost certain to ascertain someone had died. Then it would just take a small amount of research to find out who. Or, better yet, ask someone in attendance. Maybe pose as a concerned neighbor?"

"I don't really have any neighbors, and most everyone I know knows that. But it is possible that's how she found out. And another car on the street probably wouldn't have stood out. Besides, the sympathy card didn't mention that I lost my fiancée."

Bradley choked on the word. He cleared his throat before continuing. "She may not have known or cared about who died, just that I had suffered a loss."

"Alright. So, she stalked you after seeing you on the news, saw you had recently lost someone in your life, and decided to send you a card? That doesn't sound like a smart and organized perpetrator."

"No, it doesn't. But she is also obsessive and possibly believes she is an angel of mercy," Bradley said mostly to himself. Then he continued, quoting the card, "Angel of mercy. Your loved one is at peace. How do you feel now?"

Sahani could see Bradley sinking himself into the Predator's thought process. His features physically changed. As his posture straightened, his normally boyish features grew old. His eyes narrowed and his breathing slowed. Not wishing to disturb his process, Sahani sat quietly. She, too, began to contemplate the obsessive compulsion displayed by the unsub.

"She knew I lost my fiancée!" Bradley blurted minutes later.

Sahani looked up and saw understanding on Bradley's youthful face.

"What is it?" Sahani asked. "What makes you say that?"

"Angel of mercy. Who is she saving? The husbands? The children? I don't think so. She said my loved one was at peace.

"Follow me here, Sahani," Bradley continued. "These women are each the consummate partner—intelligent, beautiful, healthy, and attentive mothers. I think, in her mind, she is saving the women. She thinks she is putting them at peace."

"From what?"

"From their husbands. She asked me in the sympathy card, how do I feel now? Why ask that?"

"She focused on you, the man left behind. How do *you* feel now? It isn't over for the Predator once the victim is dead," Sahani said excitedly.

"No, it isn't. She may be watching what happens to the husbands after losing their wives. Like she's watching me. It might also mean that the Predator considers the husbands as much victims as the wives," said Bradley.

"Let's take it a step further. Is it possible the Predator considers the men her real victims? In that case, the husbands would be the target, made to suffer, as she uses the murder of the women as her weapon."

"It's possible. It would also explain the sexual penetration and the defeminization. What better way to send a man into agony if not by brutalizing his wife and leaving him behind to see it?"

"So, you're saying the use of the object for sexual penetration was not to throw off law enforcement but to torment the husbands?" Sahani asked.

"It's a good theory. Maybe she believes the women are treated as objects by their spouses, so she uses an object to make her point. And, to make a further point, she takes the women's right nipple. She steals a very personal part of her body, a part of her body that the husbands would feel deeply connected to," Bradley speculated.

"It is a good theory but still just a theory."

"She doesn't make the women suffer. If she got any satisfaction from the actual murder, past research tells us she would kill her victims slowly. The Predator first knocks them out and then quickly cuts the carotid. Her victims, caught by surprise, barely knew what hit them."

"Thank God. Yes, that supports the theory," Sahani suggested. "Bradley, if we're right, do you think the Predator would still be watching Grace-Ann's husband?"

"There's only one way to find out," Bradley said. "Let's take a break. I'll go talk to Nick and see if we can put someone on the Colson house."

Bradley rolled out from behind his desk, but Sahani stood in his path.

"Derek was right. You are incredibly good at your job," she said before she stepped aside.

Without a word, Bradley pushed the joystick on his chair and rode past Sahani down the hall to Nick's office.

"Is he in?" Bradley asked Hazel.

"Yes, Agent Whitman. I'll tell him you're here," Hazel replied.

After hanging up her phone, Hazel told Bradley he could go in to see Nick.

"Listen, Nick, I think I . . . we may have found a course of action on the Predator. We think there's a chance she may be stalking her victims' husbands. Do you have anyone who could sit on the Colson house and monitor the activity?"

"Yeah, I'll let Tony know. He can put someone on that. But why would she stalk the husband after she already killed her victim?"

"It's a working theory, but the husbands may be her ultimate victim. She wants to see them suffer. We're still working it out, but because so much time has passed already, we need to act quickly just in case we are right. We don't have any idea if or how long she watches them before moving on to the next couple."

"Alright, I'll take care of it. Did you fill Derek in?" Nick asked.

"No. That's your job, not mine. Unless Sahani beats you to it. She's his own personal office mole," Bradley said. "Be careful with her, Nick."

"Oh, come on, Bradley. You can't be serious?"

Bradley met Nick eye to eye but didn't speak.

"No way. Derek wouldn't do that," Nick said.

"But he has, hasn't he? Why is she here, Nick?"

"To help with the case. To help us deal with the extreme violence of the Predator."

"Sounds like those words came directly from Derek's mouth. Really, Nick, why do you think she is here?"

"I . . . I think she is here to help."

"Okay. If that's what you believe, fine. I'm just saying you should watch what you say around her, that's all."

Bradley began to leave when Nick asked, "Bradley, are you alright? I mean, is there anything I can do?"

"I'm fine, Nick. Let me know if we get any hits on the house."

Bradley left Nick's office and returned to the bullpen to look for Mara. Her desk sat empty. He looked over to his desk, happy to see Sahani had vacated it. Once at his desk, he dialed Mara's phone.

"Hey, Bradley, what's up?" Mara asked.

"How are you making out on the gym and yoga angle?"

"I've started with the first known victim and have spoken with seven of the husbands so far. Five out of seven of our victims belonged to an organized exercise group of some kind. The first victim, Janet Marston, didn't work out with a group but had a strict jogging routine. Barbara Baker, the second victim, didn't belong to a group either, but she walked her dog at the same time on the same trail every day. It wasn't until a week after her dog passed away that she went for a walk again. That's when the Predator struck. Either the Predator was very patient and waited for Barbara to get back to her routine, or it was an attack of convenience."

"Not convenience. She is patient and thorough," Bradley stated.

"The other five women belonged to different gyms or exercise groups. It seems the Predator figured out an easy way to find her preferred type of victim."

"Yes, it does. Can you do something for me?" Bradley asked.

"Of course. What do you need?"

"I want you to also ask the husbands if they ever felt or saw anyone watching them after their wives had been murdered. You'll want to soften the question, obviously, but I have reason to believe the Predator is watching these men."

"That's creepy. Why would she do that?"

"It's a long story, and I'll fill you in when I see you, but it is important," Bradley explained.

"Okay. I'll see what I can find out," Mara said.

"Thanks. Call me with anything interesting, will you?"

Mara agreed to keep Bradley informed of her progress.

Mostly out of curiosity, Bradley followed the hallway heading to Sahani's office directly across the hall from Derek's new office.

Derek's office door was closed. Sahani's door lay open, and her office sat empty. Bradley could hear muffled voices coming from behind Derek's closed door.

As Bradley turned to leave, Derek's door opened and Sahani emerged.

Surprised to see him, she asked, "Were you looking for me?"

"I wanted to let you know that it looks like we were right about how she finds her victims. I just spoke with Mara. Other than the first two, each victim belonged to an organized workout program. I've asked her to find out if any of the husbands felt as if someone watched them after the murders."

"So, it seems we're on the right track."

"Yeah."

"Are you ready to get back to it?" Sahani asked.

Bradley sat silent for a moment before replying, "No."

Only half over, the day had taken its toll on Bradley. His body sat heavy. Sadness and anger choked his heart, and he felt alone, extremely alone. He left the office without informing anyone. That wasn't unprecedented, considering he worked from home most days. But it was unusual. When working a big case, Bradley inevitably informed his boss and co-workers where they could find him. This time, he just didn't wish to be found.

Instead of going home, Bradley went to see Zayt. He hadn't seen him since the memorial, but he knew Zayt watched over him. Perimeter cameras at Bradley's home had caught Zayt multiple times jogging by the house. Zayt also had a key to Bradley's home so he could take care of Rusty when Bradley needed to be away. If he thought of Derek as his brother, Zayt was his best friend.

He drove his truck via the access road down into the old sandpit. Sitting on that ocean of sand, a community of tiny homes connected by wooden walkways lined the sunken village. The main building housed the kitchen, dining room, and recreation center. Cate, who did volunteer work for the community, managed the kitchen and dining area. As it was late in the day, Bradley hoped she had already finished her work and gone home. As much as he loved Cate, he wasn't ready to see her. His frame of mind required a more aggressive outlet.

Before he saw anyone else, he saw Rusty frolicking among the small buildings. The dog looked happy which placed an involuntary smile on Bradley's face. It lasted only a few seconds.

He parked his truck alongside the wooden walkway that led to the main building. Zayt had added the extended walkway to the access road specifically to give Bradley access to the ramp.

When Rusty heard Bradley's truck coming, he immediately ran to it and jogged beside until Bradley parked and lowered himself to the walkway where Rusty waited.

"Hey, buddy. You look like you're having fun. Where's Zayt?" Bradley asked Rusty.

The Doberman flashed his eyes toward the main building.

"Thanks, pal. Go have fun."

Rusty bounded off to finish his daily visitation rounds.

Bradley found Zayt alone in the kitchen changing a light bulb.

Standing on a stool with his back to the door, Zayt heard the quiet whirr of Bradley's chair.

"Hey," Zayt said.

"Hey."

"Nice to see you out of the house."

"Yeah, well, it wasn't by choice," Bradley said.

Zayt stepped off the stool, folded it, and stuffed it under the commercial kitchen sink.

"Something wrong?" Zayt asked.

"Huh, besides my life, you mean?"

Zayt got two bottles of water from the refrigerator and motioned for Bradley to follow him. He led them to the empty dining room where Zayt took a seat at one of the tables. He handed a bottle to Bradley.

"Spill it," Zayt said.

"Forget it. It's nothing."

"Something's got you tied up in a knot. It's all over your face. What happened?"

"Derek lied to me," Bradley said.

"And?" Zayt asked while lowering his eyebrows.

"And what?"

"So. Derek lied to you. That's what's got you in a bunch?"

"You don't understand. He deceived me. He fucked me over," Bradley blared.

"How so?"

Bradley explained how he felt deceived and hurt by Sahani's deception and Derek's willingness to go along.

Zayt took a big swig out of his water bottle, placed it on the table, leaned toward Bradley, and said, "So you're telling me that Sahani tricked you into getting you out of your house and back to work."

"Exactly."

"And Derek found out about it later and did . . . what?"

"Nothing. He backed her. He said she did what she had to do."

"And how, exactly, did he fuck you?"

Bradley's voice began to rise. "He let her. And they made Nick go along with it, too. I was their fucking dupe."

"Hold on," Zayt said as he put his hand up. "What you just told me is Sahani fooled you and both Derek and Nick found out about it after she did. Is that right?

"Yeah."

"I don't think you're angry at Derek and Nick. I think you're pissed off because you fell for it. What should Derek or Nick have done? Come to your house and held your hand?"

"They should have told me," Bradley yelled. "Derek should have fired Sahani and sent her packing. Instead, I have to work with her."

"Ahh, there it is," Zayt grinned.

"What the fuck are you smiling about."

"He's back."

"Who's back?"

"That arrogant prick who thinks he is the only one who can make things better for everyone. Remember that guy? The one who outright lied to his boss and put himself in the line of fire? The one who skirted every rule in the FBI manual? The one who doesn't play well with others? That guy."

At first, Bradley was staggered. He had expected Zayt to understand his anger and resentment. Now he saw that wasn't the case. He began to turn his chair to leave.

Zayt stood up and blocked his way.

"Oh, no, you don't. You don't get to play the injured little boy with me. Stand your ground and speak your mind."

"Get the fuck out of my way," said Bradley.

"No."

"I'll run this chair right into you."

"Go ahead. I've had worse."

"What do you want from me?" Bradley asked.

"Nothing. You came to see me, remember? You wanted me to have sympathy for you, to tell you that you were right to feel the way you do. Well, you came to the wrong place."

"I'm getting that," Bradley said.

Zayt leaned down, put his hands on the arms of Bradley's chair, and looked him square in the eyes.

"Because, deep down, you don't believe this bullshit you're spouting. But I get it. I've been there."

"What the hell are you talking about?"

Zayt breathed in deeply and exhaled loudly. "When we met, you never asked me how I ended up here, living in this sandpit."

"You were looking for your friend from your unit in Afganistan, the one you called Pantsman." Bradley replied.

"True. But I could have done that from a house, apartment, or motel room. Instead, I chose to live in a cardboard and corrugated tin shack in an abandoned sandpit. I punished myself."

"You said you liked it."

"Don't be stupid. Nobody likes it. When I lost my best friends in that roadside bomb in Afghanistan, I didn't think I had anything left. I felt responsible, helpless, and lost. I believed if I had been with them, I could have prevented their deaths. For the next two years, I lived on the edge of sanity. The only thing that kept me going was finding my friend, Pantsman, the only survivor of that bombing.

"Then one night," Zayt continued, "after the murder of Mamma Lise, my homeless neighbor, I met you. A kindred soul. I could tell almost from the moment we met, even after you treated me like a suspect in Mama Lise's murder. And lied to me. And deceived me. Do you remember that? I was pissed off that I fell for it, too. So, yeah, I've been there."

"I remember. You didn't talk to me for a week."

"Yeah, well, I got over it. And you will, too. Derek would never do anything to hurt you. He'd kill for you. In fact, he has, hasn't he? You'd be dead if he hadn't shown up the night Joshua came for you."

Bradley sat silent, shoulders slumped, and eyes lowered. He thought, *Am I that thin-skinned? Have I lost my perspective?*

A man walked through the side entrance of the dining room and headed to the kitchen.

"Hey, Baxter, how are you doing today?" Zayt asked.

"Right as rain, Zayt," the man replied before walking through the kitchen door.

"Am I really that much of a prick?" Bradley asked.

Zayt laughed. "At times, man, yeah."

Bradley's face softened. "Thanks, Zayt. I knew I came here for a reason. Not quite how I saw this playing out, though." Bradley grinned.

"Kindred souls, dude."

"Hey, do you want to come up for dinner tonight. I haven't cooked in a long time. I feel the need," Bradley said.

"Ah, sorry, I can't. I've got a date," Zayt grinned.

"What? Since when? Who would go out with a chump like you?"

"Maybe when you stop being such a dick, I'll bring her to meet you. Rusty already loves her."

"I'll work on it. Thanks for the talk." Bradley began to leave.

"Bradley."

"Yeah?"

"Don't beat yourself up about this. And work it out with Derek."

"Yeah."

ANGEL WINGS

She pulled her Camry into Blue Hills Reservation at 12:30 p.m. on Wednesday. Hers was the only car in the parking lot. She seized the dog leash from the front passenger seat and stepped out of the car. The road leading up to the parking lot was visible from where she stood. It was early, but she wanted to make sure the vicinity was clear.

While she watched for Cecile to drive up the road, she scanned the area. The piece of torn cloth she had hung from a bush earlier that day swayed in the light breeze. She saw no one. Her excitement rose.

She thought of Wheelchair Man, *Agent Bradley Whitman*, she corrected herself, and her body tingled. Surely, he will come. The thought that Cecile's husband, Jake, will suffer did give her joy. But the anticipation that Bradley would come to see her labors somehow surpassed hers for Jake's suffering. *And this time she would leave a special message for Wheelchair Man.*

The SUV approached the parking lot.

"Here we go," the Predator whispered. She positioned herself near the space where Cecile always parked—not too close to scare her off but not too far away that she couldn't get to her before she let the dog out.

Cecile's car came to a halt.

Looking anxious and worried, the Predator turned in circles as if looking for something. She approached Cecile as she opened her car door.

"Please, can you help me? Did you see my dog on your way in? He's a Golden Retriever. He took off before I could get the leash on him. Oh, my God. I can't find him," she said, almost in tears.

"No, I didn't see him on my way in," Cecile replied. "Which way did he go?"

"Over that way." The Predator pointed toward the bush with the dirty piece of cloth hanging from it.

"I can help you look. How long has he been gone?" Cecile asked.

"Just a few minutes. He couldn't have gone far, right?" the teary eyed woman asked.

"No, he's probably doing his business in privacy, just inside the tree line," Cecile said, trying to calm the woman.

The two walked through a small opening between the bush and a pine tree.

"Jake!" yelled the woman. "Come here, boy!"

"His name is Jake? That's my husband's name," Cecile chuckled.

About twenty feet into the tree line, the woman stopped and said, "Did you hear that?"

"No, I didn't hear anything," Cecile answered.

"It sounded like a yelp. Oh, my God." The woman began to run further into the woods.

Cecile followed but lost sight of her. She found herself in a small clearing when she heard a faint rustling behind her. She turned just in time to see the softball-sized rock before it cracked her skull.

Cecile fell on her back, her head striking another rock partially buried in the ground. Not waiting to see if Cecile remained alive, the Predator pulled her knife from a backpack that sat against the base of a tree and slowly sunk the blade through Cecile's neck.

With Cecile dead, the Predator went to work. She undressed her, leaving on only shoes and socks. She used Cecile's clothes to wipe off the bloody knife and then placed the clothes and rock in the backpack.

From the bag, she pulled a wire whisk, a cooking tool she had found many years before in her kitchen drawer and had no use for until her third kill. She straddled Cecile's abdomen, facing her feet, and placed Cecile's left hand inside her own leggings to cup her. As she violated Cecile with her kitchen tool, she pleasured herself with Cecile's manicured hand.

After using a disinfectant cloth to wipe the DNA from Cecile's hand, she continued with mutilation of Cecile's breast, then placed Cecile's left hand over the open wound. *He will no longer take joy in her body,* she thought.

As much as she had enjoyed herself, it was what she did next that she had most anticipated. Something new, just for Wheelchair Man. She found she enjoyed trying new things. One at a time, the Predator took each of Cecile's limbs and swung them back and forth, scraping the ground to leave the image of an angel.

She carefully backed away from Cecile, packed the knife into the backpack, scoured the area to make sure she hadn't forgot anything, then donned the backpack. As she backed away from the site, she erased her footprints using a downed tree branch she found nearby.

Before she emerged from the tree line, she scoured the area. She saw no one. She retrieved the dirty cloth from the bush and headed to her car. The bark of the Bichon Frisé coming from the partially opened window of the SUV made her smile.

"I need you," Nick spoke into the phone. "We got a call from the Weymouth Police Department about a missing woman. Nobody has seen her since late this morning. The police hadn't opened an official investigation right away because it was inside twenty-four hours, but, because of the previous Predator case, the sergeant who took the original call unofficially delved into her disappearance. He found her abandoned Escalade with the dog inside. It's now an official investigation."

Bradley looked at his clock. 5:04 p.m.

"What makes you think it's the Predator?" Bradley asked.

"Brunette in her early forties, physically fit, and keeps to a schedule. Today's schedule included walking the dog at Blue Hills Reservation in Quincy. Her SUV is parked in the Blue Hills parking lot.

"I'll meet you there," Bradley said.

Since he left the office without so much as a goodbye, Bradley hadn't talked to Nick. He knew he hadn't been working at his best, and the feeling was disconcerting.

By the time Bradley arrived, the parking area had nearly filled with local police, the FBI Predator task force, and two media trucks. The search of the reservation had taken only fifty-five minutes before they found Cecile's body. As Bradley looked for a place to park, officers cordoned off an area to the north side of the parking lot with yellow caution tape. Inside the tape sat a black Escalade.

Nick saw Bradley pull in and ran to meet him at his truck.

"Stay put for a couple of minutes, Bradley. We're clearing everyone out and setting up perimeter lights. The park manager told me there is an easier way to access the area where the body is. I'll send him over to you."

"Have you seen her yet?" Bradley asked.

Nick hesitated, "No. But one of our people found her, so the crime scene should be mostly undisturbed."

"Have you called Maria Reyes?"

"I just did. She's on her way," Nick said.

Fred Chambers managed Blue Hills Reservation. He introduced himself to Bradley and climbed into the passenger seat of Bradley's truck.

"The terrain can be tricky out here, especially now that the sun is starting to go down. Lots of rocks and some steep inclines. I can show you the best way in, but I can't promise you a smooth ride," Fred said with concern.

"Which way?" Bradley asked.

Fred directed Bradley to a dirt road that took them east of where Cecile's body lay. The road narrowed to a footpath, and Bradley could hear tree branches scraping his truck panels.

Three hundred yards in, Fred told Bradley to make a U-turn along the edge of a steep incline. Once they headed in the opposite direction, thinning foliage allowed for a panoramic sunset view of Furnace Brook below and an eighteen-hole golf course in the distance. Fred made one more course correction, leading them down a narrow cart trail before telling Bradley to stop.

"This is a far as you can get this vehicle. From what they told me about where she was found, we need to go about thirty yards that way." Fred produced a flashlight and pointed northwest. He got out of the vehicle and watched with curiosity as the truck's side panel opened. The platform holding Bradley slid out from the driver's seat then lowered him to the ground.

"That's a hell of a thing, isn't it?" Fred said.

"It is," Bradley replied.

Once on the ground, Bradley hit a switch on the control board of his wheelchair to prompt the two heavy back tires to engage while packing the small wheel away.

"Son of a gun, that's cool," Fred smiled. "How does it handle uneven ground?"

"I guess we'll find out," Bradley said. It never occurred to Bradley that he might not be able to travel to the crime scene.

Not wanting to accidentally disturb evidence, he asked Fred to stay behind him. Fred had been correct about the landscape. If Bradley were in his old wheelchair, the uneven terrain would have prevented him from getting more than twenty yards in. But his gyro-equipped PW-4x4Q all-terrain power chair could not only handle the slopes, but his seat also adjusted to each separate incline to keep him from bouncing back and forth. Only twice did he ask Fred to remove debris from his path, not because he didn't think the chair could handle it, but why put wear and tear on the chair if he didn't have to?

It wasn't long before he saw yellow tape with his colleagues Tony and Jim standing outside of it.

Out of respect for the deceased, Bradley sent Fred back to the parking lot via the lighted path. Bradley tucked the flashlight into his chair's side pocket to use for his return trip to the truck. He navigated his chair alongside Tony and Jim and got his first good look at the body. It lay more than thirty feet away from their high ground position. When Bradley looked down, he saw it immediately.

"Jesus Christ," he muttered.

"It's a fucking snow angel!" Tony said.

"Without the snow," Bradley replied. "Any news on when Reyes will get here?"

"All I know is she was on her way," Tony said. "Quincy PD wanted to bring their own guy in, but Nick took care of that. No one has touched the scene."

"Who found her?" Bradley asked.

"Mara."

"Jesus. Nick didn't tell me. How is she?" Bradley asked.

"I haven't seen her. I think Nick whisked her away pretty quick. You know, away from the media and shit," Tony said.

"Yeah, I saw Nick put her in his SUV. I'm not sure if she's still here but she looked a little pale," Jim explained.

"She's tough. She'll be alright," Tony added.

Bradley pulled out his cellphone.

Are you alright? he texted Mara.

I'll be fine. I just need to shake this chill, Mara texted back.

I know the feeling, Bradley replied. *Call me if you want to talk.*

Thank you, Mara came back.

Doctor Maria Reyes and her assistant approached from the opposite direction, the lower side of the crime scene. The assistant set up additional lights focused directly on the body. The lights made the body look like a glowing angel.

"Hello, Maria," Bradley said.

"Hey, Bradley. When are you going to catch this bastard?"

"Soon, Maria. You just need to do your magic. Give me a little something to work with."

"I'll see what I can do," the doctor replied.

Carrying her medical bag, she carefully ducked under the yellow tape. Her assistant, a newly hired thirty-something man carrying a camera, followed her. Bradley listened as Maria instructed the man on how to approach the body, which pictures to take, and when to back away. Bradley knew the assistant would know such things already, or she would not have hired him, but Maria liked to keep a tight rein on her crime scenes.

Bradley waited ten minutes before asking Maria, "First thoughts?"

"This angel thing seems to be catching on."

"Yeah, she's making it personal now," Bradley said.

Maria stopped what she was doing and looked at Bradley.

"Did you say she?" Maria asked.

"I did, but keep it under your hat, okay? I just thought it might help you with your examination."

Bradley, Tony, and Jim waited patiently. They knew better than to try to rush Maria.

Bradley knew Maria was making progress when she sent her assistant back to the vehicle to retrieve a body bag.

"Hey, Bradley," Tony asked after some time, "what did you mean when you said she is making it personal now?"

"You've seen the updated profile, right?" Bradley asked.

"Yeah. You think she could be stalking the husbands. But the profile didn't say why you think that."

"Jim, would you excuse us for a couple minutes, please?" Bradley asked.

"Sure. I'll head back to the parking lot. Nothing going to happen here anyway."

Bradley waited for Jim to be out of earshot, but he didn't seem to mind if Maria overheard.

"The Predator sent me a sympathy card. I didn't see it right away because I didn't open my mail, but she is, or was, watching me. You see that angel down there?" Bradley pointed to Cecile. "I think that's meant for me. The card said, "Take comfort in knowing an angel is watching you.""

Bradley noticed Maria snap her head toward him. He met Maria's eyes. They conveyed sadness and understanding. Maria seemed to go back to work with even greater commitment.

"It's a detail we'd rather the press never gets hold of," Bradley said.

When Maria finished her examination, Bradley and Tony ducked under the yellow tape. Bradley waited for Tony to do a thorough walk around the body before he moved his chair closer.

"We're clear," Tony said. "Just watch out for the angel wings. Don't walk or roll over them. I'm going to want more pictures of those just as the Predator left them."

Tony called for the FBI photographer to take additional pictures of the crime scene. The photographer arrived within minutes.

"I want every detail caught on camera. Get the surrounding area also. She had to leave some sign somewhere," Tony said, frustrated.

"Other than the full-blown angel imprint, there's nothing new to see here. I don't see any physical evidence. Unless Dr. Reyes can come up with something at the lab, all we have is the profile to work with," Bradley said.

"You're right about this one. She's smart," Tony said.

"Yeah, but so are we. I'm going to leave the victim with you Tony. I want to speak to her husband. Talk to Nick. We should have someone watch the house."

Bradley made his way to his truck then back to the parking lot. He found Nick dealing with the local police and press. When Nick saw Bradley return, he rushed to Bradley's driver's side door.

"Her name is Cecile Boulanger. She lived in Weymouth with her husband, Jake, and two children. The Weymouth PD is on their way to tell her husband now."

"I'm going to go speak with him," Bradley said. "Nick, why didn't you tell me Mara found her?"

"I don't know. I was worried about her, I guess. I just couldn't wrap my head around it yet. I didn't want to say it out loud."

Bradley sighed. "Yeah, I get it. Is she still here?"

Nick replied, "No. I sent her home."

"Good. I'll check in with you after I talk to Jake Boulanger."

On the way to Weymouth, Bradley called Mara.

"Hey," Bradley said, "how are you doing?"

"I'm okay, thanks. You don't need to worry about me, Bradley," Mara replied.

"Well, I'm glad you went home, glad you're taking a little time away from this thing."

"Actually, I came to the office. I'm with Derek right now. I'll put you on speaker," Mara said.

"Bradley, what have we got?" Derek asked.

"Not much new to go on, except . . . "

"Except what?" Derek asked.

"She left an angel imprint in the ground. She used Cecile's body like a snow angel," Bradley explained.

"Jesus. Do you think that's for you?"

"Yeah, I do. I think she may be obsessing over me for some reason. There's no other explanation why she would make this personal unless she's just taunting us. But I don't think that's the case. This could work to our advantage."

"Or put you in danger," Derek said.

"Doubtful. As far as we know she only kills women." Bradley paused, wondering if that were true. *Does she only kill women because she wants to torment the husbands? Or does she only kill women because she knows she can handle them easily. Maybe she sees me as an easy target because of my physical limitations.*

"Bradley, are you still there?" Derek asked.

"Yeah. Just thinking. I'm going to speak with Jake Boulanger, the victim's husband. I'll stop by the office after. Mara?"

"Yes, Bradley?"

"Call me if you need anything, alright?"

"I will. Thanks, Bradley."

Bradley parked his car in front of the Boulanger house behind two Weymouth police vehicles. One police officer stood on the stairs by the front door. There were two cars parked in the driveway, a Mercedes Benz and a Cadillac. The doors of the Cadillac stood open.

Bradley watched as an older couple emerged from the house. The police officer held the door for them. A young boy clung to the woman while the man carried two suitcases. Behind them, another boy and a man followed the couple out to the Cadillac. The boy held a fluffy white dog. The man hugged each child before they got into the car. As the older couple got the boys settled, Bradley watched the victim's husband, Jake, turn his back to the car and break down in tears.

It occurred to Bradley that he should scan the neighborhood. He used his cellphone to take pictures of vehicles parked on the street and in driveways. Nothing looked out of place.

Bradley waited until the Cadillac drove out of sight before he got out of his truck. Jake had already gone back inside his house. Bradley rode up the driveway and onto the front walkway. The police officer came down the stairs to intercept him.

Bradley showed the officer his FBI badge. He asked the officer to bring Mr. Boulanger out to see him. When the policeman came out of the house, he instructed Bradley to follow the walkway to the right of the garage, as it would bring him to the back patio. That's where Bradley found Mr. Boulanger.

"Mr. Boulanger, I'm Agent Bradley Whitman. I'm sorry to intrude. I'm very sorry for your loss."

Boulanger could only nod his head. Bradley knew the look. He could almost feel the lump in the man's throat and the hole in his gut.

"Would you mind if I asked you some questions?"

Boulanger shook his head.

"Have you noticed anyone or anything unusual in the past few weeks? Maybe someone new in the neighborhood?" Bradley asked.

"No. Nothing that I can think of."

"Did your wife have a routine, keep to a schedule?"

"Yes. She is a . . . *was* . . . a creature of habit. Very organized."

"Did she have her schedule written down?"

"Uh, I don't know. Maybe. She had a date book in her purse. She probably wrote things in there."

"I can look into that, thank you. Mr. Boulanger, did Cecile belong to any organized exercise group?"

The question took Jake by surprise.

"What?"

"Did she belong to a gym, bicycle club, or yoga studio? Any place like that?" Bradley asked.

"She went to yoga class every morning. Somewhere in town. What does that have to do with her murder?"

"I'm just trying to cover all the bases, Mr. Boulanger. Can you run me through her schedule, as much as you know with as many details as you can remember?"

"We got the boys ready for school in the morning. I dropped them off on my way to work. Then Cecile would go to yoga class.

I think she came home before going to work. She didn't like using the showers at the yoga place. Then she either took the dog for a walk or," he paused, "ran errands. I know she went grocery shopping on Wednesdays. She picked the boys up from school and then came home."

Boulanger's voice became shakier with each answer.

"So, she went to yoga every day?"

"Yes."

"And she picked the boys up at school every day?"

"Until today," Boulanger choked.

"Yes, I'm sorry to put you through this, Mr. Boulanger."

"Jake. Call me Jake."

"Where did Cecile work?"

"At the Weymouth Nursing Home. She only worked a few hours a day, but she really enjoyed it."

"Had Cecile mentioned meeting any new friends lately? Maybe a woman from the yoga class or someone at the nursing home?"

"No, I . . . don't know." Jake sunk his head in his hands and broke down.

Bradley watched as grief took control of Jake's body. His shoulders heaved, and his torso shuddered. Bradley placed his hand on Jake's bucking shoulder.

"Jake, I'm going to leave you alone now. But I would like to come back tomorrow. Would that be alright with you?" Bradley asked.

His head still in his hands, Jake nodded.

Before emerging from the back of the house, Bradley put his cellphone in record mode. He took video of the surrounding area as he rolled from the walkway to the driveway and then to the street and his parked truck. He wasn't sure how much the camera would pick up in the dark, but to the naked eye, nothing seemed out of place.

Back at the office, Nick called everyone into the conference room. Nick stood at the head of the table. Derek sat in the back of the room. Bradley stayed in back near Derek.

"Cecile Boulanger, age thirty-seven from Weymouth, was found approximately fifteen minutes from her home at Blue Hills Reservation in Quincy. We have confirmed this as the second Pathside Predator attack in our state. The coroner is going to work around the clock to get us her report as quickly as possible."

Bradley was not surprised to hear that news. Maria could be a tenacious workhorse when provoked. The Predator had provoked her.

Nick continued. "On the table in front of you is the updated profile for our unsub. We believe she may monitor the bereaved husband, so we are going to put round-the-clock surveillance on his home. Surveillance teams will be equipped with cameras to record the activity in the neighborhood. I want every insignificant detail recorded or photographed. This is an upscale neighborhood, so try to blend in."

"Nick?" Bradley interrupted.

"Yeah?"

"Does Mr. Boulanger know we will be watching the house?" Bradley asked.

"No, not yet. I don't think it's necessary to put any more stress on the man. We can revisit that decision if we need to."

A month before, Bradley would have thought it the right decision. But now, he wasn't so sure. Jake could be a big help with the investigation just by keeping his eyes open. Besides, if it were him, he would want to know.

When Bradley noticed Derek glancing at him, Derek looked away.

"The teams and shifts will be posted on the board within the hour. Jim and Devon have taken the first shift. We'll work four-hour shifts, four shifts a day from 6 a.m. to 10 p.m. We do not believe Mr. Boulanger is in danger. We think the Predator will only observe him. Focus on your surroundings. Remember, our unsub is fit. She may decide to jog past his house or ride a bicycle. Record everything. Have you got anything to add, Bradley?"

"Nothing on this detail, Nick." Bradley answered.

"Alright, read the profile. Get a feel for who we are looking for, but suspect everyone. That's all."

Nick left the room, which emptied, leaving only Bradley and Derek.

"What did you find out from the husband?" Derek asked.

"Everything we thought we would. She had a routine. She took a yoga class every morning. And he's devastated," Bradley answered sadly.

"Tell me about the angel."

"Just like I remember making in the snow as a kid. Or at least I think I remember. It was deliberate. In fact, I would go as far as to say it was a billboard. She didn't want me to miss it."

"I want to put a tail on you and put someone at your house," Derek said.

"No way. No. I've got cameras. You know that. And the only place I'm driving is here to the office. We need everyone focused on Jake Boulanger and the Predator. I'll keep my eye out. And I've got Zayt," Bradley stated emphatically.

They sat in awkward silence.

"Are you and I going to be okay?" Derek asked.

Bradley paused.

"Just give me some time," he answered before he rolled out the door.

Mara had been in the conference room, but now Bradley could not find her. He needed to see her to make sure she was alright. He knew she was strong, and she had seen bad things before, but this was different. He worried about her.

He met Nick in the hallway.

"Do you have time to fill me in?" Nick asked.

"Yeah, I was just coming to see you, but I wanted to check on Mara first. Do you know where she is?" Bradley asked.

"Ah, yeah. I do."

"Well?"

"I can't really say," Nick said as he averted his eyes from Bradley's.

"What are you talking about? Either you . . . Oh, Sahani."

Bradley's first instinct was anger, then hurt. Mara always came to him with her worries and questions. But his concern for Mara overshadowed his guardian instincts. He worked to put aside his feelings, something he found difficult to do these days.

"Well, then," Bradley continued, "should we go to your office?"

"Yeah," Nick said.

With little to add from his interview with Jake, Bradley assured Nick he would speak with him again the next day.

"But I did take a little video, just in case. I haven't looked at it yet," Bradley said.

Nick came out from behind his desk to watch the video on Bradley's cellphone.

"This is when I first got there," Bradley explained as he played the video taken with his phone's camera.

Bradley had scanned the immediate neighborhood. There were a few cars parked on the street, but most of the vehicles parked in driveways.

"Okay, this is when I left," Bradley said.

"It's hard to see," Nick said. "Maybe the guys in the lab can enhance it."

"Yeah, good idea. I'll forward it to them and ask them to check it out in the morning," Bradley said. "I'm going to head home. Tell Mara . . . ahh, never mind."

She had watched as Jake hugged his boys and loaded them into the shiny black Cadillac. She took great pride when he broke into tears. Once again, she had chosen well. *Now,* she thought, *this self-indulgent man will understand what he's done. No longer will he enjoy a hedonistic life, using his wife as a toy. Let's see how he feels now.*

But she knew she wasn't the only one who watched. Moments before, Wheelchair Man had parked his truck on the street and did not get out. Her body tingled when she saw him drive up. She wondered if he got her message. *Could he be so self-absorbed that he missed it? Of course, he could. He's a subjugator—never introspective, just like the rest. Or, is he?*

Curious as to how long he would be there and despite the risk, she had decided to stay and watch the house. She had imagined the two men sharing their despair, sulking together, falling apart.

Self-satisfaction had filled her heart. *Cecile is happy now. And her captor will pay the price.* The Predator had felt good about that. But uncertainty lay beneath, and she didn't know why.

He had stayed for forty minutes. Mesmerized by him, she watched until his truck drove away. *I'll come back in the morning.*

A package awaited Bradley when he got home. The box measured approximately a foot square and two inches deep and leaned against his door. The silence from his house indicated that Rusty was not there.

Bradley picked up the package and entered his empty home. He habitually turned on the backyard light to let Zayt know he was there. He would expect to see Rusty or both Rusty and Zayt arrive soon.

The return address on the package read Amherst, Massachusetts. The only people he knew in Amherst were Holly and John. He opened the cardboard box. Inside he found a framed photo of him and Laney taken two years before at the *Maker's Mark* movie premiere in Boston. He wore a tuxedo. Laney wore a light blue gown. Holly had taken the picture on the red carpet leading into the theatre. Bradley found a note attached to the photo.

"She lives in our hearts."

Bradley's eyes grew moist as he stared at the photo. He found himself smiling from memories of that night. He reached for his cellphone and found Holly's contact. He texted, ***Thank you!***

Almost immediately, he received a red heart emoji in response.

Bradley placed the photo on his desk, then booted his computer. His workday hadn't ended yet. On the drive home, thinking about the Predator watching her victim's homes, he was reminded of something Sahani had said. She speculated that the Predator may have been at Bradley's house the day of Laney's memorial.

He brought up the camera video from that day, beginning at the point when the limousine brought them home. He set the surveillance machine to copy the contents to his computer. Then he watched the video show the day unfold. He recognized most of the people and vehicles, but not all. He focused his attention on the unknown vehicles.

Then, something on the video took his attention away from the cars. He watched as Derek came and sat beside him. Then the rest of his friends, one by one, gathered. It didn't look like any of them spoke. They just sat there. With him. In silence. He had no recollection of it.

A tear escaped his eye. He wiped it away before returning his focus to unknown people and vehicles on the video.

Using the face-to-face calling application, he picked up his cellphone and dialed his father's number.

"Bradley, hey, is everything alright?" Doug asked as his face appeared on Bradley's screen.

"Yeah, Dad. Everything is fine. I have some questions for you if you have a minute."

"Always."

"I'm looking at the footage of Laney's memorial and I see people that I don't know. Did you and Mom have friends there that I wouldn't recognize?"

"Bradley, why are you doing this to yourself? You've got to give it some time, son," Doug said, worriedly.

"No, it's not like that. I promise. It's a long story, and I don't want to bother you with the details, but I'm trying to identify every person and vehicle that was there that day. I promise, I'm fine."

"Oh. I'm sorry. It's just that the last time . . ."

"I know. I was in rough shape. I'm working on it."

"That's great to hear, son. So, to answer your question, yes. Some of our neighbors and church friends came to Laney's memorial. I can get you a list if you want," Doug offered.

"I don't think that's necessary. Would you mind looking at a few pictures right now?" Bradley asked.

"Not at all."

"Here's the first couple." Bradley held his phone to the screen so his father could see the couple in question.

"Yes, that's Roger and Sarah Oustman. They go to our church. Sara sings in the choir with us."

"Do you know what kind of car they drive?"

"A tan Buick sedan. What's this about, Bradley?"

"You'll just have to trust me that everything is fine, and I just need to know who was here."

"And what they drove?"

"Yeah."

"Okay. Who's next?"

Bradley went through everyone he didn't know and matched them to a vehicle.

"That's everyone. Every person is accounted for. Thank you for your help, Dad."

"Anytime, son. You'll have to explain to me what we just did sometime."

Bradley chuckled. "Yeah, I will. Give Mom a kiss for me, will you?"

"I will. I love you, son."

"I love you too."

Bradley saved the copied version of the surveillance video to his computer, then printed out still black and white photos from two separate camera angles. Convinced he had each vehicle in the pictures that had parked either in his parking lot or on the street, Bradley began to eliminate them one by one.

He was left with one. A dark-colored Toyota Camry followed the procession of cars to his home and parked on the street rather than pull into his parking area. No one got out of the car. Using the clock on the surveillance machine, he determined the Toyota stayed for just under an hour before making a U-turn and leaving.

He tried to zoom on the vehicle, but the picture became too blurry.

"Great! One of the most popular cars sold in the United States," Bradley muttered to himself.

The front door opened, and Rusty ran in.

"Jesus! Give a man some warning, will you?" Bradley said to Zayt.

Rusty ran to Bradley, jumped on his lap, and licked Bradley's face, then ran to his bed.

"You're getting lax, man. Rusty has made you sloppy. You depend on him to save you from someone like me," Zayt said.

"Dude, there is no one like you," Bradley responded.

"That's true. Why create another once you hit perfection."

Zayt recognized the pictures on Bradley's computer monitors. "Why are you watching this? Haven't you beaten yourself up enough already?" Not one to hold anything back, Zayt sounded concerned.

"It's not what you think," Bradley replied. Then, remembering he had seen Zayt jog by his house on numerous occasions, he asked, "Hey, you've been keeping an eye on the place. Have you noticed a dark colored Toyota Camry skulking around?"

"Skulking? Is that your uptown word for stalking or spying?"

Bradley smiled. "No, seriously. Do you remember seeing this car," Bradley showed him the printed photo, "at any time in the last couple of weeks."

Zayt grew serious and took a good look at the picture.

"Yeah, I think so. Some lady with a dog was parked there recently, I can't remember when exactly."

"The dog!" Bradley shouted. "How could I have missed that? I saw her. She was parked on the other side of the street. I thought she was lost."

"She who?" Zayt asked.

Before Bradley could stop himself, he blurted, "The Predator!"

Zayt stood, open-mouthed. "The Predator is a woman?"

"Shit, Zayt. You're not supposed to know that. Forget I said anything."

"Wait a minute. Why would the Predator be watching you?"

"I didn't say that."

"Yeah, you did. What the hell is going on?"

"You're not going to let this go, are you?" Bradley asked.

"You're goddam right, I'm not. Not if you have a serial killer stalking you."

"She doesn't want to hurt me. My theory is she is obsessed with me, but I don't know why. I think she saw me on the news, then she found out about Laney somehow. I guess I remind her of the husbands she leaves behind."

"How do you know she doesn't want to hurt you?" Zayt asked.

"Because it's not in her profile."

"Seriously, dude? So, because you didn't put it in her profile, then she won't kill you? How close to God do you think you are?"

Thinking Zayt overreacted, Bradley shook his head.

"Don't you have a date tonight or something?" Bradley changed the subject.

"Yeah, I do. I was just dropping Rusty off."

Hearing his name, Rusty jumped to his feet.

"Settle down, buddy. Zayt's got better plans than hanging out with us," Bradley smirked.

"Now that's the most sensible thing you've ever said."

Zayt headed for the door. Then he stopped, turned, and said, "Just do me a favor. Keep your eyes and ears open."

"Absolutely," Bradley replied.

After Zayt left, Bradley picked up his phone and tapped Nick's name.

"Nick, I think we're looking for a dark-colored Toyota Camry. The surveillance teams need to know they shouldn't approach the vehicle, but we need a license plate number and pictures of the driver. And I think I know how she lured Cecile off the path and into the woods."

"Christ, Bradley, you just left here an hour and a half ago."

"Sahani suggested that the Predator may have been watching me the day of Laney's memorial. I just pulled my video camera feed. All the guest vehicles are accounted for except one, a dark-colored Toyota Camry. Then, the day I came back to the office, I saw a woman in a dark—maybe dark blue or black—Camry with a dog in the back seat. I didn't think much of it then, but it makes sense now. She used a dog to get to Cecile."

"The lost dog con. Dog lovers fall easily for that one."

"Especially if she had set it up properly," Bradley said. "There's no way the Predator owns a dog. She must have stolen one or picked it up off the street. If Cecile had seen her walking the dog once or twice, she would have no problem believing the Predator's ruse."

"We might have her!" Nick said excitedly.

"Only if we're very careful. Remember, we don't have any physical evidence. Even if we find her, we need to make sure we can nail her."

"I'll have someone track down reports of missing or stolen dogs. Any idea what breed it was?"

"I know exactly what it was. A Golden Retriever," Bradley said.

Bradley couldn't sleep. When he wasn't thinking about the Predator, he thought about Laney. Rusty sensed Bradley's anxiety and tried to comfort him by snuggling up to him in bed.

"Nice try, buddy, but I don't think I'm getting any sleep tonight."

The clock read 2:00 a.m.

He moved from the bed to his wheelchair. Rusty, however, decided to stay in bed. Bradley poured himself a glass of orange juice before moving to his desk.

Once the computer came to life, Bradley satisfied the questions in his head by typing them into a document.

Who is the Predator?

How does the Predator choose her victims?

How does she lure her victims?

How does she choose killing locations?

Why is it important to her to hurt the husbands?

Why would she be interested in me?

"Alright, Bradley. Let's see what you've got," he whispered.

Under the typewritten words, *Who is the Predator*, Bradley

added, *A smart, detailed woman with a deep-seated need to punish married men. (Or men in a serious relationship with a woman?)*

He wanted to add more, but experience told him to keep it simple. After all, the exercise wasn't meant for details but only to give him direction.

He continued with the next question about how the Predator chose her victims.

She frequents gyms, yoga studios, exercise classes, or clubs.

Bradley stopped there. Without thinking of the time, he texted Mara to suggest she jump ahead to Cecile Boulanger's case in her investigation of the murders rather than continue in sequence.

He immediately got a reply.

Already planned to do that. Will talk to Boulanger tomorrow.

Surprised he got a response, he texted, *What are you doing up?*

Mara: **Same as you, I guess. I can't sleep.**

Bradley: **Yeah, I get it. I'm going to see Boulanger tomorrow, too. Why don't we go together? Then we can both go to the yoga studio.**

Mara: **Perfect. What time?**

Bradley: **How about I pick you up at your apartment at 8:30?**

Mara: **I'm at Nick's. I'll meet you at your house at 8:30.**

Bradley: **Okay. Promise me you will shut your phone off and try to get some sleep.**

Mara: **Only if you do, too.**

Bradley: **Deal! Goodnight.**

Mara: **Goodnight.**

Mara followed her last text with an emoji of a sliver moon wearing a sleeping cap.

Bradley smiled, but he didn't go back to bed as promised. He continued with his guidance exercise.

How does she lure these women and make them comfortable?

In Cecile's case, he felt all but certain she used a dog. He typed that into the document. He also wrote that she could have used the same ruse for Barbara Baker, as the Predator may have known that Barbara's dog had passed away. He made an additional note to find emotional soft spots in the victims such as children, lost pets, or a rescuer—someone who had experience with injuries and would come to the aid of someone in need.

He moved on to how she chose her kill locations. Obviously, the victims frequented the areas of their attack. The women most likely felt a certain sense of safety because of familiarity with their surroundings. The Predator took advantage of that and may have made an effort to become a familiar presence in the areas prior to her kills. Bradley made a notation to canvas regular visitors of the properties for information on new faces or vehicles.

Why does she want to torment certain men? That, he concluded, required a deep psychological profile. *An incident from her past, probably as a child,* he wrote. His list continued: *abused, sexually assaulted, abandoned?*

He could speculate all he wanted, he thought, but the exercise had convinced him of something he did not wish to admit. He would need Sahani's help to figure out the answer to the question, Why.

The thought of asking for Sahani's help, needing her help, made Bradley feel ill.

What does that say about me? The question crept into his mind before he could stop it. He pushed it aside and moved on.

The last gnawing query on his list concerned why she would fixate on him. None of the previous police or FBI reports suggested the Predator paid any attention to the investigations into her murders. So if she weren't interested in him professionally, it had to be personal. Was it as simple as he had lost his fiancée and was left to grieve like the husbands of her victims? He wrote it down, but the answer didn't give him a sense of direction about where or how to find a more definitive reason.

He woke at 5:30 in his chair and slumped over his desk. Much like him, his computer had put itself into sleep mode. Bradley punched the power button to wake the desktop machine.

As he scanned the document displayed on the monitor, he determined that the new day might be an extremely important day. Today he might discover the identity of the Predator.

With that thought in mind, Bradley sent a text to Sahani Kumar. *Nick has additional information regarding our unsub. I think you should get with him first thing and ask him about the car and dog. We will need a deep psychological profile. You may want to focus on why she is taking a risk by watching me. As far as I can tell, this has been her only mistake, so it must mean something to her.*

Jake Boulanger met Bradley and Mara in the driveway as he had expected them.

"Let's go around the back," Jake said.

Bradley glanced at Tony's black Ford sedan parked two houses away on the opposite side of the street. He also scanned the neighborhood for a dark Toyota Camry. He saw none.

Once settled, Bradley introduced Mara to Jake Boulanger, and she expressed her condolences.

"Mr. Boulanger, I understand that your wife frequented a yoga studio in town. Do you have the name or address of that facility?" Mara asked.

"Yes, after you left last night . . . I'm sorry, I don't remember your name," Jake said to Bradley.

"It's Bradley."

"After Bradley left last night, I looked it up in my bank records. It's called East Side Yoga and Fitness. It's on East Main Street here in town."

Mara made a note. "Thank you. Have you remembered anything else? Maybe Cecile talked about a new friend or someone she met while walking the dog?"

"No, she didn't mention anyone new," Jake said.

"I'm going to show you a picture of a car. It's a generic photo of the type of car someone saw in the parking lot at Blue Hills," Bradley lied. "Have you noticed a car like this? Maybe in your neighborhood?"

"It's a Camry," Jake said. "Nobody in this neighborhood owns one. I don't think I've seen one recently, either, except maybe on the highway driving to work."

"It may be nothing. You said your wife stuck to a routine. Can you think of anything that might have happened in the last few weeks to change that routine? Did she get a flat tire? Or have to work late? Anything at all?" Bradley asked.

"A few weeks ago, we went to her aunt's funeral," Jake said.

Mara made a note, then asked, "When was that?"

"Um, it was a Friday, so that would have been three weeks ago tomorrow. It was . . . wait . . . the car. There was a blue Camry parked there. Our limousine passed it on our way out. I remember it because it was parked on the lawn at a strange angle. There weren't any graves in that area. Most people park next to the grave they are visiting."

"Was there anyone in the vehicle?" Bradley's voice raised an octave.

"A woman. That's all I saw. I just got a glimpse," Jake said.

"That's good, Jake. What about any markings or stickers on the car? Or license plate numbers?" Bradley asked.

"Like I said, we just rode by, and I happened to notice it. I didn't pay that much attention."

Mara was making notes of the conversation when she asked, "Where was the funeral held?"

"Green Living Cemetery in Malden."

Bradley snapped his head to look at Jake. "Where did you say?"

"Green Living Cemetery. It's off Route . . ."

"Yes. I know it." Bradley spoke softly. "What time was the funeral, Jake?"

"First thing in the morning. I think we were there at nine o'clock, something like that. Do you think that's where she saw us? Is that how she found Cecile?" Jake's eyes began to moisten.

"No, Jake. That's not where it started for Cecile. She may have been following her, though," Bradley managed to choke out.

Mara had made the connection with the cemetery. She kept her head down as Bradley noticed her wipe her eyes.

"Thank you for your time, Jake. If there's anything we can do for you, or if you remember anything else, please give me a call," Bradley said.

"You'll keep me updated, right?" Jake asked.

"As much as possible, yes," Bradley replied as he handed Jake his business card. "This is my direct number. Call me anytime."

Mara packed her notes. They left Jake sitting alone at his patio table.

Before reaching the sidewalk, Mara said, "I saw it, too."

Bradley stopped. "Saw what?"

"The car. I saw it the day of Laney's memorial. I'm pretty sure it was the same car. It was parked in front of the industrial building across the street from your home. I'm sorry, Bradley. I didn't know."

Bradley reached for Mara's hand. "Of course you didn't know, Mara. None of us did. You've got nothing to be sorry for."

"How did you know?"

"Know what?" Bradley asked.

"About the cemetery."

"I didn't know. I thought I was eliminating possibilities. We just got lucky."

As the platform positioned Bradley into the driver's seat of the truck, Mara said, "So, the Predator saw you at the cemetery and recognized you from the newscast. She followed the procession back to your house and watched for a short time, thus becoming obsessed with the FBI agent who was working her case and experiencing the same effects of loss as her victims' husbands."

"Thus?" Bradley grinned. "Thus committing her fatal mistake."

Bradley's phone rang.

"Yeah?" Bradley answered.

"Hey, it's Tony. I'm across the street."

"Yes, Tony. We saw you when we pulled up."

"I thought you would like to know that a dark blue Camry backed into one of the neighbors' empty driveways at 6:45 this morning and stayed until 7:30."

"Did you get a plate number?"

"Clear as day. Already sent it to Nick."

"How about a photo of her?"

"Not as lucky."

"Stay put. Maybe she'll be back. You might want to move the car. We wouldn't want anyone getting suspicious."

"Already did. This ain't my first rodeo."

"We're going to nail her, Tony. I can feel it," Bradley said.

"Abso-fuckin'-lutely," Tony replied.

Bradley hung up and turned to Mara. "We got a license plate."

Bradley headed straight for the office instead of the yoga studio as intended.

Mara and Bradley found Nick, Derek, and Sahani seated in the conference room.

"Well?" Bradley asked. "Have we got a name yet?"

"Amanda Lessing, age thirty-two, born in Delaware. The photo on her driver's license is almost five years old." Nick slid a copy of her license photo toward Bradley and Mara.

"Well, here's another confirmation. Jake Boulanger saw her Camry at Green Living Cemetery while he and Cecile attended Cecile's aunt's funeral three weeks ago, on a Friday."

Bradley waited for the three of them to absorb what he told them.

Derek got it first. "That's where she saw you!"

The realization spurred action.

"I'm going to get to work," Sahani said as she rushed out of the room.

"I'm getting her picture out to state and local police with instructions to observe and report but not to apprehend the suspect," Nick said.

"She's not done with Jake Boulanger yet," Bradley stated. "She wouldn't go through all this planning and execution and then abandon her prize. Unless we scare her off."

"But she will also be looking for her next victim," Nick said.

"Yes, but not here. If she follows her own routine, she's going to move to another part of the state," Bradley added.

"Maybe not," said Derek.

"What do you mean? Why not?" Bradley asked.

Derek answered, "Because of you, Bradley. Sahani was just running a theory by us. After you texted her this morning, she began concentrating on the Predator's obsession with you. She said the Predator may see you as some sort of cosmic or angelic sign. Our unsub seems to be conflicted by you. At least that's what Sahani thinks."

"But why?" Bradley asked.

"She doesn't know, but she doesn't think the Predator is comfortable with her feelings about you. That's what has prompted her to make these mistakes," said Derek. "I want to put added surveillance around your house."

Derek stuck his hand up before Bradley could protest. "Not agents. Just add some cameras on the buildings across the street to get a wider view. Something with infrared that we can monitor 24/7. Maybe we could get a good look at her."

Bradley thought about it. "Only if you promise to take them down the minute this is over," Bradley said.

"Agreed," Derek nodded to Nick.

Nick left the room to make the arrangements.

"What's next?" Derek asked.

"Mara and I are going to the yoga studio where Cecile worked out," Bradley told him. We'll show the picture around and see if we get a hit. Maybe someone will know where she's living."

"Alright. I'm going to be in meetings for the rest of the day, but text me if you need anything or you get a break in the case," Derek replied.

Amanda had dreamed about him that morning. She sat naked on his lap in a winged wheelchair as they soared through the clouds. She wrapped her arms around his neck, his arms wrapped her waist. He smiled at her and offered her a knife. She took it. He placed his left hand on her disfigured right breast and massaged her until her left nipple grew hard. She arched her back. His tongue tickled the tip of her hard nipple and, just as she was to thrust the knife into his neck, she woke aroused and unsatisfied.

She needed to see him. She longed to see him. Then, as the sleepiness wore off, she recalled the last time she felt that way.

Amanda Lessing was fifteen years old. Nathan Cornwell lived across the street with his wife, two children, and a dog. People remarked what a handsome and happy family they made. But Amanda knew better.

Every day during the summer, telling herself that the front yard received more sun than the back, she donned her bikini and sunbathed on the front lawn. She had seen the way Nathan looked at her. She watched his manhood swell, filling his white cotton shorts as he mowed his lawn. He wanted her, and it made her feel powerful.

Living without a father and with a mother who earned her money lying on her back, Amanda learned early in life the power of sex. She also learned that most of the power lay with men.

At fifteen, sunbathing in her front yard, she found herself in control.

She knew Nathan and his wife's schedule. On Saturday night, the wife and kids visited the in-laws. Every week, Nathan refused to join them. Instead, clenching a beer, he sat back in his recliner, and gazed across the street into her bedroom window as she slowly removed her bathing suit and slipped into a skimpy lace nighty.

One Saturday night, with her mother gone for the weekend, Amanda set her plan in motion. Shirtless and sweaty, he had lingered over his lawnmower that afternoon and glanced at her often as he pretended to perform maintenance on the machine. She knew he was ready.

Having put much thought into her intentions, she chose the red lace, as it best accentuated her slender body and blossoming bosom. The backlighting of her bedroom lamp provided just enough to tempt an onlooker but not so much as to give away the prize. Before she moved from her bedroom to the laundry closet, she closed the window shades. Then the entire house went dark.

Nathan Cornwell sat up in his chair and peered out the window. The streetlight shone on her front door. The door opened, and a robed Amanda stepped out of the house and raced toward his front door. His doorbell sounded.

She told him that, as she plugged something into her bedroom outlet, the whole house went dark. She didn't know what to do. Could he help?

Cornwell jumped at the opportunity as he explained the cause as most likely a tripped fuse. An easy fix, he told her.

Grateful, she led him into her house and to her bedroom to show him the offending instrument, a pink and purple object whose shape resembled his own swelling shaft that he tried desperately to hide.

He quickly turned his back to her and walked to the kitchen while he mumbled something about a fuse box.

She followed.

Nathan located the box in the laundry closet, quickly found the tripped fuse, and reset it. The hall light came to life as well as her bedroom. From where he stood, Nathan heard buzzing and glanced down the hallway into her room. The purple shaft slowly skipped across her bedside table in tune with the hum.

Feigning embarrassment, she ran to her room and gripped the vibrator's shaft with her right hand.

Nathan licked his lips as he watched her hand pulsate.

Heat rose through her body with an intensity like never before. She knew she had him. She knew she was in control, and to prove it she allowed the robe to slip from her body and beckoned him with her index finger.

Without hesitation, he did as expected. She threw the bedroom into darkness as he entered, leaving only enough light from the hall to guide them. They bounced on the lumpy mattress as she pulled him toward her.

He moved with fury, ripping his own clothes from his body, then hers. She abdicated her power and allowed him to relish her breasts, abdomen, and thighs. She made only one request before slipping her legs apart: that he have no mercy. When she asked him to make it hurt, he smiled.

With each manic thrust, she took back her sovereignty. With the first, she reclaimed her independence. With the second, her authority, and with the third, her supremacy. For with the fourth thrust, she would transform that self-proclaimed king into a fool.

She reached for the kitchen knife she had stashed under her pillow. Grasping the wooden handle with her right hand, she raised the knife. But she had miscalculated the speed of his fourth thrust. His shoulder caught the shaft of the knife to force the blade into her right breast and carve her with the weight of his body. She let go a savage scream.

He couldn't react quickly enough to the knife and her obvious intention, and his motion drove him in for a fifth and fatal time. She had readjusted the position of the blade, and the forged steel speared his neck without a hint of mercy.

Covered in blood, she rolled his lifeless body off her, careful not to expunge any of his blood from her body, for she knew first impressions would stick with the responders.

The authorities arrived within minutes of her call. She sat naked, shaking, and covered in blood on the floor, and clutched the telephone with her right hand as the EMTs raced through her door. Her left hand covered her nippleless breast.

The newspapers reported that an unnamed, underaged female had been assaulted by a neighbor, Nathan Cornwell, a married father of two. The attacker used a knife from the victim's kitchen to subdue her, but according to authorities, the young woman managed to distract her attacker and use the knife against him, killing him quickly.

Townspeople immediately called for Nathan Cornwell's damnation, and his wife and children never returned to their home.

Although technically he was not her first, since her mother had shopped her out since her thirteenth birthday, Amanda considered Nathan to be just that, the first of her choosing.

It would take only days before she realized how anticlimactic her plan turned out to be. Nathan could suffer no more. He was at peace while his poor wife bore the brunt of his narcissism. To Amanda, that hardly seemed fair.

Three weeks later, she moved to Connecticut.

After awakening that morning from her dream, she sat on the edge of the bed. *I can't stop thinking about Wheelchair Man,* she told herself. *It's as if I have manifested his tortured soul just by being here. All of my actions affect him by proxy. He's miserable, and it's exhilarating! But he's also quite different from the others.*

PSYCHOLOGICAL INSIGHT

With Amanda's picture, Mara and Bradley visited East Side Yoga Studio. Several women recognized the woman in the photograph, but no one knew anything about her. She had originally shown up six weeks before, an employee recalled. She signed in as Janet Marston and paid cash for her classes. She hadn't been seen back in class for five days.

"Janet Marston," Mara mumbled. "Her first victim."

"We need to go back to Janet Marston's case. If she really was Lessing's first victim, history tells us that they knew each other. Knowing Lessing's penchant for active women and knowing Janet Marston did not belong to a gym or other organized exercise group, we have to wonder how the two women did know each other. If we find the answer to that, maybe we will find some concrete evidence, because she's leaving us nothing," Bradley sighed.

His phone rang.

"Yeah?" he answered.

"Bradley, it's Sahani. I know you are busy, but I could really use your help on this psychological profile. I need to run it by you. Are you coming back in today?"

"Mara and I are heading back now. I'll stop in and see you when I get there," Bradley replied.

Bradley hung up and sighed.

"Is everything alright?" Mara asked.

"Huh? Oh, yeah. It's just Sahani. She's working on the psych profile and wants to run it by me."

"She's amazing, you know. I had a nice long talk with her yesterday. She knew just what to say to get me back on track."

"Yes, she is a master at manipulating people," Bradley said.

"No," Mara snapped, "it's not at all like that. She is excellent at reading how people think. Like how sometimes they put too much pressure on themselves that they forget to be human."

Bradley searched Mara's face to determine to whom she referred.

"Are you talking about you or me?" he asked.

"I was talking about me, but now that you mention it, the same could be said for you, too."

"It's a hazard of the job," Bradley said.

"Exactly. That's why she's here. And I, for one, am grateful for her."

"Then I'm happy for you. I just don't like her methods."

"Even if they work?" Mara asked.

Bradley didn't answer, but the immediate response that entered his mind had been, *Especially when they work.*

Bradley tapped his knuckles on the frame of the open doorway. Sahani, engrossed in her work, looked up from her desk.

"Bradley, come in. Thank you for agreeing to see me."

"We still have work to do." Bradley's cold reply was meant to sting.

"Yes, we do. I'll get right to it. I've been thinking about Amanda Lessing's mental state. It is almost without question that she suffers from a personality disorder, possibly schizoid personality disorder. She seems to be a loner who is focused on one task, killing the wives of men she wishes to punish. Would you agree?"

Bradley nodded.

"Although she has used similar patterns in the execution of her task, the killings are not ritualistic. She has continued to modify her message as time passes."

"Message?" Bradley asked.

"Yes, I'm getting to that. Bear with me, please. I'm working through some thoughts as I speak."

"Okay. I'm listening."

Sahani continued. "Now, the marring of the breast is the only consistent action from the first to latest victim. Am I right?"

"Well, there's the knife through the throat, although that went from slashing to stabbing—and the removal of their clothing," Bradley replied.

"Yes, the throat. And they were all naked. It would follow that these three details are extremely important to Amanda Lessing."

"Of course they are. This is nothing new, Sahani," Bradley barked.

"You're frustrated. I get it. But what I'm suggesting is that these three details are her entire motivation for the killings. I think we are looking for a woman who, at some point in her childhood, was stripped of her clothing and maimed."

Sahani stopped for a moment to gauge Bradley's reaction.

Bradley turned the idea over in his mind but did not respond.

Continuing, Sahani said, "It's highly possible Amanda Lessing, as a child, was abused, disfigured, and left naked somewhere, most likely by a man. An assault of that level would almost certainly result in post-traumatic stress disorder, which is common in personality disorder cases."

"Okay. I can see that. But what did you mean when you said she was leaving a message?" Bradley asked.

"Right. We know she is intelligent and organized. Everything she does has a reason. I believe that reason is to tell us her story. The sexual assault with an object, the leg spread, and then the angel. They all tell her story."

"I assumed the angel was for me," Bradley said.

"Yes. I think it was. I think she wants you—you specifically—to know her story."

"Why?"

"That I don't know," Sahani admitted.

"Have you found anything on record to back up this theory?" Bradley asked.

"No. I thought I would leave that to you. But there is one more thing."

"What's that?" Bradley asked.

"I understand you and Mara are trying to figure out how Amanda chooses her victims."

"Yes, that's right. It seems she uses physical fitness venues to surveille and possibly befriend these women," Bradley explained.

"But I don't think she chooses the women," Sahani told him.

"What do you mean?"

"My guess is she chooses the man. Then if the wife meets her criteria, she begins her process."

"Son of a . . . that makes sense. Of course. We've been thinking about this backwards."

For the first time since he entered Sahani's office, Bradley looked her square in the eyes. "We need to find out what these men have in common."

"How can I help?" Sahani asked.

"You already have, but stay close," Bradley said as he rolled out of the room.

Sahani lifted her chin and shoulders, and her face brightened. When he had finally faced her, she saw a spark in Bradley's eyes. A spark that had been missing. She hoped it would ignite the fire that Derek so often spoke of.

"Who's looking into Amanda Lessing's juvenile records?" Jim heard Bradley bark as he rolled into the bullpen.

"I am," Jim answered.

Bradley headed straight for Jim's desk.

"What have you got?" Bradley asked.

"She grew up in New Castle, Delaware, but I can't find any school records after sixth grade. She lived with her mother, Myrna Shore, who has a thick rap sheet of solicitation arrests. Lessing does have a sealed juvenile record. I've already put the paperwork in to access that. I should have the information shortly. After the age of twelve, she either dropped out of school or was home-schooled. But I'm guessing her mother wasn't interested in her daughter's education, since she only made it to sixth grade herself." Jim said.

"What are the odds? Have you done an internet search?"

"I'm just getting to that. I'll let you know when I have anything."

About to leave, Bradley stopped and said, "Jim, do a search for reports of assaults on minor females in her hometown area between the time of Lessing's twelfth and eighteenth birthdays."

"I can bet it's going to be quite a list. Can you narrow it down for me?" Jim asked.

"Try sexually assaulted minor females who were found naked and slashed with a knife."

"Ahh, I see what you're getting at. I'll get right on it."

"Thanks, Jim. Hey, how are the wife and kids?" Bradley asked.

"Um," Jim's mouth dropped open before he replied. "They're great, Bradley. They're getting bigger every day. The kids, I mean. Not my wife," Jim chuckled. "Thanks for asking."

Bradley smiled. "You're a lucky guy," he said before he rolled away.

Yes, I am, Jim thought as he watched Bradley return to his desk. Jim's sense of gratitude overpowered an initial feeling of empathy.

An alert appeared on Jim's monitor announcing that Amanda Lessing's juvenile report was available for review.

The more Jim read, the bigger the pit in his stomach became. Lessing's first arrest came at the age of twelve years old, the same age as Jim's daughter, Betsy. The juvenile report listed charges of solicitation, petty theft, burglary, and truancy. Amanda Lessing had also been arrested in the sting operation of a film pornographer when she was just thirteen years old. Jim found it hard to believe she never spent more than three months in a juvenile detention facility.

He forwarded the report to Bradley.

Using the National Criminal Database, Jim searched for assaults in Amanda's hometown area committed on female minors between the dates that Bradley specified and resulting in knife wounds. He got more than six thousand hits. He added another filter to search for victims found naked, and results dropped to just under thirty-seven hundred. He reduced the number even more by limiting the search to the town of New Castle. He still got more than thirteen hundred reports of assaults fitting the description. Out of pure desperation,

Jim typed the name Amanda Lessing into the filter search. As expected, he came up empty.

Knowing it would take him days to gather the facts from all the reports, Jim decided to use the internet. In his search bar, he typed the words "new castle minor female sexual assault knife."

Realizing he forgot to narrow down the search with a date, he added the decade 2001-2010.

Jim became frustrated with the process when the first page of results were stories from local newspapers about a man who had died of a knife wound. "Local Man Knifed," "Husband and Father Dead," and "Neighborly Love?" were some of the headlines from stories printed seventeen years prior.

On the second and third pages of results, he found more intriguing reports of incidents and began delving into the stories. After two hours of getting nowhere, he gave up and returned to the first page of results. His curiosity got the best of him, so he clicked on the article headlined, "Neighborly Love?"

June 20, 2004 — New Castle police responded to a 911 call on Blackbird Lane last night reporting the rape of a minor female. On arrival at the designated address, police discovered the dead body of the alleged perpetrator in the victim's bedroom. The reported cause of death was a stab wound to the neck.

The victim was transported to New Castle Hospital with injuries and is said to be in stable condition.

According to a source close to the investigation, Nathan Cornwell, 36, who lives across the street from the victim, reportedly entered the home, retrieved a knife from the kitchen, and assaulted the minor at knife point. The victim managed to momentarily distract her assailant, gain control of the knife, and kill her attacker.

"This young woman did what she had to do," said Chief Robert Ingman. "She is lucky to be alive."

Public records reveal that the home is owned by Myrna Shore, age 32.

The investigation is ongoing.

Jim read the remaining articles concerning Nathan Cornwell, then printed them out and raced to Bradley's desk.

"I think I've got what you're looking for," Jim said excitedly.

Bradley read the stories, then picked up his phone and dialed Sahani's extension.

"Can you come out to the bullpen?" Bradley asked.

She reponded, "I'll be right there."

Sahani had barely planted her feet when Bradley shoved the printouts into her hand, saying, "Her mother's name is Myrna Shore."

When finished reading, Sahani looked up. "Well, this would certainly do it," she stated. "And I'm outraged that a newspaper would do so little to protect the identity of the victim. I can't imagine what she must have gone through as a result of this article."

"I think it's safe to say nothing good came from it," Jim stated.

"I've got more," Bradley said. "While Jim was running down this information, I spent time looking into her juvenile record. The thefts and solicitations didn't tell me much, but I looked into the pornographer she got arrested with. His real name is Charles Harker, but he's gone by the names Pierre de Lust, Michael Dickman, and a few others," Bradley said, shaking his head.

"He's been arrested multiple times, served just two years, and prefers youthful subjects," Bradley continued. He is credited with more than eighty pornographic films, but here is the interesting part. With the help of the DOJ's Child Exploitation and Obscenity Section, I was able to find out that between 2001 and 2004 he made a series of seven films that have become quite popular in that market. Would you care to guess who starred in each of those films?"

"Amanda Lessing," Sahani sighed.

"Except she had a stage name. Just a single name like Cher or Zendaya. They called her Angel." Bradley smiled as the name spilled from his mouth. "You were right, Sahani, she's telling us her story."

"We need to fill the others in," Sahani said.

After Sahani left, Jim turned to Bradley and asked, "How do you know Amanda Lessing starred in the porn movies if her real name wasn't listed?"

Bradley replied, "I watched them."

Stunned at his reply, Jim asked, "How are they still available if the DOJ knows about them."

"Someone is selling pirate copies of the originals. I just had to search the dark web."

"You downloaded porn from an illegal site on a government computer? And then watched it?"

"How else would I know if it were her. As it was, I had to watch multiple videos to know with absolute certainty that it was. She was much younger then than what her current license photo depicts."

"Can I be in the room when you tell Nick what you did? I've got to see this," Jim smiled.

"You probably should be. I downloaded them from the website using your name." Bradley smiled before shifting his chair into gear and heading to Nick's office, leaving Jim with his mouth agape.

"Derek is hung up in meetings. I'll have to fill him in later," Nick said. "This is all important information, but what we need is solid evidence against Amanda Lessing. We need to find out where she is and who she is planning on taking out next. If we can't do that, all this means nothing. If she shows up at Jake Boulanger's house again, I think we should have the surveillance teams follow her."

Bradley disagreed. "That's risky, Nick. If she finds out we are on to her she'll dump any possible evidence and disappear. You've got the local and state police watching for her vehicle, right?"

"Right."

"It's just a matter of time before they find her. We also have her picture in every gym and yoga studio in the state. I think we need to be patient," Bradley suggested.

"I wish I had your confidence," Nick said. "Alright, we'll give it a little more time. What's your plan?"

"Mara and I will start at the beginning again. The key may be in finding out what the husbands have in common. Something in their behaviors incurred the wrath of Amanda Lessing. We need to find out what that was," Bradley replied.

"Okay, but I want you to take Sahani with you," Nick said.

Bradley opened his mouth to protest but stopped himself. He quickly realized that Sahani could be an asset. And it was her idea to connect the husbands in the first place.

Bradley nodded.

"Alright. Tony, you and Jim find out everything you can about the New Castle assault. Interview the police, neighbors, media, and family members. I want to know every detail about the case," Nick said. "Let's finish this."

Before leaving the office, Bradley printed photos of Amanda Lessing from the porn videos he had downloaded. He tried his best to use uncompromising poses but found few.

Mara, Sahani, and Bradley agreed they should speak first with the husband of the most recent known victim, Jake Boulanger. Bradley called ahead to arrange with Boulanger for them to meet at his house.

Sitting on the Boulanger back patio, Bradley began, "Jake, we need to ask you some personal questions, and I apologize for the bluntness, but you need to be completely honest with us." He paused. "We don't think the Predator chose your wife to be the victim. We think you may have been the prime target."

Jake's back stiffened while his eyes narrowed in anger. "What are you talking about? The bastard killed my wife. He mutilated her, raped her, and left her to rot. How is she not his victim?"

"Jake," Bradley asked sternly, "were you having an affair?"

Equally as stern, Jake replied, "No. Goddam it. I love my wife."

Sahani said, "Please, Mr. Boulanger, believe me when I say your wife certainly was the Predator's victim. But we are investigating why she was chosen." Sahani inched closer to Jake and spoke in a soft, sympathetic tone. "But we think you were also chosen. The Predator wanted you to suffer, as you most certainly are right now. And we need to know why you were singled out."

Sahani could see Jake Boulanger's muscles tense. Anguish filled his face. He choked on his next words.

"Are you saying this was somehow my fault?" he asked.

"No, absolutely not," Sahani responded. "The only person responsible for your wife's death is her assailant. And we need your help to apprehend the Predator."

"How? How can I help? I don't know anything," Jake whimpered.

Bradley said, "Maybe you do." Bradley reached in his pocket and took out the driver's license photo of Amanda Lessing. He showed it to Jake. "Do you recognize this woman?"

Sahani watched his reaction closely.

Jake examined the photo for a moment, then furrowed his eyebrows. "I don't know. She looks a little familiar, but I don't know why. What does she have to do with this? Did he use her to get to my wife?"

"Mr. Boulanger, you hesitated before you answered. Please, look at it again. And know that whatever you tell us will be kept confidential," Sahani promised.

"I don't know her," Jake replied.

"How about her?" Bradley pulled another photo from his jacket pocket. The photo showed a naked Amanda Lessing at the age of fourteen, straddling an equally young male.

Sahani saw it immediately. A flushness spread across Jake's face like the closing curtain of a Broadway play. Then his chin gave way to the gravity of his guilt.

Mara, who had been sitting quietly, reached for the notepad in her bag. She was right to assume that she should take notes from that point on.

"What's going on? What does she have to do with my wife's death?" Jake asked.

"So, you do know her?" Bradley asked.

"No. I mean, I don't know her. I've seen her . . . in some movies," he replied cautiously.

"What movies would those be?" Bradley urged.

Jake's Adam's apple dropped deep in his throat as he swallowed hard.

"Let me explain. After giving birth to our last child, things were different. I love my wife. I would never cheat on her, but I needed an outlet," Jake was on the verge of tears.

"We aren't here to judge you, Mr. Boulanger . . . Jake," Sahani said. "We can discuss the reasons at a later time. What we would like from you now is details such as where you got the videos, how you paid for them—that kind of information."

"I found them online. I've never done anything like this before, so I didn't know where to look and I wanted to be discreet."

"How long ago did you do this?" Bradley asked.

"Maybe seven or eight months ago," Jake answered.

"And how does it work?"

"The first website I found sold videos only from this one actress. Angel. I didn't want to spend much time searching the web, because I knew the more I looked, the more shit I'd get for advertisements. So I bought from that first site using a credit card that my wife didn't know I had."

"And did they deliver the video to you, or did you download it?"

"I downloaded them. That was the only option," Jake said.

"Them? You bought more than one?"

Jake nodded.

"So, you had to give your name and address to use your credit card?" Bradley asked.

"Yes, but I assumed the purchase went through a third-party payment system like most purchases do, you know, so it's secure," Jake said sheepishly.

"Why would you assume that?"

Jake's shoulders sunk. "I . . . I guess I wanted to believe it."

"What are the names of the movies you purchased?" Bradley asked.

Jake couldn't bring himself to say the names out loud, so he reached for Mara's notepad and wrote three titles: *Angel of the Horde, Angel on My Rocket,* and *Angel Flings.*

Then Jake said, "You still haven't told me what she has to do with my wife's death."

"No, we haven't," Bradley said as he turned his chair and left.

Mara followed Bradley, but Sahani stayed behind.

While waiting for Sahani to return to Bradley's truck, Mara said, "I can't imagine having to live with that guilt—if we turn out to be right, that is."

"Oh, we're right. I can feel it. She's punishing these guys for buying the porn that she's selling them. And, in some twisted way, she thinks she is saving these women from sexual deviance."

When Sahani returned to the truck, Bradley asked her why she stayed behind.

"I gave him the name of a psychologist friend of mine. He's going to need to talk to someone. I believe him when he says he'd never bought pornography before. I don't think he knew what he was buying."

"You mean child pornography?" Mara asked.

"Yes," Sahani replied.

"But he still watched it, didn't he?" Bradley added.

"Yes," Sahani sighed.

Next, they visited with Todd Colson, husband of Grace-Ann, the Predator's first Massachusetts victim. After some coaxing, Todd admitted to purchasing and watching several of Amanda Lessing's pornographic videos.

Before the day finished, Mara, Sahani, and Bradley had spoken with four of the husbands of victims who lived in New

Hampshire, and all of them confirmed they had purchased from the porn website.

It was after nine o'clock when they arrived back at Chelsea headquarters, but the lights were still shining on the eighth floor, so the three decided to go upstairs instead of getting into their respective vehicles and going home.

As they got off the elevator, they saw Tony and Jim huddled around Tony's desk. The two looked up when they heard the elevator doors ding open.

"Hey, how'd you make out?" Tony asked.

"We got what we were looking for," Bradley replied. "How about you?"

"More than we bargained for," Tony said.

"Good. I look forward to hearing what you've got. Are Nick and Derek still here?" Bradley asked.

"Yeah. Nick will be out in a couple minutes. Who knows about Derek? He is one busy SOB these days," Tony said.

"I guess that's what you get when you play with the big dogs. No time for the pups anymore," Bradley said with a smirk.

"Bradley, while we wait for Nick, may I talk to you in private?" Sahani asked.

"Ah, yeah, sure." Bradley shrugged his shoulders and followed Sahani to the empty conference room.

Once the door closed behind them, Sahani turned on Bradley with eyes glaring and said, "I don't think it's right that you denigrate Derek in front of the others."

"What the hell are you talking about?" Bradley replied.

"You implied that Derek doesn't care about the people in this office anymore. And you, of all people, know that is not the case."

"I didn't imply anything except that Derek is a busy man. I agreed with Tony, that's all," Bradley said defiantly.

"I'll give you the benefit of the doubt that you didn't mean to imply what you did, in fact, imply. Let's say the current difficulties between the two of you clouded your judgement and leave it at that. But don't take me for a fool."

Bradley was about to reply, "As you did me," when he thought better of it. Sahani was right. He had taken a cheap shot at Derek.

Instead, Bradley said, "Point taken."

Sahani stood, poised to continue the argument until she realized there wouldn't be one.

"Oh. Okay, then. Let's get back to work," she said and walked out of the conference room.

Nick joined them in the bullpen and asked that they wait a few minutes before briefing him because Derek wanted to be there, and there was no need to go through everything twice.

Ten minutes passed before Derek walked into the room.

"I apologize. I didn't mean to keep you waiting this long."

Just as Derek finished his sentence, the elevator opened and an FBI security guard, holding four large pizza boxes, stepped out.

"Over here." Derek pointed to an empty desktop. He thanked the guard and said, "I don't know about the rest of you, but I haven't eaten all day" before he opened the boxes and reached for a slice.

The others did the same.

"Bradley, why don't you go first?" Nick said.

"We know how she is picking her victims. We have confirmation from six of the husbands that they downloaded multiple pornographic videos starring Amanda Lessing, alias

Angel. We think she is selling the movies from her own website which allows her to collect the names and addresses of her buyers. Mara is going to coordinate the follow-up with the rest of the husbands with help from local FBI and state police. But I'm convinced this is how she decides who to target."

"What's your next move?" Derek asked.

"We're going to get help from the DOJ's Child Exploitation and Obscenity Section and Cyber Crime Unit to put pressure on the website host to give us access to the website. Those two departments have much more experience in these matters and will be more effective," Bradley stated. "If we can get a list of men from Massachusetts who have purchased from the site, we might be able to get ahead of her. We know what she's looking for."

"Let's hope," Derek said.

"What have you got, Tony?" Nick asked.

"Conflicting reports, depending on who you talk to," Tony answered. "We've confirmed that the minor involved in the New Castle assault was Amanda Lessing. The police department stands by the original story that Nathan Cornwell entered the unlocked home, took a knife from the kitchen, and used it to assault then fifteen-year-old Amanda Lessing. During the attack, Amanda was somehow able to distract Cornwell and turn the knife on him. He died instantly. Amanda suffered a severed right nipple from her breast, and the examination showed signs of what the doctor noted as "brutal genital penetration.""

"Was she naked when they found her?" Sahani asked.

"According to the police report, she was naked and covered in blood," Tony said. "But there's more. We also talked to Cornwell's wife. She is adamant that her husband would not have done such a thing. She painted the picture of Amanda Lessing enticing her husband by sunbathing in her front yard whenever Nathan worked outside. She also said Amanda kept her shade open when she undressed. The wife says she did it intentionally to tease men."

"Most women would have a hard time believing their husband could do such a thing," Sahani said.

"Yeah, that's what Jim and I thought, too. But we talked to some of the neighbors, and they told us the same thing. Some, including the wife, went as far as saying they think Lessing lured him there and killed him."

"Is there any evidence to support that theory?" Derek asked.

"Only that Amanda weighed about 95 pounds at the time and Nathan Cornwell checked in at 250. It's hard to imagine her getting the upper hand in a situation like that," Tony said.

"What did the coroner have to say," Bradley asked.

"He remembered the case well. He recalled initially being impressed with the victim and how she was able to fend off her attacker. But," Tony said, "as the years went on, the doctor found himself doubting her story. Then, of course, no one was ever charged. Cornwell was dead and couldn't defend himself, and the authorities never opened a case to investigate further."

"Either way, it would have been a defining moment in Amanda's life. It is the story she is telling," said Sahani.

Nick's ringing cellphone interrupted the conversation. He looked at the caller ID and said, "I should take this," before walking to the other side of the room.

Sahani continued in a thoughtful tone. "It's almost like she's reliving her life every time she murders these women. Maybe she thinks she is saving them by killing them because she wishes someone had done the same to her. Possibly Nathan Cornwell."

"On behalf of the seventeen women who have died at her hand, I wish he had, too," Tony said.

Sahani shot him a disapproving glance, but Tony did not back off his statement.

From across the room, Nick yelled, "We got her! That was Sergeant Doyle of the Revere Police Department. One of their off-duty officers spotted the blue Toyota Camry at the Crosstown Motel in Malden. He's watching the place now." Nick slammed his hand on a nearby desk in satisfaction.

"We'll need to work fast," Bradley said.

"I'll take care of the search warrant," Derek said. "Nick, text me the address of the motel." Derek hurried to his office.

Within minutes, three of their vehicles sped out of the Chelsea parking lot and screamed toward the Malden motel. Bradley drove his truck with Sahani in the passenger seat. Nick and Mara traveled in Nick's SUV, and Tony and Jim rode in Tony's sedan. They parked a half mile away from the motel and waited for Derek to arrive with the search warrant. The area was deserted, the perfect spot to stay if one didn't wish to be seen.

"Don't think too poorly of Tony," Bradley said. "I doubt he was the only person in the room thinking that."

"It's never okay to wish someone dead," Sahani replied.

"What if it's yourself?" Bradley said as he stared out the pickup truck window.

Sahani wondered if they were still talking about Amanda Lessing.

"Especially if it is yourself," she answered.

Sergeant Donovan Doyle pulled his Revere Police Department vehicle along the driver's side of Bradley's white Silverado and rolled down his passenger window.

Bradley rolled down his own window. "What brings you out this late, Doyle?"

"I came to watch the show," the sergeant replied. "Should be a good one. One for the books. Tell me you have enough to nail this son-of-a-bitch."

"Let's just say we know what we're looking for. How did your officer find this place?" Bradley asked.

"He wouldn't come right out and say, but I gather he spent a couple of hours here with a companion that wasn't his wife," Doyle said.

Bradley chuckled. "I can see the headline now. Serial killer thwarted by sleazy sexual encounter. Soon to be a major motion picture."

"We do whatever it takes," Doyle laughed.

"Speaking of doing what it takes, whatever happened with you and Reyes?"

Doyle smiled.

"Good for you, Doyle. I'm happy for you. Just don't do anything stupid," Bradley laughed.

"Now that's a promise I could never make," Doyle chuckled.

Bradley saw Derek's vehicle approach followed by two Malden police cruisers. Derek pulled up to Nick's SUV for a moment, then both proceeded toward the motel.

"It's showtime," Doyle said.

The caravan pulled into the motel parking area. Derek headed to the main office while the other vehicles surrounded the blue Toyota Camry. Nick directed Tony and Jim and one of the Malden police cruisers to go around the back of the motel just in case there was an exit they didn't know about.

A few minutes later, Derek and the owner of the motel walked toward them. The owner carried a large key ring.

Derek pointed to Room Number 17. Nick, Mara, and the two Malden police officers got out of their vehicles to join Derek and the motel owner. Bradley and Sahani stayed in the truck with the engine running.

Derek instructed the owner to stand aside immediately after unlocking the motel room door. With guns drawn, the officers, Nick, and Mara entered the room. Derek stood outside with the motel owner.

It was less than a minute later that Bradley and Sahani watched the four of them walk out the front door without Amanda Lessing. Nick said something to Derek, who then went inside the room. When he came back outside, he looked at Bradley and shook his head side to side.

Derek walked over to Bradley's truck and said, "You're going to want to see this."

Bradley turned off his truck and initiated the ramp system to lower him to the parking lot. He found a paved ramp leading onto the sidewalk and made his way to the room.

The stench of an old, wet gym bag smacked him in the face. Bradley had the sense that anything he touched in the room would either be sticky, grimy, or slimy. The tan walls used to be pale yellow, and the green shag carpet was right out of the 1960s. Other than a double-sized bed, the room had a wooden chair with a split down the middle of the seat, a rickety table with a television and DVR player on top, and a bedside table with lamp. The small bathroom boasted a window the size of a breadbox high on the wall over the sink.

Bradley knew instinctively that Amanda Lessing hadn't spent one night in the room. There would be no fingerprints, no incriminating evidence, and no trace of where she went from here. It was all for show. Especially what she left on the bed.

Lying on the unclean bedspread was a photograph of Bradley leaving Jake Boulanger's home with his cellphone raised as he took video of the neighborhood. Bradley remembered the moment. His video had been too dark to capture details, but without touching the photograph, he noticed it was clear as day. *She must have enhanced it herself,* he thought. On the bottom right of the photo, in black marker she wrote, "I hope someday you'll find me."

Sahani and Derek entered the room.

"I blew the case," Bradley said, pointing to the photo. "I should have known she was watching me, and I tipped our hand."

"There's no way you could have known," Derek said.

"Sure, there was," Bradley said as he exited.

"The lab guys are on their way to go through the car and the room. But I don't think they're going to find anything," Nick said to Bradley when he got outside.

"No. She's too smart for that. She's gone, and we're back to square one, thanks to my mistake," Bradley replied.

"We don't know that. She could have picked up one of our teams long before she took that photo. Don't beat yourself up. And we're not back to square one. We know how she chooses her victims and where she does her surveillance. Go home, get some rest, and I'll see you in the morning. There's nothing else to do here," Nick commanded.

Bradley headed to his truck and rode the electric ramp into his driving position. Then he saw Sahani hurrying to catch up to him.

"You weren't just going to leave me here, were you?" she asked.

"I figured you could hitch a ride with one of the others," Bradley replied.

"In my world, if you bring a girl to the dance, you drive her home," Sahani smiled as she stepped up into the passenger seat.

"Well, it wasn't much of a dance now, was it?" Bradley said.

"Are you always this hard on yourself?"

"When I fuck up, yeah."

"What about when someone else fucks up? Are you this hard on them?" Sahani asked.

Bradley didn't answer.

They drove in silence for miles until Sahani finally spoke.

"I've been thinking about what you asked me earlier—if it's wrong for a person to think about killing themselves. It's an interesting question on many levels. For instance, if a person is terminally ill and decides to take their own life instead of enduring immense pain themselves and exposing their loved ones to feelings of helplessness, I would oppose societal ideologies and understand, maybe even condone the idea.

"Or," Sahani continued, "someone who is unable to comprehend the consequences and finality of the decision to take their own life, I could certainly understand, however tragic. But for all others, yes, I think it is wrong and, dare I say, selfish to kill oneself. But to think about killing yourself is a far cry from actually doing so. And I would be willing to bet the average adult has thought about it more often than you might think."

Bradley remained quiet.

"As for Amanda Lessing, outwardly she believes she is killing these women for their own good, which would imply that she doesn't understand right from wrong. But I don't think that is the case at all. I think she is hiding behind her schizoid tendencies. Deep down, I think she knows full well what she's doing is wrong.

"So here is my final psychological profile of Amanda Lessing. She is killing these women because it's the only thing that keeps her from killing herself. She sees it as her only means of survival. She's chosen to punish the men who objectify her when they take pleasure in watching her films by symbolically killing herself using their wives. She is sick, but she is not insane."

"Remember that last part if this case ever gets to court," Bradley said.

They again rode in silence until Bradley pulled alongside Sahani's car in the headquarters parking lot.

Bradley waited for Sahani to step out of the truck and close the door before he rolled down his window and said, "Your position on suicide doesn't take into consideration those who believe in life after death, those who believe they belong to a group of souls who will continue to return to this earth time and time again, those who consider the idea as hitting life's reset button. It still may not be ideal, and it probably is selfish, but to them it's not final."

Before Sahani could respond, Bradley drove away, leaving her to wonder if she would see him again.

ALL THINGS GREY

She used Cecile Boulanger's name to purchase and register her new, used black Toyota Camry. She knew it too soon for the Social Security Administration to have flagged her Social Security number as belonging to someone deceased. By the time that took place, she reasoned, it would be too late. She would already have stolen a license plate to replace the one she received.

She drove west on Route 2, choosing the northern toll-free route instead of traveling the quicker Massachusetts Turnpike paralleling Route 2 to the south in order to avoid the turnpike cameras.

She knew she was getting close to her destination when she started spotting signs for moose crossings. After traveling the busy road for seventy-five miles, she turned south onto the picturesque Route 202. What little research she had done on the college town of Amherst told her she would pass through an area known as the Lost Towns of the Quabbin Valley. Her Camry followed the winding road rising in elevation until she came upon Pelham Overlook, a scenic viewpoint. She stopped her car in the small parking area and admired the vista. Below lay a large lake dotted with forested islands.

This must be it, she thought.

The story of the reservoir intrigued her. Back in the late 1930s, the Massachusetts government seized the land of four farming communities and forced families to leave their homes so they could flood the area to create the reservoir to serve residents of Boston and some suburbs.

As she looked at the beautiful Quabbin Reservoir, one thought occupied her mind. *Only a group of narcissistic men would displace so many families so they could have a drink of water.* Lessing then continued on her way.

On the cusp of summer giving way to fall, the college town burst with youthful exuberance. In early evening, the sidewalks were alive with students, teachers, and residents alike. Restaurants were at capacity, and bars braced for a big night. Amanda found a parking spot on Main Street near the center of town at the intersection with North Pleasant Street where most of the activity seemed to be. She slipped into a pizza place, ordered a slice, and sat on a bench to observe behaviors—her favorite pastime.

Her eyes were drawn to a couple in their late twenties holding hands. They strolled like they had no destination in mind. They talked and laughed while gazing at each other.

Amanda quickly snapped her head away as she felt her anger rise inside. But then it occurred to her that their happiness wouldn't last. *If I come back in five years and watch that same couple, they won't be holding hands or chatting happily. And they certainly won't be laughing.* A warm feeling spread through her body and tamped down the anger as she told herself, *He may even end up on my list.*

Licking her fingers after she placed the last bite of light and airy pizza crust into her mouth, she thought about Wheelchair Man. She hated to leave him, but she knew she would see him again. Their connection was a strong one. *Too strong, maybe.*

In the light of a new day, Nick's optimism had deteriorated.

"She'll need a car," Nick said as he paced the bullpen.

"I'm monitoring all stolen car reports within a sixty-mile radius," Tony responded.

"Goddam it, why don't we have the coroner's report yet? I thought she was putting it on the fast track?" Nick scowled.

Mara responded, "She is, Nick. Some things you just can't rush."

"Well, push her harder! Where the hell is Bradley?" Nick barked.

Everyone shrugged their shoulders.

"I'll call him again," Sahani said as she picked up her cellphone.

"Jesus Christ, we had her. We fucking had her," Nick screamed as the elevator dinged.

"We did. But we don't anymore. We'll just have to find her again," said Bradley as he rolled out the elevator doors.

Sahani breathed a sigh of relief. She had been trying to reach him for an hour.

"Sorry I'm late," Bradley said. "I stopped in to see Maria Reyes."

"And?" Nick asked.

Bradley smiled as he pulled a sheet of paper from his jacket pocket.

"We got DNA," he said.

Nick closed his eyes and put his hands together as if in prayer.

"Thank you," Nick said, just above a whisper. "Is she positive?"

"She's positive it isn't Cecile Boulanger's DNA. She doesn't know who it belongs to. The report says she found it under one of the fingernails on Cecile's left hand, the hand that had been wiped with the disinfectant cloth. It looks like she missed a little." Bradley continued to smile.

"Why the big smile?" Mara asked.

"She's making mistakes. As far as we know, the only two victims to have their hands wiped clean are the last two Massachusetts victims. If that's the case, it means she added something to her story that could come back to bite her in the ass."

"So, where are we with the website seizure?" Nick asked.

They each looked at the other waiting for a response.

"Jesus Christ, someone get on the phone with Child Exploitation and find out where we're at," Nick yelled.

"I got it," Bradley replied as he moved to his desk.

Sahani followed him.

"You had me worried. Was that your intent?" she asked.

"Not at all. I just thought you needed to see a different point of view. Not everything is black and white or right and wrong. Some of us live in the grey area from time to time."

"Oh, I'm quite familiar with the grey area. I'm just happy to know you recognize it when you go there," Sahani grinned.

"As do you," Bradley replied.

Sahani could not suppress her laughter. She felt at that moment that Bradley would be alright because, whatever name you put to that grey area—depression, grief, guilt, deceit—if you recognize you are there, there are infinite options to find your way out. On the other hand, if you think in terms of black and white, your options become limited.

Sahani rejoined the other agents while Bradley made his phone call.

"Hello, this is Agent Bradley Whitman. Could I speak with Agent Christine Woods, please."

After a brief pause, a voice answered, "Well, if this is how long it takes for you to decide to ask a girl on a date, then you've got some issues."

Bradley chuckled, "Hello, Christine. How have you been?"

"Hello, Bradley. It's nice to hear your voice. How did you track me down?"

"I always keep tabs on the special ones," Bradley said. "I heard you went to child exploitation in Washington. I thought that a much better fit for you than white collar crime."

"And you were right, of course. But I'm guessing this isn't that social call I hoped for way back when."

"Had I only known," Bradley said, as if his voice smiled. "No, you're right. This isn't a social call. I put a request in late last night and wanted to follow up. We have a situation involving pornographic sales of images of a minor. But there's a twist. The minor is now an adult selling the videos through her own website. She is also involved in another investigation we are working, a high profile one. We need access to the website sales records without the suspect knowing we are on to her. How possible is that?"

"It's possible, but it could take some time. Have you contacted the cybercrime unit?"

"Last night, the same time I contacted you folks. They are my next call."

"Ask for Ben Sojourn. He's the best. I'll see what I can do on my end and coordinate with him. Send me whatever information you can as soon as possible."

"Thank you, Christine."

"No, you don't get off that easy. You owe me dinner, someplace nice, here in the city," said Christine.

"It's a date," Bradley promised before he hung up the phone. For the first time in months, Bradley didn't feel like a wounded puppy. Christine obviously had not heard nor even known about Laney. He sat for a moment and ruminated on how nice it was to have a conversation that wasn't draped in a black veil. Then he picked up the phone and called Ben Sojourn.

When finished with his call, Bradley sent pertinent information to both Agents Woods and Sojourn then rejoined Nick, Mara, Tony, Jim, and Sahani.

"Well?" Nick asked when Bradley came back.

"We've got both child exploitation and cybercrime working on it as a high priority case. Agent Sojourn from cyber said if all goes well, he could have something for us in a few hours. It seems he has dealt with the website hosting company before and has some bargaining power. Agent Woods from child exploitation will apply pressure as well. But they warned that if the company digs in their heels, it could take weeks."

"Shit," Nick muttered.

"Keep the faith, Nick. Put those hands back together and pray. Because you can be sure that Amanda Lessing has already begun the process for number eighteen."

"Right," Nick moaned. "In the meantime, Tony and Jim, continue to try to find where Lessing stayed while she was here. Get the names of single women who checked out yesterday from every hotel, motel, bed and breakfast, and YWCA within a sixty-mile radius. Mara and Bradley, see if you can figure out where she went after dropping her car at the motel. Maybe she called an Uber or a cab."

Bradley turned to Mara. "Do you want cab companies or Uber drivers?"

"I'll take Ubers. I'll check the bus lines, too," Mara said.

"Okay," Bradley said, returning to his desk.

After an hour of phone calls, Bradley was getting nowhere, and he could tell from across the room by Mara's body language that she had made no progress either. He had just decided to take a few minutes and go to the break room for an orange juice when the elevator doors pinged and Cate walked out.

"Bradley," Cate screeched, as she tended to do when excited. She threw her arms around him like she hadn't seen him in years.

"Hi, Cate," Bradley laughed.

"I didn't know you were back to work yet," Cate said.

It became obvious at that moment that Derek hadn't mentioned anything about the falling out they had.

"You know me, Cate." Then Bradley noticed a beautiful red-haired woman standing behind Cate.

When Cate saw Bradley's change of expression, she turned to the woman and said, "Oh, Madelyn, I am so sorry. Bradley, this is Madelyn Cross. She is Derek's executive assistant. She just flew in from Washington. Madelyn, this is Bradley Whitman."

"It's nice to meet you, Madelyn," Bradley said as they shook hands.

"And you, Bradley," Madelyn replied.

"Did you have a nice flight?" Bradley asked.

"Yes, I did. But the best part was finding Cate waiting for me at the airport."

"She always brightens my day, too." Bradley flashed a smile that Cate hadn't seen in months. It melted her heart so much that she leaned down and gave him a big kiss.

"Bradley Whitman, you are the second most wonderful man in this world," Cate smiled. "Don't make dinner plans for tonight."

Before Bradley could protest, Cate and Madelyn disappeared down the hall towards Derek's office. Forgetting about the orange juice, Bradley went back to his desk to make more calls.

Before he could pick up the telephone, he noticed a large shadow looming over him. Tony and Jim stood in front of Bradley's desk.

"Who's the gorgeous red-head?" Tony asked.

"She's Derek's executive assistant. She just flew in from Washington," Bradley answered.

"How is it that Derek is surrounded by so many beautiful women? What's his secret?" Tony asked rhetorically.

Bradley took Tony by surprise when he snapped at him. "He is a gentleman who respects women for who they are, not what they look like."

Tony held both his hands up in front of him, palms out. "Okay, forget I asked." Then he and Jim ambled back to Tony's desk, both a little red in the face.

Bradley was unsure why he hammered Tony for his comment. But the truth was, for a moment, he wondered the same thing. And he hated himself for it.

Alone, Cate came back down the hall and stopped at Bradley's desk.

"So, Bradley, tonight we are buying you dinner," Cate said.

"Cate, I really don't . . . "

"Nope." Cate shook her head. "Uh, uh. I won't take no for an answer. And it's not what you think."

"What is it I think?" Bradley asked.

"You know. Before you met Laney, I used to try to get you to dinner to meet some of my women friends. But this isn't like that. Madelyn has a boyfriend. She's dating the personal assistant to the President of the United States, Robert Harris. So, see? It's not what you think it is," Cate said, triumphantly.

"Ah, huh. So, what is it?" Bradley asked.

"Madelyn is going to be staying with us for a few days, and I thought it would be nice if she had someone closer to her own age to talk to."

"Sure, because you two geriatrics don't know how to converse with a thirty-something? Come on, Cate. What gives?"

"Okay, look. I love Madelyn. I think she is great. But she gets Derek to herself at least two weeks every month, and now I'm supposed to share him with her when he's home, too? I mean, I know it's just a professional relationship, but it is still a relationship."

"Why Cate Wayland Richards, do I detect the faintest bit of jealousy?" Bradley teased.

"Please, Bradley. Come to dinner," Cate begged.

"Alright, I will. Unless something happens with the case. Then all escort duties are voided." Bradley said.

"If something happens with the case, I'm sure Derek won't be going to dinner either. Thank you, Bradley."

"Cate, you're not really bothered by her, are you? You know Derek would never . . ."

"I do know, in here," Cate tapped her chest. "But in here?" She tapped her right temple and shrugged. "I'm not getting any younger, and everyone around me seems to be."

"You are as stunningly beautiful as the first day I laid eyes on you, inside and out."

Cate smiled. "Could you call me first thing every morning and repeat that to me?"

"I'd be happy to. But I don't think you really need me to," Bradley said.

Cate leaned down and kissed Bradley on the cheek. "I'll see you tonight," she said, then left.

Bradley got nowhere with his phone calls, and Mara had the same results.

As they sat at Bradley's desk, Mara commented, "Maybe she hitched a ride?"

"However possible, it would be out of character for her. She is a detailed planner. She wouldn't leave anything to chance. No. Someone picked her up."

"A friend?" Mara asked without much conviction.

"No, she doesn't have any of those. Maybe a car rental company that picks people up? Or . . . what about a private service? Mara, follow me."

Bradley led Mara to Sahani's office. The door was open. Sahani looked up from her desk and waved the two in.

"Sahani, we haven't profiled Lessing's economical status. What would you say about her financial situation?" Bradley asked.

Sahani sat quiet, contemplating everything about the Predator's profile she had examined. It took several moments for her to speak confidently.

"She's got money. Enough so she doesn't have to work a regular job. It's doubtful she keeps the bulk of her money in a bank, but if she is selling from a website, the money has to go somewhere. Even if she uses an online company like PayPal to receive and make payments, she would have had to list a stable bank account to begin with," Sahani stated.

"And she wouldn't necessarily have to use her own name to open a bank account. All she would need is a Social Security number for someone who has either been long deceased or . . ."

Bradley stopped. An idea suddenly struck him. "Myrna Shore. Mara, find out everything you can about Myrna Shore. See if she is still alive and if she has a checking account. If she does, we need access to the account and any online transactions going in and out.

"I'm going to check private car services," he added, "to see if she used one to pick her up at or near the motel.

Mara left the room.

"You could freeze her assets," Sahani said.

Bradley said nothing as his eyes grew wide. When he did speak, his words seemed to come from a deep place within. Even his voice sounded different. "She's smart. She has cash stashed somewhere. Besides, I don't want her to go underground. I can't let her. I need her to continue doing what she's doing. I can't tip my hand, again. She needs to succeed for me to succeed. I have to . . ."

"Bradley," Sahani barked as she held her hand to her breastbone and grimaced.

Bradley stopped and looked up, as if returning from a trance.

"What?" he asked.

Sahani's eyebrows drew close as she leaned into her desk and glared at Bradley. "Please tell me you didn't mean what you just said."

Bradley's face contorted.

Sahani repeated, "Please tell me you didn't just say that Amanda Lessing needs to kill another human being so *you* can be successful."

Bradley looked dazed, as if he took a proper right hook to his cheek.

"That's not what I said. What I said is she needs to continue her process, thinking she is safe, to give us time to catch up to her," Bradley replied unconvincingly. The truth was, Bradley didn't remember exactly what he said.

"After speaking with you this morning, I thought you had turned a corner. I thought you were thinking clearly. But now I'm not so sure," Sahani said, her eyes furrowed and her face stern.

Bradley grew angry. "I'm doing my job. It's what I do. It's who I am. So if you'll excuse me, I have a serial killer to catch." Bradley turned his chair sharply and left the room.

Back at his desk, he found it difficult to shake his anger. Unable to concentrate, he remembered his earlier desire to take a break. He headed to the break room, the first room on the left of the hallway when heading to Sahani or Derek's office.

In the break room, he found Madelyn Cross sipping a cup of coffee.

"Oh, hello," Bradley said. "I thought you would be hard at work with Derek."

"He's in a private meeting," Madelyn replied.

Bradley couldn't help but wonder if Sahani went to see Derek as soon as he left her office. He decided he didn't care if she did. Bradley reached for an orange juice from the refrigerator, then, in an effort to calm himself he placed his chair across from Madelyn's.

"So, how do you like working with Derek?" Bradley asked.

"He's great. A little too humble at times, maybe," Madelyn smiled.

"Don't let that fool you. He is humble, but he is no pushover. Derek has a way of using his words to get his point across. He never needs to raise his voice. That's not to say he won't raise his voice, but he doesn't need to."

"I can see that," Madelyn replied. "How long have you two known each other?"

Bradley chuckled. "I was twelve years old when we met. And I've been working with him since I graduated from college. Other than my father, there's no man in this world I respect more than Derek."

The words escaped Bradley's mouth before he could think about them because they were true. He began to feel guilty about the way he chastised Derek for Sahani's deceit.

"I'm sure I will learn a lot from him," Madelyn said as her cellphone buzzed. "Looks like it's back to work for me. It was nice talking with you, Bradley."

Bradley nodded his head and took a sip of his juice. He decided he needed to apologize to Derek.

Back at his desk, Bradley placed calls to several private limousine and car service companies before he hit paydirt. Executive Auto reported picking up a woman in her thirties from the area of the Crosstown Motel the previous morning. The driver revealed that he dropped her off at a car dealership in Somerville only five miles away.

Bradley informed Nick of his intent then left the office and drove to the Somerville Auto Emporium. Although sympathetic to Bradley's needs, the manager of the company did not make it easy. After several phone calls between the business owner and Nick, the manager handed over the information Bradley had requested.

The cash purchase had been made using the stolen identity and address of Cecile Boulanger. A quick search of the department of motor vehicles revealed that the used black Toyota Camry had been registered in Cecile's name and issued the Massachusetts license plate number CN1126.

Bradley forwarded the information to Nick. An all-points bulletin was issued throughout the state for the whereabouts of the vehicle.

"I'm going home, Nick. I'll work from there for the rest of the day unless you need me," Bradley said to Nick after their business was done.

"Yeah, okay, Bradley. I'll let you know if anything comes up," Nick replied.

Bradley went to his truck and headed for home.

Rusty, happy to see Bradley so early, placed his front paws on Bradley's lap while his tail swept the hardwood floor where he sat. Bradley didn't try to move. As the two remained in the pose, Bradley realized just how wound up he had been. He took pleasure in Rusty's unconditional happiness and wished he could immerse himself in it. But he knew that, for him, it could never last.

"Alright, buddy. Time to go outside," Bradley finally said.

When Bradley slid the door open, Rusty rushed out. Bradley stared into the tiny village below. He wondered how Zayt's date had gone. He wondered if Cate sat at home feeling jealous. He wondered if Mara had been sleeping better. He wondered what, if anything, Sahani had said to Derek. He wondered why he still sat there wondering such things.

Bradley crossed the room to his desk and booted his computer. Without thinking, he opened his desk drawer and glanced at the sealed letters that lay inside. He reached down to touch the top letter addressed to *Cate*, as if to make sure it was really there. As he closed the drawer, his eyes focused on the photograph of him and Laney at the *Maker's Mark* movie premiere, but this time, he didn't smile.

Rusty returned a short time later and settled in beside Bradley.

A little after noontime, Bradley got the news that Tony and Jim had discovered where Amanda Lessing had been staying. It confirmed to Bradley that Lessing had plenty of financial resources, because the rooms at the Everett casino were not inexpensive, but they are the perfect place to blend into a crowd. They were also kept extremely clean, so the lab crew was unable to lift any fingerprints or usable DNA from the room.

Not long after, Mara called Bradley and reported that Myrna Shore was seemingly still alive and held a checking account with Delaware Bank & Trust. The account had originally opened in 2004, seventeen years prior. Bank records showed little to no activity in the first eight to ten years, but since then the money flow had picked up, especially in the last five years. Mara noted that the website selling the Angel videos had gone live seven years before. She confirmed that funds from the purchase of Amanda's videos were deposited into the Myrna Shore account.

"The money goes into the bank via a third party, so there is no record of where the purchases originated," Mara stated.

"So we really need the website host to release that information," Bradley said.

"Yes," Mara agreed. "That seems to be our best chance. Have you heard anything yet?"

"No. Nothing yet."

"Why aren't you here, Bradley? I thought we were working on this together," Mara asked.

"We are. I just had something to take care of, that's all," Bradley lied.

"Oh, okay," Mara said. "Sorry. I don't mean to sound needy, but I work much better when you're here." Mara let out a little laugh.

"Well, you've got Sahani now," Bradley said before he hung up.

Bradley felt a twinge of guilt for his lie and his last remark. Once again, he spoke without thinking, something he rarely did, but the last few days seemed unavoidable.

No sooner had Bradley hung up with Mara, Cate called.

"Can you meet us at Grill 23 on Berkeley Street at seven o'clock?" Cate asked.

"Okay. I'll wear my tails," Bradley joked.

"Wear your pajamas for all I care. Just, please come," Cate said.

"Seven o'clock. I'll be there," Bradley replied before he hung up.

What the hell is wrong with me? Bradley asked himself, knowing he had no intention of going to dinner. *You're a terrible friend, that's what's wrong with you,* he answered himself. *You're a fucking self-absorbed heel. When did that happen?*

Once again, Bradley was saved from his thoughts by his telephone ringing.

"Bradley, it's Christine. I just emailed you the sales report from the website for the year."

"You are the best, Christine," Bradley said.

"And you owe me dinner. Let me know if there is anything else you need," she added.

"I will, thank you."

Bradley immediately opened his email and found the report. He downloaded it to his hard drive, then opened it. His excitement waned as he examined the document at length. Amanda Lessing sold approximately 1,200 units per month at $49.99 per unit, averaging nearly $60,000 a month.

He exported the report into an Excel file and sorted by state. Then he alphabetized the states.

It only took minutes to confirm that both Massachusetts victims of the Pathside Predator were married to a man on the list.

The same was true for one of the New Hampshire victims. He knew if he had earlier sales records, he would find the names of all the Predator's victims.

As he inspected the report more closely, he found that Massachusetts boasted the eighth highest number of state sales in the country with a total of 357 for the year to date. When Bradley considered how many other websites were selling direct-to-buyer child pornography, he shuddered at the probable numbers.

Bradley separated the Massachusetts information and created a new file. With three of the names already accounted for—Coulson, Boulanger, and his own purchase in Jim Jansen's name—354 probable victims remained.

He then wrote a list of criteria for prioritizing the possible targets.

He wrote:

married male

age 30-45

physically fit wife (yoga, gym member, etc.)

has children
upper middle class
purchased multiple videos
Note: Predator has probably moved from this general area

Bradley divided the master into ten separate lists, nine of which contained thirty-five names each and the tenth, which he kept for himself, with thirty-nine names. He emailed the nine lists, along with the criteria, to Nick so he could assign them to other agents. He also suggested they should meet in the morning to review the results.

"9 a.m. meeting," Nick responded.

Before Bradley delved into the names, he texted Cate. Even though he had warned her it could happen and even though he hadn't planned to go to dinner with them anyway, he felt guilty.

Cate, I'm sorry I can't join you tonight. Development in the case.

Cate didn't respond.

Bradley used every FBI source available, including marriage certificates, birth records, IRS documents, department of motor vehicles information, and credit card activity. He also delved into the world of social media when available. The afternoon turned to evening and then early morning before Bradley had researched every name on his list.

He whittled thirty-nine names down to five, then cut it to just two names for his short list—the Predator's more likely targets. Using the law of averages, Bradley surmised the team would compile a short list of between seventeen and twenty names.

Bradley printed out a map of Massachusetts and, using a red marker, placed an x where each of the two short list names lived. With a green marker, he added the other possible targets. He would add the rest of the x's at the 9 a.m. meeting.

A thought occurred to him while he added names to the map, and it kept him from getting more than two hours sleep that morning.

With Rusty snoring at his feet, Bradley printed out maps of Connecticut, Rhode Island, and New Hampshire. He marked each map with the victims' home locations using the numbers one through five, the order in which they were killed. He'd hoped to find a geographical pattern, and he did.

The conference room filled with weary faces as the coffee pot made its way around the table. Bradley had brought himself an orange juice. Derek was not present.

"Let's get right to it," Nick said. "We'll start with Tony and then move clockwise around the table. Tony, you have our attention."

"Using the criteria provided, out of the thirty-five names given me, I determined three possible targets, the third name being possible but not probable. I am of the opinion that one name stands out above the other two: Matthew Collins of Pittsfield."

Bradley marked Pittsfield with a red x on his map.

Jim sat to Tony's left and added two names to the list. By the time the ten agents finished, Bradley had placed eighteen red x's on the map. The red marks spread across the state.

"Okay. Great work everybody. Give Bradley a copy of your report on your way out. There are bagels and doughnuts in the break room," Nick said.

While the rest left the room, Bradley and Nick stayed behind. Nick watched as Bradley switched from the red marker to the green, understanding Bradley did not wish to dismiss even the least possible of targets.

"Well? What's this map telling you?" Nick asked.

"Looking back on the previous cases, state by state, Lessing's first two victims lived within a fifty-mile radius of each other. The third and fourth victims did also but they were approximately a hundred miles away from the first two kills, except in Rhode Island because of its limited size. But, Lessing's third and fourth Rhode Island victims were about as far away from the first and second as she could get. The last victim in each state lived within twenty miles of a state border. So, she does have a pattern."

"So," Nick said, "if she continues with that pattern, we can count out anyone within a hundred miles of Revere and Weymouth."

"Theoretically, yes. But she will also want to give herself the largest number of possibilities. There's only one area on this map that suits every criteria."

With a black marker, Bradley drew an oval to encompass the area he thought Amanda Lessing would be found. The top of the oval cut through Sunderland, Massachusetts. The western edge caught Easthampton and went to Chicopee in the south, Belchertown to the east, and back to Sunderland.

"And Interstate Route 91 cuts through the middle of the area in case she needs a quick getaway," Nick observed.

The oval captured six x's, two red and four green. The red x's landed on Amherst and Holyoke, while the green x's sat on Chicopee, Northampton, South Hadley, and Belchertown.

A feeling of uneasiness invaded Bradley when he saw that someone in the town of Amherst was most likely a Predator target. He knew the town well because of his friends Holly and John who lived there. They always spoke of how quaint the town felt even though it is a college town. He quickly rummaged through each agent's report to find the name connected to the possible Amherst target and sighed with relief when he didn't recognize it. Then he chastised himself for thinking it possible he might find John Davidson's name on the list.

"Mara and I can take the Amherst couple, Stephen and Andrea Edwards. I can get some insight into where Lessing might stay from Holly. She knows the area well," Bradley said.

"Okay. Tony and Jim will watch the Holyoke couple"—Nick searched the report for their names—"Timothy and Bonnie Franklin."

"Tell Mara to pack her running shoes. The report says Andrea Edwards is a jogger," Bradley said before leaving the room.

Three hours later, Bradley and Mara cruised down the Massachusetts Turnpike at a steady eighty miles per hour. Bradley made arrangements for Zayt to take care of Rusty while he was gone. He packed enough clothing for a week. Amherst was only two hours away, but he didn't want to waste time driving back and forth.

Mara read aloud from the information they had gathered about the Edwards couple, which included photographs from their driver's licenses. They talked strategy for the first half hour. Then Mara asked, "Where are we staying?"

"That's a good question. Let's find out," Bradley said. "Call Holly."

Bradley's hands-free calling system lit up on his screen, and a computer voice said, "Calling Holly."

The phone rang four times before Holly picked up. "Bradley, is this really you?" Holly sounded surprised.

"Yes, it is darlin'. Why so surprised?" he asked.

"Because I can count on one hand how many times you have called me in the twenty years we have known one another."

"Well, start another hand, because here I am. And you're on speaker. I've got Mara here with me. We're on the pike heading your way. Unfortunately, it is a business trip, so I don't know if we will have time to get together, but I wanted to pick your brain about a good place to stay between Amherst and Holyoke."

"Here, of course. John and I have plenty of room. And Holyoke is only fifteen miles away." Holly said.

"That's very nice, Holly, but we will be keeping horrible hours, and the office is paying for our stay. So, I thought you might be able to steer me to the most expensive and luxurious hotel nearby."

"That's easy. The Inn on Boltwood. They've got a great restaurant on site, beautiful rooms, and wonderful staff."

"Perfect. Now, what if we wanted to be nice to the agency and stay at a decent hotel without breaking the bank?"

"Then I would go with the Courtyard by Marriot on Route 9. It's pretty basic, but you would have plenty of restaurants to choose from. Of course, neither one will be better than staying here," Holly said.

"I appreciate it, Holly. But, trust me, it would be a major disruption, and we still wouldn't have time to catch up. If I have time once we wrap this case up, I'll let you know." Bradley said, realizing once again that he would not do that. "Give John and your dad my best."

"You are a stubborn man, Bradley Whitman."

"And you are a lovely soul," Bradley said as he hung up.

"So, you think Amanda Lessing is staying at the Inn on Boltwood?" Mara asked.

"We'll find out," Bradley answered. "Call Nick."

Bradley asked Nick to find out if Lessing had a room booked at the Inn.

"She's probably using Cecile Boulanger's name, but it could also be under her mother's—or someone else's entirely," Bradley warned.

"I'll get back to you," Nick said.

"To the Courtyard then," Bradley stated when he hung up.

"But if Lessing is staying at the Boltwood, it doesn't necessarily mean she is going after Andrea Edwards. Bonnie Franklin could still be the target, right?"

"Right. They are close enough together that it could be either one or both. I think she likes to keep her options open. My guess is she looks for couples who project happiness. In her mind, that would mean deception on the part of the husband. To Lessing, that would make perfect sense. She would then rationalize that she is doing these women a favor, saving them."

"That's very sad. I imagine she's never had a single person in this world that she could trust," Mara said.

Bradley didn't respond. He couldn't feel sorry for Amanda Lessing after what she had done. He wondered how anyone could. *How can a person find compassion for someone so inherently bad?*

Bradley had just steered the truck into the Courtyard parking lot when Nick called.

"She's there, goddam it. You nailed it. She's using the name Myrna Shore. She checked in yesterday," Nick said. "I'm going to call the local and state police to prep them so they'll be ready when we need them. How do you want to play this?"

"We'll watch Andrea Edwards from a distance. Lessing has most likely started her surveillance already. Tony and Jim should do the same with the Franklins."

"Why don't we just take her at the inn?" Nick asked.

"Too risky. This is a busy little town. I don't want to rush this, Nick. We have time. I think we should do this as safely and quietly as possible. We know Andrea Edwards is a jogger. That will appeal to Lessing. And hopefully it will give us an opportunity to grab her without putting other people in danger."

"Alright. We'll do it your way. I'll update Tony and Jim. Keep me posted." Nick hung up.

"Let's get settled in our rooms. Get your running gear on. We'll need to be ready in case Andrea goes for a jog tonight. You'll still be able to conceal your glock while you run, right?"

"Of course," Mara said. "My running pants have a built-in holster at the nape of my back. I never leave home without it."

"Me neither. Okay, let's meet back in the lobby in 30 minutes," said Bradley.

Information about Andrea and Stephen Edwards came in rapidly. Nick had the Chelsea team find out as much as they could about the couple and passed it along to Bradley and Mara.

Professor Stephen Edwards taught literature at the University of Massachusetts while Andrea worked part-time weekday mornings at a daycare center. They had two children in elementary school, a beautiful home on Pelham Road, a Lexus and Cadillac. On paper, Bradley thought, they looked like a perfectly happy couple, just what Amanda Lessing would look for.

Bradley drove Pelham Road, which ran from the town of Pelham to Main Street in Amherst. The country road provided a stark difference from the neighborhoods in eastern Massachusetts. Homes occupied multiple acre plots with large yards and trees protecting each households' privacy in contrast to the postage stamp lots in the city. The Edwards home sat diagonally across the street from Amethyst Brook Conservation Area.

After scouting the area, Bradley parked his truck among the eight other vehicles in the conservation area's parking lot. They watched as people came and went. Some came for a jog or a hike, but most came with their dog, or in some cases, dogs. But there didn't seem a time when the park wasn't bubbling with activity.

"There is a lot of action in this park," Mara said.

"Yeah. It hardly seems like the ideal place to attack someone. There are way too many people," Bradley added.

"But it would be the obvious place for Andrea to take a jog. It's so convenient."

"I know. If this is where Andrea comes, it's doubtful Lessing will try anything here. It's very public. It might scare Lessing off. She might not go after the Edwards."

"I'm going to go for a jog. I want to see what the park looks like, just in case." Mara said as she jumped from the truck.

"Okay. See if there are any secluded trails. But put your radio earpiece in. I don't want to be out of contact at any time," Bradley advised. "It's going to be dark soon. And the internet says the park closes at 8:30 so we have little more than two hours. Do you have a headlamp?"

"Right here," Mara tapped her left hip where her fanny pack sat. She put the radio earpieces in her ears. "Testing. Can you hear me?"

Bradley gave Mara a thumbs up as he heard her voice through his own earpiece. Mara walked to the beginning of the Robert Frost Trail and did some stretching exercises as she perused her surroundings.

"It looks fairly open. I can see at least four people, three with dogs, walking back toward the parking lot. The placard at the beginning of the trail says the main trail is only half a mile long. It follows along a stream. I'm going to run that trail."

"Okay. Could you describe the area to me as you go?" Bradley asked.

"Alright."

Bradley watched as Mara set out on the trail. Moments later, all four people Mara had mentioned appeared from the trailhead and headed back to their vehicles. Four cars remained in the lot, none of them a black Toyota Camry.

Bradley had been watching for the car since getting to town. He estimated that he had seen close to sixty black Camrys so far. None had the license plate CN1126. Bradley knew it was possible Lessing would change her plate, but he thought it too soon for her to have done it.

"I've reached the end of the open area," Mara reported. "There's a field in front of me. The trail takes a right-hand bend into the tree line, and I can see the brook ahead. It's beautiful. There are a few more people headed to the parking area. So far, everyone here is walking or jogging by themselves or with a pet. I haven't seen multiple people together. That tells me people feel very safe here," Mara said.

"That could be good or bad. If people feel safe, they let their guard down," Bradley responded.

"Okay, I'm going over a brid . . . a woo . . . to wa . . ."

"Mara? Can you hear me?" Bradley asked.

"I hear . . . me?" Mara's voice sputtered.

"Dammit. If you can hear me, keep talking. Maybe it's just a bad spot."

Bradley's attention got pulled away as he noticed Andrea Edwards appear across the street from the front door of her home. She wore jogging clothes.

Bradley watched her pass by the two vehicles sitting in her driveway, stop at the street to look for traffic, and jog across the street to the parking lot.

"Mara. Can you hear me? Andrea Edwards is here. She is about to enter the park. Can you hear me?"

"I hear y . . . can . . . if . . . th . . ."

Bradley watched as Andrea stretched before entering the trail. She wore a headlamp.

Mara said the main trail was only half a mile long, Bradley thought. He used his cellphone to find a map of the trails in the Amethyst Brook Conservation Area. The Robert Frost Trail crossed the brook three times before coming to an end a half mile away. The state owned and maintained the trail.

Another trail, called simply the local trail by those who used it, was not managed by the state and, according to the park website, was less traveled. That path did not follow the brook, but it did traverse the more densely wooded area and ended at the same point at the end of the state trail.

The local trail also allowed for hikers to make a large loop midway along the path. Someone had forged a U-shaped footpath on the southside of the local route. One could conceivably walk the state trail to the local trail, then make a loop on the U-shaped path before returning to the local trail leading back to the parking area, resulting in a two-mile trip.

As Andrea disappeared into the park, Bradley decided to get out of the truck to see which trail she planned to run. By the time he hit the pavement and rolled to the trailhead, she was out of sight. What he did see was four people, two with dogs, heading back to the parking lot. He nodded politely as each came through the opening in the fence that edged the paved area.

One by one, the last of the automobiles pulled out of the lot, leaving his white Chevy sitting alone. The sun was about to make its final descent, and Bradley already had a hard time seeing clearly into the park. He returned to his truck to retrieve a flashlight.

"Mara. Where are you now?" Bradley asked through the radio. He waited.

"Mara. Can you hear me?" he asked?

Dammit, Bradley thought, *these damn radios are shit*. He vowed to talk to Nick about getting some new equipment.

There was nothing for Bradley to do but wait. Surely, it wouldn't take Mara more than ten minutes to finish her run, assuming she went to the end of the Robert Frost Trail and came directly back. But if she decided to shadow Andrea, Bradley had no idea how long she would be gone, or which trail she traveled.

Ten minutes passed. Then fifteen. With his impatient nature, Bradley's heightened anxiety of late had him reeling. He moved his chair to the front of the fence opening, turned around, and went back. He did it again and again and again, his version of pacing.

Bradley's impatience turned to irritation, then annoyance, and finally landed on anger. Mara knew he waited to hear from her. He found it unacceptable that she would not come back and report to him. Sure, he knew she would track Andrea to examine her habits and her running pace. She would not be doing her job if she didn't. But it still pissed him off that he was out of the loop. He didn't like it. He tried to reason with himself, but it didn't help.

When thirty minutes passed, Bradley decided he'd had enough. Just as he was about to head into the park, he saw a figure to his right, jogging down the sidewalk along Pelham Road. The figure stopped, bent over, then straightened. With the dim illumination that shone from the streetlight Bradley could see that it was Andrea Edwards. She must have come out of the park from a point further up the road. She crossed the street and went into her house.

Bradley breathed a sigh of relief. Not that he was worried, but he was tired of waiting. Sure that she had been tracking Andrea from a distance, he watched for Mara.

"Mara. Can you hear me?" Bradley said into his radio.

No response.

"Goddamn radios," Bradley whispered irritably.

Minutes passed.

"Jesus Christ, Mara. You couldn't have been that far behind her," Bradley said to no one.

Five more minutes passed.

Bradley began to worry. *What if she tripped and broke her ankle?* He looked around hoping someone would drive into the lot. It had gotten very dark, and he doubted anyone would come to walk their dog or go jogging in the park for the rest of the evening.

With his flashlight guiding him, Bradley headed into the park through the opening in the fence and onto the Robert Frost Trail. The path was wide and well kept. He made it to the tree line quickly, then turned with the pathway into deeper darkness.

He heard the water ahead before he saw it. A wooden bridge spanned the brook, but Bradley's hopes of crossing it dashed when he saw the two stairs he would need to navigate. Although Bradley's chair could climb stairs, Bradley had only operated that function once at the store where he bought the chair, and then it was on wide, sturdy cement stairs. He did not feel confident enough to try to mount the thin wooden planks of the bridge stairs. He would have to go back.

As he traveled back to the parking lot, he noticed the small opening to the local trail that he hadn't seen on the way out. He looked at the park map again, and it showed no water crossings on that trail. He ducked into the tree line once again.

The path was wide enough for his chair with little room to spare, and although it was not kept as neatly groomed as the state trail, he could navigate it easily enough. His flashlight seemed to illuminate brighter because the trail itself had become much darker.

"Mara," Bradley called out.

He heard nothing but distant rushing water.

He continued on the path for a few hundred feet before he noticed another small opening in the tree line to his right. That must be one end of the U-shaped trail that he saw on the map. Bradley continued straight. His plan was to go to the end of the trail. If he didn't come upon Mara by then, he would go back the way he came and take the loop. He feared that Mara lay on the state path and he would not be able to reach her to help her. He considered calling local police for assistance but decided to finish searching the local route first. He passed the other end of the U-shaped loop and continued for another quarter mile before he saw a dark shadow on the path ahead.

The closer he got, the harder his heart beat, because the closer he got, the easier it was to see that the shadow was a body. He leaned into his chair pushing the throttle to its limits and raced toward the figure.

"Mara!" he yelled.

In the dirt, Mara lay motionless on her right side with her headlamp illuminating the path. Bradley leaned down to touch her, positioning himself so he could feel for a pulse in her neck.

"Thank God," he whispered as he felt the blood rushing through her veins.

He examined her head, noting a blotch of blood on the left side. Bradley's eyes furrowed as he processed the situation.

Why would she have blood on the left side of her head if she fell on her right side?

"It doesn't make sense, right?" a woman's voice came from behind him.

Bradley sat upright, his back stiff. With his flashlight sitting in his lap, he turned his chair toward the voice. From the darkness, Amanda Lessing appeared to glow.

"She's not dead," Lessing said. "I barely tapped her on the head."

"Why?" Bradley asked.

Amanda laughed as she circled around him and stood next to Mara. "To see you, of course. I knew if I left you subtle clues, you would come. Now, please back away from her," she said as she pulled a large knife from behind her back.

"Well, here I am. You don't need her anymore," Bradley said.

With a chuckle, Amanda replied, "Always the savior. I knew it. I could tell from the moment I saw you. It radiates from you."

Bradley turned his chair to face her and slowly began to move his right hand toward his chair pocket where he kept his Glock.

"I'm not an idiot like most people you deal with," she said as she knelt down beside Mara and placed the point of her knife on Mara's neck. "Throw your gun into the woods." She nodded her head toward the darkness. "Go ahead. Give it a good chuck."

Bradley weighed the options, pulled the gun from his chair pocket, and threw it into the woods.

"I know you're not an idiot. In fact, you're very smart. That's why this," Bradley swiped his hand in front of him, "doesn't make any sense."

"Well, you're right about that," Amanda sighed as she produced two large plastic zip ties from a fanny pack and bound Mara's hands and feet. "I just couldn't help myself. I missed you."

"Me? Why me?" Bradley asked, sincerely wanting to know the answer.

Amanda stood and went to Bradley. She knelt in front of him and looked him in the eyes. "Because we are soulmates, you and me. I felt it the first time I saw you. I hoped you felt it, too, but you being a man, it may have been too much to expect."

Mara moaned. Bradley glanced at her, hoping she would not make any sudden moves prompting Amanda to hurt her again.

"I don't believe in soulmates," Bradley said.

Lessing smiled as she stood and stepped back. "That's alright. You don't have to. Men just don't have the capacity for understanding the way women do. Men mostly serve themselves. But you're different. You have promise. You are more like me."

"What makes you say that?" Bradley asked. He inched forward toward Mara as he spoke.

"That's close enough," Amanda commanded. "You don't need to worry about her. Not yet, anyway. Seriously, Bradley. You must see the similarities by now."

Bradley shuddered when she called him by name. It felt menacing even if it didn't sound menacing.

"But I don't," Bradley replied.

Another moan escaped Mara's lips, and Lessing saw the pain it caused Bradley. Wishing to capture his full attention, Amanda stepped forward and sat on Bradley's lap on top of the flashlight. She placed her left arm around his neck, dangling the knife with her right hand beside the chair.

"At first, I wasn't sure how deeply we were connected. But the more I read about you, the more I understood. We both live our lives with the same goal. Protect the innocent and punish the guilty for as long as we can. We are smarter than most, and we do whatever it takes to accomplish our goal."

"But I don't kill innocent people," Bradley stated.

Amanda Lessing huffed loudly. "Men," she sighed. "You, of all people, know that death is peace. Otherwise, why would you consistently put yourself in its path? Why would you wish for it? You think about it all the time, just like me."

"No. I . . ."

"You can deny it all you want. It won't change anything. I know you better than you know yourself, because I am you and you are me. We know better than others how to protect those in need, and we know how to punish those who deserve it. But we also wish upon ourselves what we do to punish others," Amanda said as she gazed into Bradley's eyes.

Suddenly, it seemed as if Amanda had lifted the black veil that draped over Bradley's heart and saw the chips and cracks that lay underneath.

Mara let out a holler as she came to and found herself bound. "What the fuck?"

Amanda's attention turned to her bound captive. Bradley grasped Lessing's right arm with both hands and tried to wrestle the knife free. Lessing tightened her grip around Bradley's neck with her left arm as she attempted to strangle him. Her neck hold forced Bradley to remove one hand from her knife wielding arm to release the hold she had on his neck.

Mara wiggled in the dirt trying to free herself. When she could not, she used her bound feet to inch toward Lessing and

Bradley. She kicked at Lessing, hoping to help free Bradley from the chokehold.

Lessing lost her grip on Bradley's throat but managed to break Bradley's hold on her right arm and plunge the knife into his upper thigh.

As Amanda pulled the knife out of Bradley's leg, she jumped out of the chair, putting a little distance between herself and Bradley.

The blood rushing from his leg felt like lava from a volcano. The knife had struck close to his groin where his nerves remained healthy, so he felt every ounce of the searing pain. He placed his hand on the wound and pressed as he let out a roar.

Lessing watched as his distress morphed to determination. She shifted her attention to Mara, who frantically wiggled at Bradley's feet. Mara's eyes caught Lessing's glare, and Mara knew what would come next. She saw the knife, held in both hands, come toward her.

The rage in Lessing's eyes glowed as the flashlight Bradley threw at her hit her square in the face. Lessing stumbled and fell on her back.

Bradley pushed himself out of his chair onto the ground directly behind Mara. Mara rolled back on her right side in time to see Lessing regain her stance and charge toward them, the knife catching what little moonlight trickled through the trees.

In one quick move, Lessing landed on her knees and thrust the knife toward Mara's throat.

The gunshot echoed off the trees. Amanda Lessing seemed to hover over Mara and Bradley as her knife-wielding arm dropped onto Mara's stomach, the blade upright as if standing at attention. As Lessing's body collapsed toward Mara and Bradley, the blade pierced her own maimed breast and left her torso propped like a tent with her chin resting on her chest. The three lay in a heap for several moments before Bradley could speak, the gun still smoking in his hand.

"Are you alright, Mara?" he asked.

Mara lifted her head and shakily replied, "Yes. You?"

"Yes."

Mara glanced at Bradley. "Never leave home without it," she sighed and dropped her head back onto the ground.

Covered in Lessing's splattered blood, the two rolled her lifeless body off them.

Bradley reached for the knife and pulled it from Lessing's chest. He cut the zip ties from Mara's legs and hands. Mara fashioned a bandage out of Lessing's clothing and wrapped it around Bradley's knife wound. Then the two sat in stunned silence. It took only minutes before they heard a siren closing in from a distance.

VOWS

Bradley sat by himself next to the last row of chairs arranged in Derek and Cate's living room. It was two weeks since Amanda Lessing surprised them at the park. The incident convinced Nick and Mara not to wait any longer to finally get married. Neither wanting a big wedding, they invited immediate family and a few friends. Derek and Cate offered their spacious home for the ceremony and reception. Nick asked Bradley to be his best man.

Derek came out of the kitchen and sat next to Bradley.

"How's Nick doing?" Derek asked.

"Not well. He's a train wreck. I had to get out of that room."

"Cate said Mara is flying on a cloud, whatever that means," Derek chuckled.

"Nick will be fine once he sees Mara. It's the idea of the whole thing that's got him rattled," Bradley said.

"And how are you doing?" Derek asked.

"I'm good. I already wrote the toast. That's the hardest part, right?"

"That's not what I meant," Derek said. He poked his finger into Bradley's chest. "How are you doing?"

"I'm fine. Everything's good," Bradley replied.

"Look, I know things have gotten tense between us, and I'm sorry. I . . ."

"Derek, it's okay. We are okay. Brothers have arguments all the time, but they get over them. And that's what we are. Brothers. And we always will be."

Derek nodded in agreement.

Cate entered the living room and announced, "We're ready to get started. Everybody, please, take your seats."

"She looks amazing," Bradley said about Cate to Derek.

Derek looked lovingly at Cate with the look Bradley envied most. "Well, remember. You get the first dance, because she is the maid of honor and you are the best man, but I get the rest of them," Derek laughed.

The short ceremony took place in front of the large stone hearth. Mara looked like a princess in her beaded white wedding gown, and Nick looked uncomfortable in his black tuxedo. But once he saw Mara walking towards him, he looked like a child in a candy store and full of pure joy.

The living room doors opened to a large outdoor patio where a tent had been erected. Portable heaters managed the cool autumn air. Speakers crooned with songs from the Sinatra era while guests feasted on the catered meal of spit-fired prime rib, baked stuffed shrimp, roasted baby red potatoes, and asparagus with hollandaise sauce.

With the meal finished, it was time for the best man to make his speech. Bradley moved from behind the table while Cate clinked her champagne glass to capture everyone's attention.

Bradley cleared his throat.

"Well, this day has been a long time coming. And for those of us who know Nick well, we held our breath through the ceremony wondering if he was going to become the runaway groom."

The group chuckled.

"No, seriously, I never thought anyone would ever be able to win Nick's heart, except of course, Nick."

More laughter.

"The first time I knew Nick was a goner was at my home. Mara and a male friend of mine were enjoying a nice chat after dinner and Nick couldn't get out of his own way."

Chortles.

"I had never seen him so jealous. But that's also the night I felt I knew the real Nick. He is as tenacious in love as he is in his work, and I mean that in the best possible way. He cares deeply and he loves deeply. And I am grateful he considers me his friend."

A collective "Ohhh" came from the guests.

"Now, as for his beautiful bride, Mara, I am grateful you got Nick to comb his hair."

Laughter erupted.

"You are not only one of the best agents I've ever worked with, but you are also one of the few people I would trust—and have trusted— with my life. You are grace personified. And you radiate strength, kindness, compassion, and integrity—all of which you will need in your marriage."

Another round of laughter.

"They say we should tell our loved ones every day how much we love them because we never know what tomorrow will bring." Bradley's voice choked.

"I would like to end this toast with a message not only for the bride and groom but for all of those present," he said. "I love you all, and I'm grateful to have had you in my life. And to Mara and Nick, may your lives be full of happily-ever-after. Cheers!"

"Cheers!" the guests said in unison, then clapped as Bradley resumed his spot behind the table.

Cate turned to Derek with tears in her eyes and said, "That was a beautiful toast, wasn't it?"

But Cate noticed a concerned look on Derek's face.

"What is it?" Cate asked.

"Nothing," Derek forced a smile. "Nothing at all. It was beautiful."

As promised, Bradley got the first dance with Cate, and his chair swirled around the dance floor like it did the first night Bradley ever danced on the cruise ship where they met many years before.

As for Derek, he sat and struggled with a phrase Bradley used in his speech, *"I'm grateful to have had you in my life." Why did he use past tense?* Derek thought.

Derek tried to engage him in conversation, but Bradley managed to avoid it. Bradley wasn't sure he would be able to go through with his plan if he spent too much time with Derek. It would hurt too much.

He left the party early, sighting his leg injury as a reason to get home and relax. He had lingered over his good-byes longer than normal, his decision weighed heavy on him even though he knew it to be the right one.

On the way home, Bradley stopped in front of the post office and fingered through the envelopes, seven in all. He double-checked the addresses and made sure each had a stamp. He drove to the drive-up mailbox, took a deep breath, and tossed them in.

Then Bradley went home.

Two days later, a letter addressed to Cate was delivered to her home. Unbeknownst to Cate, the same letter had been sent to her sister Sheila, Holly, Mike, Zayt, Mara, and Bradley's parents.

Cate opened the letter.

Dear Cate & Derek,

By the time you read this, I will be gone! Please know that this was not an easy decision, but it was a necessary one.

Cate's hand began to shake.

"Derek," she screamed.

Derek ran into the room at the sound of Cate's distress.

"What is it? What's that?" Derek asked of the letter.

"It's from Bradley." she answered.

Derek's heart sank. The fear he had felt at the wedding filled his gut. He remembered Bradley's words just as he spoke them, past tense: *I love you all, and I'm grateful to have had you in my life.*

Cate handed Derek the letter.

Derek read aloud:

Dear Cate & Derek,

By the time you read this, I will be gone! Please know that this was not an easy decision, but it was a necessary one."

I've spent my life believing I knew who I was, what I wanted from life, and how to go about getting it. But I've come to realize that is not the case.

I doubt this will surprise you.

I don't like the person I have become. I need to find a way to release the old and embrace the new. I've decided it is time for me to do some soul-searching. I don't feel I can do that in the environment I have created.

Rusty and I are on the road.

Derek stopped reading and breathed a sigh of relief. "He's okay, Cate. Thank God, he's okay."

He continued reading.

Rusty and I are on the road. To where? I don't know. I have left my cellphone at home, and I did not bring a computer. I left instructions and information about my house on the kitchen table. Do with it what you will.

I will not be in touch, and I ask that you not try to find me. This journey I must do alone.

Please don't be sad. Know that I am doing the right thing for me, as you should continue to do for yourselves.

I love you with all my heart.

Bradley

With the letter feeling heavy, Derek dropped his hand to his side. Cate sobbed.

"Jesus, I thought he killed himself," Derek said as he collapsed into a chair.

"What are we going to do?" Cate cried.

Derek thought before speaking. "Cate, I don't think this is a bad thing. This might be exactly what Bradley has needed all these years. We'll have to trust that he is doing what's best for him. So we're going to do what Bradley wants us to do. We're going to live our lives and be happy and hope that someday we'll see him again."

Derek wrapped Cate in his arms and held her tight. "Have I told you today that I love you?"

Bradley gave his passport to the guard in the shack. Rusty sat beside him and looked up at snow-capped mountains.

A single phrase had haunted Bradley since the night he killed Amanda Lessing, and he found himself thinking about it now.

And we wish upon ourselves what we do to punish others.

Maybe she had been right, Bradley thought. *But it's time for me to make some new wishes.*

"Here you go, sir. Enjoy your stay in Canada," the guard said as he handed Bradley his passport.

Looking ahead, Bradley replied, "Thank you. That is my hope."

ACKNOWLEDGMENTS

I am thankful for the incredible support and encouragement I continue to receive from friends, family, devoted readers, and spirit guides. I treasure every moment we have together.

To my fellow author and sister, Paula Francis, thank you for allowing me to interrupt you at any time to discuss plot, or ask for cover design advice and for whisking me away for a much-needed break from my computer to play cards.

Thank you, Richard Bruno, for proofreading my manuscript. I appreciate your expertise and thoughtfulness. And to Brenda Anderson, thank you for your helpful and thorough review of *Pathside Predator*. I appreciate your keen eye for detail.

And to my editor, publisher, and very good friend, Marcia Gagliardi of Haley's Publishing—thank you for continuing to love and nurture my fictional family as much as I do.

photo by Paula Francis

ABOUT the AUTHOR

You can't always plan where life will take you.

That certainly proved true for Christine Noyes. Growing up a tomboy in Shrewsbury, Massachusetts, she spent her youth building forts, playing sports, and enjoying the perceived innocence of the 1960s.

Without a clear vision of what her life should be, she went where she felt most comfortable: to the kitchen. At the age of eleven, she began her work life as a dishwasher in her grandfather's restaurant. She spent the next several decades reinventing herself, becoming an accomplished chef and then a sales representative, an entrepreneur, and eventually a writer and illustrator.

Chris never chose her professions. They chose her.

Few people say that going bowling changed their lives, but it did exactly that for Chris. She met the one person she never expected to meet, the man she calls her husband and soulmate, Al.

from the next Bradley Whitman novel
by Christine Noyes

REAPING REDEMPTION
OMINOUS DEVELOPMENT

Although he didn't reveal a weapon, he dressed as a warrior. He stood with his arms crossed on his puffed-out chest, his shoulders drawn back to accentuate his thickly corded neck, and his square chin thrust toward the camera. He held his head high.

Derek Richards, FBI executive assistant director of criminal, cyber, response, and services, studied the man in the video—the latest of several that Ali al-Haqani had produced. Derek found each one more ominous than the previous.

"What have you got so far, Sam?" Derek asked his National Security Branch counterpart.

Sam Houghton shook his head. "Not much. He's a relative newcomer but seems to be quickly gaining a following. He's an Afghan citizen, grew up in Asadabad, but went to college at the Massachusetts Institute of Technology here in the states. He graduated nine years ago with a master's degree in chemical engineering. After graduation, his passport shows him traveling to Saudi Arabia, Pakistan, and then back to Afghanistan."

"And the messages you intercepted? Have your guys been able to decode them yet?" Derek asked.

"No. That's why I'm here. We know this threat is imminent and the chatter we're picking up suggests they will attack in either New York or DC. But the truth is, we just don't know where or when. All we know is it's going to happen soon."

"Are we looking at a dirty bomb?" Derek asked.

"Only speculation at this point," Sam answered. "That guy you told me about, the analyst, can you get him here?"

Derek paused. He didn't know how receptive Bradley would be. It had been a year since he abruptly took a leave of absence from the FBI and disappeared.

Derek responded, "I'll do my best."

Derek returned to his office and stopped at his executive assistant's desk. "Madelyn, I need you to get a message to Agent Bradley Whitman. He's in India."

"I thought he disappeared. Your wife told me you didn't know where he was," Madelyn exclaimed.

"Cate doesn't know that I know." Derek explained. "I was able to track him down not long after he left, and I've been keeping tabs on his travels."

"Oh. It's best you keep that to yourself. Cate will be furious with you if she finds out," Madelyn said.

"She's not the only one who's going to be furious," he replied, thinking of Bradley's request that no one try to find him. "I'm going to need the plane. I also have a classified folder that's got to get on the jet before it leaves. Tell the pilot I want it in the air in an hour. I'll have the go-ahead of the director by then."

"Classified?" Madelyn asked.

"Bradley still has clearance. I just need to officially reinstate him before he looks at it," Derek said. "Madelyn, I need to talk to him as soon as possible. Even if someone on the ground has to track him down. We can't wait for a messenger."

"Do you know where in India he is?" she asked.

"The Sterling Darjeeling hotel, Ghoom, West Bengal."

Madelyn peered over her notepad. "That's quite specific."

"I just wanted to make sure he was okay," Derek said, noting her questioning gaze.

"I'll get right on it," she replied.

BALANCING ACT

Watching the sun rise over the peak of the Himalayan mountains may have been the most spiritual experience of Bradley Whitman's thirty-five years. For all the trouble it took to get him there— waking at 2:30 that morning and bouncing in the passenger seat of his driver's Jeep while navigating the thin, cratered winding road through the darkened pine forest—it was worth it.

"Rajesh, you were right," Bradley spoke softly.

His driver responded, "There is nothing more beautiful on this earth."

The orange glow awakened the deep blue sky and cast a golden hue on the valley below. Bradley could discern no beginning or end to the panoramic masterpiece.

Darjeeling, in the state of West Bengal, India, was known for growing tea and for the sunrise view from its highest point atop Tiger Hill. Among the snow-capped mountains basking in the early morning rays were Mounts Kanchenjunga, Makalu, and Everest.

Bradley could not think of a time when he felt more serene than he did in that moment. *This is what I've been searching for, this is where I need to be,* Bradley thought. He reached for his traveling companion, a black-and-rust-colored Doberman Pinscher named Rusty, and stroked his head.

"What do you think, boy?" he asked the dog.

Rusty gazed at the sun, cast a quick glance toward Bradley, then back at the sun. Much like Bradley, it seemed Rusty did not wish to interrupt the harmony.

A stillness overtook Bradley. He couldn't sense time nor the weight of his own presence but allowed himself only to be there in the moment. He no longer felt separate from his surroundings. Instead, he became part of them. He and Rusty sat quietly for an hour before Rajesh reminded Bradley of their next destination.

Bradley, stirred. "Ah, yes. Batasia Loop and the N gauge toy train." He engaged the throttle on his PW-4x4Q all-terrain power wheelchair, and the electric motor lightly whirred as Rusty walked alongside.

Bradley had hired Rajesh and his Jeep for the duration of his visit in India. After his difficulty maneuvering through Bhutan, for his trip to India, Bradley had planned ahead. *Strange*, Bradley thought, *that Bhutan,—a country so forward thinking as to develop Gross National Happiness as a measurement of its citizens' happiness as an indication of the nation's health—would be so far behind in supporting the needs of disabled individuals.*

"Jump in, Rusty," Bradley said when they reached the Jeep.

Wearing his red therapy dog vest, Rusty leapt into the passenger seat, then into the back seat. Rajesh easily lifted Bradley and placed him on the passenger seat. Then he used a ramp to load Bradley's chair into the short truck bed of the vehicle, where he strapped it down.

Bradley enjoyed the bumpy daylight ride back through the pine forest. "I've been looking forward to this train ride. I hear the views are spectacular. Have you ever been on the train, Rajesh?"

"No, I never found the time."

"Come with us today. No sense in you waiting around for me."

"I've made plans to meet my son while I wait," Rajesh explained.

Bradley smiled. "That's nice. Family is important."

A stitch of guilt snuck through Bradley's happiness armor as he thought about his parents.

Rajesh's cellphone rang.

"Yes. . . . Who? . . .When? . . . Okay, give him the number." Rajesh hung up the phone and handed it to Bradley.

"Someone is trying to get in touch with you. They said it was important," Rajesh said as he continued to drive.

Ten minutes later the phone rang. Bradley answered.

"Bradley, it's Derek."

Bradley paused. "How did you . . . what's wrong? Is everyone alright?"

"Yes, everyone is fine. But we do have a . . . situation."

"What kind of situation?" Bradley asked.

"A classified one. I need you, Bradley."

"Derek, I don't think . . . "

"I know, but I need you," Derek stated.

Bradley closed his eyes and sighed. After a moment, he replied, "Alright. I'll catch the next flight home."

"I've got a plane on its way. It will arrive tomorrow at Bagdogra International Airport at 3:30 p.m., your time. I'll email you what I can now, but the classified material will be on the plane with Agent Noor. She can answer any questions you have. And Bradley?"

"Yeah."

"I'll have to reinstate you," Derek said tentatively.

Another pause. "I understand."

The line went dead. And just like that, Bradley was back in. But he couldn't say no. Derek was like a brother to him. And Bradley knew Derek would not have called if it weren't of the utmost importance. After thinking about it, it didn't surprise Bradley at all that Derek knew exactly where to find him.

"Rajesh, I'm afraid we have a change of plans."

Back at the hotel, Bradley booted his laptop. Along with what little history they knew about Ali al-Haqani, Derek had sent a password protected link leading to a file containing Ali's thesis for his degree in chemical engineering, his MIT transcripts, and four videos from Al Jazeera television for Bradley to view.

He read and re-read the documents and watched the videos multiple times as he followed along with the translated documents. He didn't know exactly what the situation was that the FBI faced, but he was certain it was deadly.

Ali al-Haqani's body language as he stood tall and rigid was all Bradley needed to see to know the man posed a threat. He didn't rant and rave like some extremists tended to. He spoke slowly and methodically, enunciating each word to impress its importance. *If he had a speech writer,* Bradley thought, *that person was very good.* But Bradley did not get the impression that al-Haqani would ever speak someone else's words. His manner was such that he could have easily been reciting his dissertation—except for his imposing posture. *Although that's not the typical garb for a fellow MIT graduate,* Bradley thought. *This looks more like a CIA problem than FBI. Unless he's on American soil.*

He felt the familiar sensation of darkness within. A heaviness seeped through his chest like thick black sludge enveloping the sun and snuffing out the light.

Rusty instinctively came to his side and placed a paw on Bradley's leg. Although Bradley's paralysis prevented him from feeling the weight or the texture of Rusty's limb, he could feel the sentiment behind it, and it made him smile.

"I'm okay, buddy. Thanks," he said as he stroked Rusty's head.

Bradley put the laptop aside and began to meditate, something he had recently learned in Tibet. His eyes closed and his arms resting palms up on his chair, he concentrated on his breathing.

Rusty quietly lay down beside him.

After a brief period of quietude, Bradley imagined himself alone on a beach at sunset. He felt the heat from the sand on the bottom of his bare feet as he stood and looked to the sea. Just as the sun dipped below the horizon, she appeared from the ocean and walked toward him. She looked beautiful in a white, flowing gown that was somehow dry. It blew in the breeze with her long brunette hair. They outstretched their arms to each other.

That is where the vision always ended. He never gets to hold the hands of the woman he loves, the woman he was supposed to marry nearly ten months before. She fades before his eyes and eases him back to reality.

His eyes still closed, he sighed, "Laney." Then he smiled. The heaviness in his chest swept out to sea, Bradley picked up his laptop and continued his work.

The following afternoon, Bradley and Rusty boarded the Cessna Citation jet and, within minutes, were on their way to DC. As promised, Agent Noor, tall and slender with caramel skin and long black hair tied in a ponytail, was on board and provided Bradley with a file folder containing classified documents.

After introductions, Bradley asked, "What can you tell me about the case, Agent Noor?"

"We have confirmed intelligence reports that an attack on American soil is imminent. Our information points to two bombs. We nearly intercepted a couple of al-Haqani's men at the Port of Houston, but they managed to slip away. We missed them by minutes," Agent Noor gritted her teeth and shook her head.

"You were there?" Bradley asked.

"Yes. We found the abandoned warehouse where the bombs were built. The building scanned positive for radioactive substances. There are pictures in the folder. It's just a matter of time before they use them."

"Do you know who these people are?" Bradley asked.

"We're pretty sure they're followers of Ali al-Haqani. They received coded messages from al-Haqani himself. When I said we just missed them, I meant it. They left in a hurry. We found these." Agent Noor pulled two pieces of paper from the folder and handed them to Bradley.

Seeing Arabic writing, Bradley asked, "Have these been translated?"

"Yes." Once again Agent Noor pulled a sheet from the folder. "It's just a list of numbers. Our people haven't been able to find any pattern, sequence, or key to unlock the code."

"How certain are you that Ali al-Haqani is behind the attack?" Bradley asked.

"He's using homegrown terrorists directed by two guys who managed to get away. We captured and interrogated one of the Americans at the warehouse. Trust me. He told us everything he knew, which wasn't much. Just that he heard the guys talking about getting the information about the targets from al-Haqani.

We are still trying to identify his two men and the other Americans. They were careful not to share their own names or personal information but didn't seem worried about using al-Haqani's name."

"I might need to talk to the American in custody," Bradley stated.

"That's way above my pay grade. You'll need to speak with my boss."

"Derek won't be a problem," Bradley said.

"Who's Derek?"

Bradley sat up straight and peered at Agent Noor. "Who exactly is your boss, Agent Noor?"

"Executive Assistant Director Houghton."

"Director of what division?"

"National Security Branch."

"Why am I here then?" Bradley asked.

"I don't know, sir."

"My name is Bradley, agent."

"Call me Zahra. You must be pretty important for them to send Cessy for you."

"Cessy?" Bradley eyed Zahra.

She chuckled. "That's just our nickname for the jet. What's your dog's name?"

"That's Rusty," Bradley said as Rusty lifted his head when he heard his name. "He definitely appreciates Cessy. The trip over on the commercial airline was much less comfortable for him."

Bradley flipped through the documents from the file folder and pulled a picture of Ali al-Haqani from the stack. He recognized the photo as a still from the latest video dated July 25.

"Zahra, what's the date today?" Bradley asked.

"Back home it's August 7."

"How long have you had this information? The codes, specifically."

"This is day thirteen."

"I'm a last resort," Bradley sighed.

"Excuse me?"

"They're running out of time, and for some reason Derek thinks I may be able to help," Bradley explained.

"Are you talking about Executive Assistant Director Derek Richards?" Zahra asked.

"The one and only."

"Yes, sir—I mean Bradley. It was his office that sent me the file folder. Can you?"

"Can I what?"

"Can you crack it?"

"I guess we'll find out. Have you got a laptop?"

"I do."

"Boot it up. Let's get to work," Bradley said as he turned on his own computer.

COLOPHON

MVB Verdigris is a Garalde text family for the digital age. Inspired by work of sixteenth-century punchcutters Robert Granjon, Hendrik van den Keere, and Pierre Haultin, MVB Verdigris celebrates tradition but is not beholden to it. Created to deliver good typographic color as text, Mark van Bronkhorst's design meets the needs of today's designer using today's paper and press. A full-featured OpenType release with an added titling companion, it's optimized for the latest typesetting technologies, too.

Garalde: the word itself sounds antique and arcane to anyone who isn't fresh out of design school, but the sort of typeface it describes is actually quite familiar to all of us. Despite its age—born fairly early in printing's history—the style has fared well. Garaldes are the typefaces of choice for books and other long reading.